MW01701361

A QUALITY MAN

KAT VINSON

KV BOOKS LLC

Edited by Monique Conrod

Cover by Fiona Jayne Media

Created with Vellum

UNTITLED

A QUALITY MAN

by Kat Vinson

PART I

WINTER

1

Sujata got to the corner across from the Indian street food restaurant she was heading to just as the Walk sign lit up. A group of her coworkers all went inside just as she started crossing, leaving Vivek Aachari alone, laughing at something someone had said. He'd stayed outside—she knew it was to wait for her. He turned before she was halfway across the street, finding her like he always did.

She waved and couldn't stop the smile that came onto her face. She loved when he let loose and let you past the shy facade he sometimes had. He was in jeans and a blue sweater over a white shirt—no jacket—that showed off the size of his chest.

Which, admittedly, was appealing.

She squashed that thought. Vivek had a huge crush on her, and she felt ... somewhat the same. But he was only two years out of grad school and young—just twenty-five to her twenty-eight. And he'd only been in the U.S. a handful of years before starting at InfoQuest, for grad school, so he might not be very progressive about women. She knew him well enough to know he wasn't a dinosaur, but sometimes people were weird once they were in a relationship.

But that wasn't even the real reason, which had to do with what her ex-fiancé had done to her. She could not risk that again.

"Hi," Vivek said as she stepped onto the sidewalk, a light coming into his dark brown eyes. He stepped closer and reached out as if to touch her, then dropped his arm. "Come on, everyone else is here. Let's go in."

"Okay, sure. Thanks for waiting for me." Before she could stop it, some weird instinct made her squeeze his arm as she said it. His arm was all hard muscle, and she couldn't help but feel a bit of lust go through her.

Down, feelings. This was not the time or place. Or the right man. Or the right ... anything.

He beamed at her and rushed to hold the door open for her.

She walked in with him. Despite her attraction, she couldn't go there. Most Indians raised in the U.S. were more like she was—fully versed in the culture of India itself, which was mostly relevant because of their parents' generation, who still followed it more closely, but more American than anything else. There was always some careful navigating to make everything work in the different worlds, but Indians born here managed it fine.

And Vivek had grown up in India. So there was always that fear—which she rationally knew was unreasonable—that if a man was still too connected to India, he might do what her ex-fiancé, Rajeev, had done to her. Which would be intolerable.

So she just couldn't do anything with Vivek. She needed to keep him in the friend compartment of her brain.

Once they were through the door, the large room buzzed with a dozen conversations. They were early, so it wasn't full yet, but there were several families and groups. An older woman in a blue and gold sari was feeding a toddler with a red plastic fork at one corner table, while a bearded white hipster and a heavily tattooed woman with dreadlocks ate quietly at the next table. It was always like this. Diverse. She loved Portland. It definitely wasn't perfect, but she was less on her guard than in Missouri.

Vivek pointed to their group. "They're in the queue."

"Oh, right." Sujata headed up to the line with Vivek right behind her. She stopped next to Kiran from work, who turned around long enough to say, "Hi, Sujata," before rejoining the raucous conversation the rest were having.

She looked around the familiar restaurant, full of wooden tables and mismatched chairs, knickknacks lining the walls and windows.

Vivek stood a tad closer to her than necessary. She thought about edging away from him, but found she didn't mind. She smelled something appealing—maybe aftershave? His grin had only now started to fade to a more subdued smile.

If she were being honest, being around him always made her heart ache. If it weren't for the battered state of said heart, she would absolutely date him. But she still wasn't over Rajeev, who was somewhere in Portland living up married life. She didn't know how to get over him.

He must be done with his residency by now. He could be sensitive and a good listener when he wanted to be, so his patients would love him. But he lacked a spine where family was concerned. She'd recently started to wonder if there was more to what had happened, but she really didn't know.

She had to get her mind off Rajeev, however. She didn't know why he was so in her thoughts tonight.

Well, it was probably for the same reason it happened every time they came here—this was where she and Rajeev had gone the night he proposed.

That beautiful ring was still sitting on the dresser. She really ought to do something about it. It was not going back to him, that was for sure. Her sister, Kavya, had told her to sell it to someone for a dollar and send him the receipt. They'd laughed about that. But she should sell it and buy herself something nice. Maybe she would.

But right now, she needed to be in the moment with her fellow Indians on a fun night out.

They reached the counter and Sujata gave her usual order—kati roll with paneer—to a woman in a sleeveless dress that revealed untrimmed armpit hair. Just saying the words out loud when she ordered made her mouth start watering. A kati roll was a delicious flatbread stuffed with Indian cheese, chutney, egg and pickled onion. As she pulled out her credit card, Vivek opened his mouth as if to say something, but didn't.

She waited for Vivek while he ordered, then maneuvered with him past a couple of tables to the two four-seaters that they'd pushed together for their group. She sat in an empty seat next to Kiran, with Vivek across from her. Kiran turned around to say hi again. He was tall and skinny and wore thick glasses, and he was also one of the friendliest people she knew.

"Hi, Kiran."

They chatted for a moment before Vivek broke in.

"Did you hear what picture we're going to, Sujata?" Vivek asked.

"No."

"*Ae Dil Hai Mushkil,*" Kiran said.

Oh heart, it is difficult. Of course it was—it was an Indian love story. Somebody probably died tragically. Despite the fact that they were often silly, she was ridiculously fond of Indian movies, a definite guilty pleasure.

"Do you know anything about it?" Vivek asked.

She shook her head. "I haven't been keeping up with Bollywood lately."

"You're such an American," he joked, dramatically putting his hand on his heart in offense. "Don't call it that. It's not a Hollywood derivative."

She laughed. "Sorry. The Hindi film industry. But how do you account for the fact that some aren't in Hindi?"

Vivek grinned, showing nice, very white teeth. One had a tiny chip she'd never noticed before and it was endearing. "Ha ha. I think we can work it out."

She should stop. Stop noticing and liking things about him.

He chattered on about who it starred and what had been said about it. "I think it will be good," he concluded.

One of the other guys broke in with, "Vivek, are you in for tomorrow?"

"Pardon?" Vivek said.

"Cricket at the park."

"*Haan*." He flashed a thumbs-up. "What time are we going?"

"I'll pick you up at eleven."

"Good." Vivek turned back to her and smiled again.

"Do you follow cricket, Sujata?" Kiran asked.

"Yes!" She was a huge fan of the Indian national team, also known as the Men in Blue for the light blue uniforms they wore. "Can you believe the financial scandal?"

Vivek's face lit up. "You like cricket?"

She shot him a look of mock indignation. "Women can like cricket too, you know."

"Yes, of course." Vivek squirmed and grimaced. "It's just—well, you know."

She smiled. "I do know. It's fine. I'm just giving you a hard time."

He took a sip of water and said, "It was good to see Mishra get a chance to show what he can do."

Sujata nodded. "That loss to New Zealand was painful, though."

"Nineteen runs!" Vivek said.

Kiran had joined a different conversation, leaving Sujata and Vivek chatting excitedly of all-rounders and centuries. Vivek's face was bright at that moment. It felt rather good to make somebody look like that.

Still, she should stop leading him on, if that's what she was doing. She didn't mean for it to be like that.

A server placed a metal tray in front of her. Her kati roll. Mmm. Slightly crisp on the outside and oozing with flavorful bits from the inside. She could smell the spices infusing the air around her.

Vivek pushed his tray of aloo tikki toward her and said, "Please, have one. I got them to share."

Oh, God. Rajeev made the best aloo tikki. The color drained from her face.

"Are you okay?" Vivek asked, concerned.

"Oh, fine."

"You look ... upset."

"I was just thinking of Rajeev." What was she doing? She never told people about him. She was frazzled. "My ex-fiancé. He loved to cook and his signature dish was aloo tikki."

"You never talk about him," Vivek said. "If he broke up with you, he must be an idiot."

She laughed. "Clearly. It was a while ago."

She would *not* think of Rajeev any more tonight. She'd concentrate on Vivek and making new memories of this place.

Two little potato patties nestled on a bed of chickpeas on Vivek's tray. Her kati roll was more than enough, but she loved anything with potato or chickpeas in it. She reached over to put one on her plate. Tonight she felt like indulging.

She just needed to keep her focus on the food, and not think too much about the man across from her. They were both appealing, and neither was good for her.

~

VIVEK FOLLOWED the guys out to the sidewalk lined with parked cars, Sujata at his side. He loved this, even though it wasn't a date, but he could almost pretend, at least for the evening.

Because it *was* theoretically possible that she could go out with him. He had scoured the employee handbook. Relationships between an employee and a direct (or indirect) report were forbidden, but he and Sujata would be fine. They were both just software engineers.

"I'm down this way," Kiran said. Ishaan, one of Vivek's other roommates, called shotgun and followed him. Before Vivek or Sujata could do anything, the other four guys had piled into a second car, leaving Vivek and her to take the back of Kiran's BMW. They were all good at this manipulation, even though Vivek had asked them not to do it.

"You guys sure parked far away," Sujata said.

Kiran glanced back at her. "Yes, there were no spaces."

She hadn't pulled away from Vivek, even though they were so

close their hands kept accidentally brushing. Or maybe not accidentally. A guy could hope.

It made him happier than it should have, although he knew it meant nothing.

"How long have you followed cricket?" he asked her.

"Oh, forever. My *baba* played Under-19s before rupturing his Achilles tendon. It didn't heal well, so he went to college instead, where he was lucky enough to meet my *maa*."

Vivek's eyes widened. "He played for the national team?"

"Yeah. He got me into it when I was just a kid." She laughed. "He challenged me to memorize stats and I was very good at it. My sister, not so much."

Kiran's silver car unlocked with a click. Vivek opened the back door for her.

"You don't mind the back?" he asked. He definitely did not mind being in such close proximity to her. And kind of alone, since the back of a car was basically its own isolated space. Which was no good when you were the only one back there, but that wasn't the situation here.

She shook her head. "It's fine."

Climbing into the back of the car required a convoluted maneuver because she was wearing a skirt. It hit mid calf, but she had to pull it up a little while getting in, and he got an enticing view of her fit legs.

Once they were buckled into the gray leather seats, Vivek turned to her. "So tell me some of these stats. Do you still remember them?"

She looked over at him and scoffed, "Of course I do. Let's see, Tendulkar's 169 against South Africa, 1997."

"Watching recordings of that is one of my earliest memories," Vivek said before he could stop himself. He knew she was older and he shouldn't be reminding her.

Kiran started the car up and pulled out onto the road.

If she noticed his accidental implication, she ignored it. "Gavaskar's multiple hundreds against West Indies in his debut."

"Wow. The seventies. That's going back."

"He made me memorize everything." She leaned toward him and said quietly, "But can I tell you a secret?"

His heart sped up. "What?"

"I vastly prefer Twenty20."

His mouth hung open for a second before he said, "You can't be serious! Cricket in three hours? It's an abomination."

Sujata laughed again and touched him lightly on the forearm, making his heart race. "My *baba* thinks that, too. I think it's the American in me. It makes it more like a TV sport, like baseball. Or football. Or football." She raised her eyebrows and gave him a sardonic smile.

He laughed at the football joke—it still threw him when people talked about football and meant American football—but then had to shake his head in an attempt to clear the distracting thoughts planted by her touch. It was the second time she'd done that this evening. Did it mean anything? Had she changed her mind? And how could he get her to do it again?

She looked away from him, out the window, as Kiran merged onto I-5.

Vivek watched her, unable to tear his eyes away. Even in profile, she was beautiful. She had a slender and delicate nose that he wanted to feel against his own. He couldn't see her nose stud from this side, but when they were face to face, it always drew his attention. Her lips were pursed now, like she was deep in thought.

And then he smelled the sublest scent of lavender. It was so Sujata.

His first girlfriend had also smelled of lavender. She was like Sujata in other ways, too. Very smart, though she studied maths rather than engineering. She also laughed all the time and radiated confidence. She'd been the one who opened his eyes to sex, even if it was difficult to arrange since they both lived in the strictly segregated dorms.

But that was all in the past, and now he was sitting a few inches from Sujata.

The car cruised smoothly down the highway. The beautiful view of the city lit up in the darkness made Vivek feel romantic, like it was just the two of them rather than a carful.

"Were your parents a love match?" he asked. "You said he was lucky to meet her."

"Hmm?" She turned to face him. "Yeah. But I meant he was lucky because she's the one who got them over here, eventually. She's a professor of electrical engineering."

Vivek glanced at her very kissable lips. "That's nice," he forced himself to say.

"Plus, they're really good together." She paused. "How about your parents?"

He shook his head. "Arranged. They're quite traditional."

Sujata smirked. "So does your mom wish you were still at home to baby?"

"Yes, she does." He turned away, watching the lights of the passing cars. Sometimes that was exactly how his parents' plans made him feel. Caught in the headlights.

"I think you mentioned siblings once."

"Yes, two sisters. I was always really close to the younger one, Mishti—she's only a year older than I am. She is married and they live at my parents' house. My oldest sister is five years older and got married very young. She lives in New Delhi." He was still so mad about Mishti's marriage, because her husband was terrible. Vivek thought he was abusive.

Besides his sisters, he also missed his nieces and nephews. And to be fair, he missed his parents, but he couldn't imagine ever going back to live there. He liked the freedoms he had here. His parents were good people, but stuck in the old ways.

"How are you liking work?" Sujata asked. "You've been with us two years, right?"

"Yes, almost." He was glad to talk of something else, but this reminded him that his time there was going to be cut short.

"Isn't it your first job?"

He raised his eyebrows. "You know it is. You're one of the people who interviewed me."

She laughed, a sound he loved for its throatiness. She quirked an eyebrow and said, "Like I remember."

Ouch. He had no problem remembering her. "I worked as part of my degree at U of O, though."

"What did you do there?"

It was fine. He obviously hadn't made as big an impression on her. "I was a teaching assistant."

They were passing downtown Portland now, about to get on the highway that would take them out to Beaverton.

"Did you like that?"

"Yes." His eyes flitted down—for just a second—to her breasts. They looked as delicious as always.

Stop thinking like that.

"I worked in the university library in college," Sujata said. She was looking out the window, so he didn't think she'd caught him peeking—or read his mind. She leaned her head against the window.

He didn't want to let her wallow in whatever unhappy thoughts seemed to be plaguing her this evening. "I'm looking forward to the picture."

"Me, too."

"Good," Vivek said. He knew a lot of people considered them silly, but he always anticipated the mid-picture dance numbers.

She turned toward him. He smiled at her and she held his gaze. She really had nice eyes. He couldn't properly see them in the dark, but it didn't matter because he already knew what they looked like. Golden brown.

She turned her head away again and he was instantly sad. No matter how perfect they were for each other, they were never going to be together. He needed to accept that.

He also needed to stop delaying the inevitable with his job. Info-Quest wasn't going to sponsor his visa. David was disappointed because he wanted to do it, but the company only sponsored five a year, and this year all spots were already accounted for. Vivek was currently working on a visa that allowed master's graduates to work in the U.S. at any technical job for two years, and his two years was up in May. Less than four months to get everything sorted.

His uncle had a software engineer job basically earmarked for him at his transportation company in Atlanta, and his parents expected him to take that. If he did, his uncle could sponsor him for a green card so he could stay indefinitely. The other option was to look for a job in Portland that would sponsor him, even though his parents didn't want him to even try to stay here. Realistically, he should be able to find something local, but he was dragging his feet because he knew he should take the Atlanta job.

He glanced at Sujata, who was still looking out the window. The lights of businesses along the highway streaked by.

Every day, he told himself to get his resume out and start applying for jobs in Portland. But then he'd think of his parents, and of Sujata's repeated rejections, and he'd tell himself to just take the Atlanta job. But then his mind would say, What if it's next week that she changes her mind?

Kiran exited the interstate and drove toward the theater. They parked and headed up to the ticket counter under the rounded overhang, which naturally had a line. But the others had already arrived, and they'd bought tickets for everyone.

The group pushed through the doors into the bright lights and the smell of popcorn.

Vivek was following the group toward the skinny kid taking tickets when Sujata touched his elbow—again!—and said, "I'm going to grab some popcorn this time. Do you want any?"

"Oh." He looked at his elbow even though she'd already dropped her hand. "No, I don't really like popcorn. But I'll come with you."

"Okay, sure."

They went up to the concessions counter, with its obnoxious orange backdrop behind the menu, and Sujata bought a small popcorn with light butter and a Diet Coke to go with it. "I'm going to have to spend some extra time on the treadmill tomorrow."

Vivek laughed. "I think you can probably get away with it."

She raised her eyebrows at him as they headed to the hallway with the theaters, obviously not agreeing.

Vivek was distracted, watching her, and started to go into the first theater they got to.

"Not that one, space cadet," she teased.

He laughed. He looked ahead to find the right one, fourth on the right.

Once inside the doors, they headed toward the front of the theater, where the guys were sitting, but there weren't two spare seats next to the others.

Ishaan grinned up at him. "Sorry. Not enough seats."

Vivek swallowed, his throat suddenly dry. She had to know what they were doing. The car was one thing, but this kind of annoyed him, even though they had good intentions. She might think he was the one engineering all this, which she wouldn't like.

He motioned toward two seats in the fourth row. "Let's sit there."

They squeezed past two couples to snag the empty seats. An older woman in a pink sari smiled at him as he got settled. He wondered if she assumed they were a properly married couple. If only.

"Are you sure you don't want any popcorn?" Sujata offered the bag to Vivek after he sat down.

"No, thank you."

"Your loss."

He laughed. "It's not the same. They should sell samosas like a proper theater."

"I disagree. Popcorn is the quintessential movie food."

"No." He looked at her with a smirk. "What is it everyone says? It tastes like cardboard. Buttery cardboard. Mmm." He rubbed his stomach.

"Have you had caramel corn? It's different."

"Crunchy, sugary cardboard. Mmm."

Sujata laughed and punched him in the shoulder lightly.

His eyes fell to the point of contact.

Why was she doing that so much tonight? What would happen if he took her hand? Would she let him? And more importantly, did he have the nerve?

SUJATA SAT through the previews with her arms crossed because for some reason she couldn't seem to stop touching Vivek. She had to stop it. She could feel the heat in her face and was glad it was dark so he couldn't see her blushing. It was just hard—she wouldn't describe herself as touchy-feely, but she wasn't exactly touch-averse with her friends. And she genuinely thought of him as a friend. Even though he could be really shy, he was still fun to be around when he relaxed, which he usually did on these Saturday nights out.

Vivek's hands were on his knees like he was thinking of making a move. The seats were small enough that their shoulders were perpetually touching because of his stocky upper body. When the movie proper started, she kept her arms across her chest. She stayed that way through the whole movie, extracting her hands only to get fingerfuls of popcorn to chomp on.

Vivek was otherwise motionless except when he laughed, which involved his whole body as he leaned forward each time, usually glancing over at her to share his sexy grin.

Not a date.

But that didn't keep her mind from going over the possibilities if it were a date. They'd hold hands for sure, and probably he'd lean over at some point to kiss her. Or maybe she'd initiate it.

She finally got control of her thoughts near the end of the movie. She was the one who didn't want to date him, so she shouldn't even be thinking about it. She was proud of herself for being able to focus on the story for the last half hour.

As the credits rolled, Vivek asked, "Did you like it?"

"Yeah." As she'd expected, the film was ultimately tragic, and there were some good dance numbers. And she loved it. She'd never admit how much.

"Good."

Everyone in their row had stood up, but they weren't filing out yet. They eventually began to move, and just as she reached the aisle, she heard her name. She looked up in horror to see Rajeev. Her heart nearly stopped.

"How are you?" he asked with an awkward smile.

She stared at him open-mouthed and then looked past him to see a small and slender woman in a yellow blouse, a skirt, and gorgeous black boots. She was watching Sujata with wide-eyed curiosity.

People were having to maneuver around Rajeev and his stupid parent-approved wife because they were just standing there.

He still looked good, sporting a sexy five o'clock shadow.

Her heart started up again, but now her brain was empty. She had no idea what to say, before finally coming up with his name. "Rajeev."

They were both silent for a beat, when she felt Vivek push the back of his hand against hers, an obvious invitation. She took it. That snapped her out of it.

"I'm really great. Meet my boyfriend, Vivek. We've been together for ages. How are you? Is this your wife?"

Rajeev stared back in surprise.

God, she was making a total ass out of herself. She was so glad for Vivek's firm grip. His presence was reassuring. His posture exuded a confidence he didn't always have. He must have guessed what was going on.

After a few breaths, Rajeev stuck his hand out. "Vivek, it's nice to meet you. I'm Rajeev."

She had to let go of Vivek's hand so he could shake Rajeev's. He confidently said, "It's nice to meet you, too." But as soon as he let go of Rajeev's hand, he took hers again. It was strangely comforting, under the circumstances.

The woman took a step forward, a ridiculously overconfident smile on her face. "And I'm Leela. It's great to meet you, Sujata and Vivek."

Sujata tried to smile but she couldn't help but stare at Leela for a moment. She had an accent, but she was obviously fluent in English and educated, based on her voice and her confidence. How was this woman better than her? Sujata was outgoing and smart, too.

Rajeev was staring at Vivek with what Sujata recognized as his mildly peeved expression on his face. Jerk.

It seemed like Vivek was staring right back at Rajeev.

"Well," Leela said, still smiling. It wasn't lost on her that this was an incredibly awkward moment.

Sujata hated her. So much that she realized she had Vivek's hand in a death grip, and she forced herself to let it go. But he held on, so she closed her fingers around his again.

"Yes, we need to run," Rajeev said. "It was wonderful seeing you. We should catch up some time."

"Okay, yeah. Great. Bye." Sujata gave a wave she instantly regretted as stupid.

"Okay, well, it was great seeing you again, Sujata." With that, Rajeev took Leela's hand and turned to head up the aisle.

We should catch up some time. How could he even say that? She was dying inside.

How could he have abandoned her the way he did, thrown her to the side like she was trash? They were in love—true love. How could he just walk away from that? And all for some stupid notion of family honor.

He'd gone home for a harmless visit, and he didn't come back. The next thing Sujata knew, she'd received a wedding announcement in the mail, presumably from his hateful mother. He'd bowed to pressure to marry a local woman his family had picked for him.

Sujata of course understood the importance of family in Indian culture. But it was not okay to use it as an excuse to hurt people.

At least Rajeev and Leela were halfway up the aisle now, out of her space.

Sujata relaxed her fingers and turned to Vivek. "I'm so sorry."

"I'm guessing that was your ex-fiancé," Vivek said calmly, sympathy in his voice.

"How did you know who he was?"

"Well, I suspected it because you seemed really surprised and unable to speak. But you also told me his name earlier tonight."

So she had. Never had there been a more fortuitous time to slip up and mention him. She didn't want to imagine how much worse this chance meeting would have been if they couldn't all at least pretend that she had a boyfriend. She still wasn't sure if Rajeev believed it. But he would at least be wondering. It would rankle him, at a minimum.

They were standing still and so close that she could smell him—a subtle mix of cumin and cardamom from dinner. He smelled like India. She looked up at his dark and unreadable face, half wishing he would hug her to make her feel better.

She hadn't felt this emotionally close to him before. He'd risked their friendship by taking her hand. It could have been the wrong move and really pissed her off.

But it was exactly the right move.

Yet she couldn't let herself go down this path. Seeing Rajeev had completely thrown her for a loop, and any thoughts she'd had about being ready to date again had disintegrated. She wasn't ready to fully trust a man again. "Vivek, I'm sorry. I ... you know I like you, and I also find you attractive. But I just can't. I'm too broken. I'm sorry. If ... if you don't want to continue hanging out, I'll understand."

"It's okay, Sujata," he said in a soft voice. "We are friends. Let's go." His hand brushed her lower back, getting her moving into the aisle. Her skin tingled where his fingers were, even through her shirt and jacket.

Was she ever going to get over Rajeev? And more importantly, would she always regret not taking the risk and dating Vivek now, when she had the chance?

2

W*e are friends. Let's go.*

Sujata lay in bed Sunday morning remembering Vivek's words, her fluffy white comforter pulled up to her chin. He was so kind. She felt like a heel. She'd just rejected him again. At least she'd been totally honest with him this time. He seemed to take the admission that she was attracted to him but still couldn't date him all in stride. She hoped he would accept it and move on. He deserved someone whole.

Even though the whole thing was shitty, letting him think the incident meant something would have been worse.

The annoying thing was that she really did want to date him. There was no denying it.

She groaned and pulled the comforter over her head.

She didn't want to be so attracted to him. Why, why, why?

Suck it up, girl. It was time to get up and run this out of her system. She threw the comforter off and stood up in the chilly room. Even though you couldn't run away from your problems, you could at least try on the treadmill. She raced to her closet and pulled on thick leggings and a green long-sleeve wicking t-shirt over a sports bra. She slipped her feet into running shoes and headed over to the apartment gym, jogging to try to stay warm against the bite of the early morning freeze. As she passed a row of cars, she caught a mild whiff of exhaust from one.

Fortunately, the gym was empty. She walked for five minutes on the treadmill before cranking the pace up to six, which got some heat in her.

Leela. It meant "beauty," which just pissed Sujata off. Because that damn woman was one, no doubt.

The way she acted like she was excited to meet Sujata. Did she even know who Sujata was? Rajeev might have mentioned her name. But really, who knew. Maybe he'd completely written her out of his life.

Ugh. Why was everything so horrible? And why hadn't her own parents given her a name like that? Her own name basically meant "from a good family." Woo. Arrogant much?

That thought made her smile, because that wasn't her parents at all. She ran for a while, keeping her mind focused on her feet pounding the belt. But then her thoughts took a detour.

Rajeev. It killed her to even think his name. She'd so imagined their life together, the kids they'd have. They'd dated for five years and spent the last year engaged. But as that year wore on, his family's reservations grew into a full-scale revolt. Sujata's family was Bengali, and that wasn't good enough for a New Delhi family of their stature. But he'd always promised it didn't matter. Apparently it did, however.

He was spineless and she hated him for it, but the other truth tangled her stomach. If only she'd gone to India with him like he'd asked.

He was going to finally tell his parents they were engaged, and he'd wanted Sujata to go with him to New Delhi. But she'd been in the middle of a big project and didn't think she should take the time off, even if she'd been allowed.

That had been a huge mistake. He went alone and she hadn't seen him again—until last night.

Okay, maybe it wasn't a huge mistake. If he could be persuaded to give her up so easily, he wasn't worth keeping.

And she'd been remembering things differently lately. It hadn't always been great with him. She'd kind of retreated into her shell the longer she was with him, especially once they moved in together. Living together had been a hassle, too, because neither of them let their parents know they were sharing an apartment—that would have caused all sorts of problems—so whenever any family visited, the other person had to stay with friends and take all their stuff, including clothes and toiletries, with them.

Rajeev didn't seem to mind that she stayed in so much, even though she used to be more of a social butterfly in college. She was dancing then, as now, but that and work were pretty much the only reasons she left the apartment.

Still, knowing that things weren't perfect did not dull the pain of that rejection. Almost a year had passed and she'd really started to feel better in the last few months. But seeing him had destroyed any gains. She focused for a moment on the soft sound of her feet on the treadmill belt.

She'd heard from him the first few days he was in India, then nothing. Less than three weeks later, she'd received the wedding announcement. His mother had sent it to her work address since she didn't know she already had Sujata's home address.

It still hurt her heart to think about it. The horror she'd felt at seeing that piece of paper.

How could he have done that? And what had gone down, exactly? Had he arrived in New Delhi and been escorted off to Leela's family's house to inspect her and just immediately found her irresistible? Had he even given any further thought to Sujata? Or had he intended to do it even before he left the States? Was he mad at her for not going?

She'd been so convinced of his commitment. She hadn't doubted him for a second.

Sujata shook her head and sweat ran down her face. She licked her upper lip and tasted the salt. There was also a hint of bitterness from the tears that had escaped, which seemed fitting for her thoughts. She wiped more sweat off with a towel. She planned to run for an hour, to work off that damn popcorn, kati roll, and aloo tikki.

Of course, thinking about last night just brought her mind back to Vivek. He was more ruggedly handsome than Rajeev ever was. Rajeev had slender surgeon's hands and the rest of his body went perfectly with them, even if his face was masculine. He was tall and lean. Vivek was only an inch taller than Sujata, but he felt much bigger. Like a big sexy bear.

He made her feel feminine and petite, something that didn't happen often because of her five-seven frame. She shook her head again.

Once she finished on the treadmill, she was going to have to do some work. So she should enjoy this time and not dwell on what had happened in the past, or what could never happen in the future. Some day she was going to have to start dating. You couldn't have a family with kids if you didn't date.

Well, you could, but she couldn't imagine being a single mother on purpose.

She wiped the sweat from her brow again. Thirty-two minutes to go.

No, she wasn't going to sign up for online dating, at least not right now. She was only twenty-eight. She had some time before she needed to think seriously about marriage. A little bit of time.

She should just chill out and focus on her run.

Before she could really get mentally dialed in, her phone rang. Her sister. She slowed the treadmill down a couple notches and answered.

"Hey, girl," Sujata said.

"Hi." She paused. "What are you doing?"

"I'm on the treadmill." It wasn't unusual for Kavya to call on a weekend morning, but it was early. "You weren't out partying it up last night?"

"Ha. I just went out to dinner with friends."

Kavya was a serious student in her senior year at the University of Missouri. She was a year older than Sujata, so she was older than most of the other students. She'd suffered from major depression after graduating high school and it took years of treatment to find the right medicine to bring her out of her dark place. They were all proud of how well she'd been doing in college. She was smart. So Sujata knew she hadn't been out doing body shots.

"Yeah," Sujata said. "I went out to dinner last night, too, and ate way too much."

"Me too. I'm doing some hot yoga later."

"Everything okay? You don't sound like your chipper self."

Kavya sighed. "Maa and Baba are having a dinner and they want me to be there."

"Is that a problem?"

"Ankur will be there."

"Ah." Ankur was the guy their parents—and all the aunties, as well—wanted Kavya to marry. "But Kavya, I know you actually like him."

"It's so awkward. He's shy."

The truth was, Kavya was equally shy, which was one reason everyone thought they'd be so perfect together. Nobody knew where her height came from—she was five-eleven—and there was concern that it would be hard to find a match for her. But Ankur was six-two. Everyone thought it was so perfect.

Although Sujata felt bad for her having to deal with this, she was secretly glad it wasn't her. Besides, she was convinced that the two of them did actually like each other. She had a good feeling about the match. Their parents were still letting Sujata get over Rajeev. However, that grace period might be ending soon since they were actively working on Kavya now.

"Well, tell them you can't make the drive today," Sujata suggested. Kavya was in Columbia, a couple hours outside St. Louis, where their parents lived.

"I just feel bad saying no."

"Aw, *didi*, you *do* want to see him!"

"No, that's not it," Kavya said defensively.

"Then don't go."

"How's Vivek?" Kavya asked.

Sujata grimaced. “Oh, the worst thing happened last night.” She told Kavya all about Rajeev and Leela and Vivek. *Leela.*

“I’m sorry, *shona*. That sucks.” Kavya was quiet for a moment. “God, I still can’t believe he did that to you. What a prick.”

“Mm.” There went that stomach twist again.

“Kavya, go tonight. Just be careful driving home in the dark, okay? Talk to Ankur. Make out with him if you can get him alone.”

“No way! That’s not happening.” But she was laughing.

“We’ll see.” Sujata had a hunch. She couldn’t wait to see if she was right, especially since she’d been doubting her judgment of men in general since Rajeev.

~

SUNDAY, Vivek lay on his makeshift bed in his apartment with the blanket pulled up to his chin because he was cold. He asked the apartment’s Amazon Echo what time it was.

“It’s 9:15 a.m.,” it answered. He should really get up, even if none of his roommates had managed it. He threw the blanket off and the cold air immediately bit into his bare skin.

A splash of yellow on the coffee table caught his eye. Sujata’s scarf—she’d left it. She’d taken it off last night while she was in his apartment waiting for a car. His roommates cranked the heat up in the evening but turned it way down at night.

He picked the scarf up and held it to his nose, breathing in her lavender scent, which brought to mind her gorgeous golden eyes.

Okay, and her other parts. Those legs of hers were to die for. He wanted to run his hands up her legs and …

Kaṭavuḷē, he thought in exasperation. God. He needed to stop thinking about her that way. He was developing an issue that would keep him on the couch if one of his roommates came out.

He quickly dropped the scarf back to the table and fell onto the couch. At least she’d admitted that she liked him, which he’d known but hadn’t *known*. It was just that sleek ex-fiancé messing with her head.

One of the bedroom doors opened and Vivek pulled the blanket over his lap. Ishaan yawned, scratched his bum, and nodded at him before heading into the bathroom.

After things had settled down, Vivek got up and boiled some milk for his Weetabix cereal. As he sat at the kitchen table eating, his gaze wandered to the coffee table and Sujata's scarf. Last night had been awkward. And painful. He'd been terrified that he was doing the wrong thing when he touched her hand, but it ended up helping her. The immediate joy he'd felt when she called him her boyfriend was squashed just as quickly when she told him she'd never date him. He was beginning to think it was too difficult to be around her, despite the pull she had on him.

Kiran eventually emerged from his room and they all got ready. They'd planned to play cricket in the park that morning.

"Nice whites, Ishaan," Kiran said drily. Ishaan often wore his cricket whites when they played, even though no one else did.

Ishaan smiled and said, "Thanks," even though he had to know Kiran was teasing. He came into the kitchen and grabbed a couple of pavs, bread rolls they'd made yesterday. "Ready?"

A minute later, they piled into Kiran's car and headed over.

"Nice goggles," Vivek said when Kiran put on his expensive new Ray-Bans. Kiran just grinned in response.

When they arrived, their other friends were already there and had the two wickets pushed into the ground.

Everyone said hello, then three guys came over to join Vivek and his roommates, making six per side. It was decided that Vivek's side would bat first.

Kiran and one of the other guys went out to bat.

"When is your wedding, Ishaan?" the other one asked.

"March fourteenth."

"Wow, one month. Are you ready?"

Ishaan nodded and they watched the bowler deliver the ball to Kiran. Kiran swung and missed, and the ball struck the wicket's stumps, sending the bails—the pieces that sat on top of the stumps—flying.

"Diamond duck!" one of the opponents called while the others doubled over from laughter.

"Wow," one of the guys muttered with palpable disgust. "I have literally never seen that happen before." It was blessedly rare for the first batsman to be out on the first bowl in the first innings. The friend ran to take Kiran's place.

By the time he got back, Kiran was blushing fiercely and the other team had the wicket set back up amidst continuing chuckles.

The bowler delivered the ball to the other batsman several times with no action—no hits, no outs.

Vivek's mind stayed half focused on the game while the other half replayed last night. Holding Sujata's hand had felt so good. If only she wasn't so stubborn. Maybe dating someone would actually help her heal.

It was just fear. How was he supposed to counter that? Maybe by just being the best guy.

But she'd been very clear where she stood. He really did need to accept things and move on.

Finally, the batsman connected with the ball and Vivek snapped into action, with him and his roommate running to switch places, making it just in time before the fielder hit the wicket. He was glad to be out here. Even though it was chilly, he always found this game invigorating. His team scored twenty-two runs before it was Vivek's turn to run into the crease.

He got into his stance with his bat guarding the wicket and swung at the first delivery, missing. Fortunately, the ball didn't knock the bails off. He swung again at the next one.

Crack. The ball went flying off and Vivek and the other batsman ran, but in the end it rolled out of the group's makeshift boundary, meaning an automatic four runs.

There was more of the back and forth, and although he tried to stay focused, his mind kept going back to Sujata. He needed to do something in order to figure out if he should stay here or take the Atlanta job. He couldn't put it off forever.

Vivek was bowled out after scoring twenty-one runs and ended up in the field. Sometimes he bowled, but not today, which was good because he was still having trouble staying focused on the game. Last night, and the scarf waiting at home for him, were on his mind. How could a woman smell so nice that it made his heart ache?

The game continued for another couple of hours, and then they headed back to the apartment.

As soon as his roommates were back in their rooms, Vivek picked the scarf up again and greedily inhaled the lavender.

A wondrous thought struck him. Had she left it here on purpose? He'd have another reason to talk to her.

No. He knew it wasn't on purpose. She was obviously rattled last night.

He'd have to return the scarf tomorrow. But no more smelling the scent. He needed to forget about Sujata. Maybe he should start looking on dating sites. He'd still rather find someone on his own than go with his parents' pick.

He'd look tomorrow night.

3

Sujata was due for a break. She'd spent all Monday morning and lunch hour working on getting this tricky program running and finally had it done. Now she wanted a breather and to catch up with Gwen. She didn't want to tell her about Rajeev, but maybe she should. It might be good to get it out there and not replay it endlessly in her mind. She locked her screen and headed over toward Gwen's desk, taking the short route, which meant she would pass Vivek's desk. She needed to say something nice to Vivek because she still felt awkward about Saturday night.

Her nerves were electric as she approached his desk and she couldn't help slowing down. She had to say something, but what?

He glanced up and spotted her. Now she had no choice. But there was also this small part of her that was looking forward to talking to him. Her feelings were the poster child for ambivalence.

She stopped at his cube. "Hi." There, that was a good start.

"Hi." He reached over and held up her yellow scarf from Saturday night. "You left this at my apartment."

"Oh," she said, genuinely surprised.

He'd been so nice that night. And like usual, he'd invited her in to wait for her Lyft and even offered her a glass of water, though she'd declined.

Sujata'd had no idea the scarf was missing. She stepped toward him to take it. Their hands touched for a second and the guilt coursed through her like fire, straight to her heart, and turned into something else. Something unwelcome and not work appropriate.

She had to put a stop to this. She wasn't going to date him, despite the fact that she wanted to. She was going to have to stop going out with the group, even if she'd miss the movies.

It was for the best. For both of them.

He was looking at her, a bemused expression on his face since they'd just been watching each other while her brain went off on its tangent.

"Well, thanks for bringing the scarf." She shouldn't tell him now that she was going to stop going out with them. How was she going to do that?

"Sure."

"So how was the rest of your weekend?" she asked.

"Good. We played cricket." He smiled, apparently remembering something. Something related to the cricket he'd played, she guessed.

"What?" She shouldn't engage, but she wanted to know.

"Diamond duck." He was trying not to laugh, but failing so bad that his whole body was shaking. "Kiran."

"Ha! Seriously? Poor guy. He must be so embarrassed."

Vivek nodded and tried to recover, finally straightening his mouth.

"Okay, with that image in my head, I will carry on. Talk to you later, okay?"

Crap, why had she said it like that, all encouraging? Maybe he hadn't taken it that way.

"See you." He sounded pretty neutral and looked at his screen as she stepped away.

As she approached Gwen's desk, right across from David's office, she heard her on the phone. But Gwen saw her and motioned for her to stay. So Sujata propped her arms up on the cube wall and waited.

"I'll let him know," Gwen finished and hung up.

"Do you need to do something?" Sujata asked.

"No, not right this second. How was your weekend?"

Sujata groaned, suddenly unwilling to relive it all. Gwen's weekend was surely better than hers. "Let's not talk about that. How was yours?"

"Why? What happened? Did you do something with your *friend*?" She waggled her eyebrows.

"No, no, nothing like that." Sujata looked away, out one of the windows, experiencing the horror of the moment when she heard her name after the movie. "I saw Rajeev."

"Oh, no. That's not good. Was it bad?" Gwen only knew just enough about him to come to this conclusion.

"Pretty much. I made a total fool of myself." Sujata closed her eyes to try to focus on now and not fully relive the feelings of that night.

"I'm sorry." Gwen's voice was low and sympathetic.

Her attempt to forget him wasn't working. Needing some extra support, she opened her eyes and rested her arms on Gwen's cube wall again.

"What's that?" Gwen asked, pointing at the scarf.

"Oh, I left this at Vivek's Saturday."

Gwen arched her eyebrows.

"It's no big deal. I was waiting for my Lyft."

"Okay." Gwen's face turned serious again. "Do you want to talk about Rajeev?"

"Not right now." Right now she wanted to die all over again. Time to change the subject. "Next time we go out. But you'll have to tell me about your dates."

"Oh, there's lots to tell, but let's save that, too. It's NSFW."

Sujata laughed. "You're an inspiration."

"Let's do dinner and we can share all our sordid details." Gwen waggled her eyebrows again.

Sujata cocked an eyebrow. "Maybe not *all* the details from you, but a summary."

Gwen smiled. "Such a prude."

"I'm not! I just like it to mean something. That's different." Sujata had only slept with one man in her whole life, and it had now been a year, so she did feel she was due. But she still couldn't imagine sleeping with someone she hardly knew. It was a very personal thing. She'd never bought into the "just sex" mindset.

"If you say so," Gwen said with a smirk. "When do you want to go? Actually, I have a lot going on this week. I've got class today, an early evening study group tomorrow, yoga Thursday, and I'm seeing my architect again on Friday." She grinned saucily. "Your dance class is tomorrow, right?"

"Yes. What about Wednesday next week?"

"Yeah. Let's go to Ava Gene's. Six o'clock?"

"Mmm, that sounds perfect." An expensive but delectable Italian place. "You'll call for a reservation?"

"Sure." Gwen wrote on a green sticky note and stuck it to the side of her monitor. "So, anything from David?"

Sujata shook her head. "Nothing yet. It hasn't even been a week since I turned the proposal in. I don't know when he was going to see Krishna next. Wasn't he out last week?"

"Yeah. But everybody's back in the office this week."

"Okay. Hopefully he'll really talk to him about it."

"He will. He's a guy with follow-through."

"Okay." Sujata wasn't entirely sure about that, and glanced back at his door, which was currently open. When she turned back to Gwen, she was also looking, an odd expression on her face. If Gwen were capable of being wistful, that's what Sujata would have called it. But it was likely something else.

Gwen smiled at her and said, "Well, I'd better get back to it. Got to call boss number two." Gwen managed the whole office and regarded all the executives and managers as her sort-of bosses, even though she reported to the CEO directly.

"Okay. I'll talk to you later." Sujata headed back toward her desk, pulse quickening as she approached Vivek's desk again.

Someone was talking to him and it sounded like it was work-related. So she just gave him a friendly wave as she passed, relief flooding her.

Even though it was going to be hard, she did need to shut this down. For both of their sakes. He needed to be able to move on, and she needed to stop trying to undermine her own feelings.

~

When Vivek arrived at work Tuesday morning, Sujata's chair was empty. He spotted the yellow scarf bunched up against her cube wall next to her phone. He wanted to take it and smell it again. He stopped, about to reach for it when his rational brain finally kicked into gear and he stepped back and forced himself to keep going toward his own desk.

He knew logically that this would pass. He knew he would eventually find someone else and get married. But he'd spent an hour last night perusing a dating sight, and after he noticed that he only clicked on women who looked like Sujata, he gave up. He wasn't ready.

There was always his parents' option if he couldn't find someone on his own. But he couldn't picture anyone but Sujata in his future. How could he feel this with such certainty when she was so opposed to it?

Vivek pulled his chair out and sat at his undecorated desk. He was jealous of the men who had pictures of their wives or kids. Not that he was ready for kids, but he wouldn't mind being married.

Despite his boring desk, one nice thing about InfoQuest was that they hadn't gone with the truly open plan like a lot of tech start-ups, with everyone at shared tables. Instead, there were pods with white fabric-covered dividers that held a desk in each of the four corners, although they tried to keep them to three people max. It never got too busy in his pod because both his neighbors were introverts.

He unlocked his computer and tried to begin the day's programming. Nothing too challenging today, just some new database functionality.

But his mind kept going to the yellow scarf on Sujata's desk and the woman herself, so frazzled by her ex.

This wasn't working. It was time for tea. He grabbed his mug and water bottle.

As he neared the kitchen, he heard Sujata's voice, which instantly made his heart happy. She wasn't being loud, but his ears were especially attuned to her.

"... when we were at the movie," she was saying. "It was a disaster. I pretended I was with you-know-who, the poor guy."

Vivek rounded the corner just as she said the last bit, that little happiness gone. He couldn't tolerate being pitied.

"Oh, hi," she said, her eyes wide as she finished filling her mug with hot water.

Theresa, one of Sujata's good friends, smiled at him but avoided eye contact as she breezed off, a slightly guilty look on her face.

"Hi." Vivek headed to the water dispenser and began filling his mug with hot water. "You really don't need to pity me, you know."

She put her hand to her forehead. "I'm sorry. I don't pity you. I just feel so bad about that. It just felt like I used you."

He returned to the counter and got a tea bag out.

He still wanted to say something empathetic about how he understood her now, since meeting Rajeev. But he didn't quite have the words formulated when his roommate Kiran walked in from the other side of the kitchen.

"Vivek. Sujata."

Vivek sighed inside. Of course Kiran would have to appear right at this moment. Vivek nodded at him and dropped the tea bag into his mug before swirling it.

Sujata smiled at Kiran. "Morning, diamond duck."

"Oh, you told her?" He laughed, apparently unfazed. "Not my best moment."

Vivek was smiling, but his earlier mirth was gone.

"*Gangs of Wasseypur*'s on this weekend if you want to see it," Kiran said, blatantly changing the subject. Maybe he wasn't as unfazed as he seemed.

Vivek nodded. "Sounds great. Are you in, Sujata?" He did wonder how it would be, now that he knew she'd never give him a chance. They'd only ever be friends.

"Oh, uh, no. I won't be able to go this weekend." She wasn't looking at him. It was obvious that she was totally lying. She got the half-and-half out of the fridge and set it next to the mug.

This made him sad, even though it was probably for the best. Maybe it would be hard for him to keep seeing her socially when nothing would ever happen.

Kiran finished filling his mug and left and Vivek found himself still standing there looking at Sujata. He should say something.

"So Sujata, is that true for all future weekends, or just this weekend?" he asked, dreading the answer. To busy himself, he went back to the water dispenser and filled his bottle.

She looked at him, her beautiful eyes regretful. "I thought about it a lot over the weekend. I think it's best if we don't hang out. I think it's hard on both of us."

"Yeah, you are probably right. It's okay." It so was not okay. He checked the bottle—halfway full. He'd just have to get on with his life. "I've obviously been hoping you'd change your mind, but I need to stop delaying things. InfoQuest won't sponsor me for an H-1B, and my current visa expires soon, so I have to figure out what to do. I've been needing to look for a new job for a while." He still didn't think he wanted the Atlanta job. But he knew he should take it at this point.

Her brow furrowed. "They won't sponsor you? Why not?"

Of course she ignored the most important part of what he'd just said. "Apparently they only do five a year, and they've hit the cap for this year. I don't think it's personal."

"That sucks. InfoQuest seems to be a good fit for you." She took a sip of her tea. "What are you going to do?"

"I have some ideas. I'll figure it out." He put the lid on the water bottle. His options were basically the Atlanta job, or getting himself together and doing a mad scramble on the job boards.

"Okay. Good luck finding things. I hope you don't have to go back to India." She cocked her head. "Unless you want to, of course."

"I'm not planning to go back." He picked up his mug off the counter. "I have one definite option to stay in the U.S., even though I don't love it. But I'd better get back to my desk."

"Yeah, same here."

They started walking towards their desks, not saying anything. It felt like something was really over this time. She had officially pulled back, and he could no longer pretend he had a chance. It didn't matter that she clearly did want him. He'd always wondered why she wasn't willing to try. It was that jerk's fault.

They got to her desk. "See ya," she said as she veered off for her chair.

Vivek nodded and continued on.

Maybe he should convince the guys to go out to a bar and find himself a—what did they call it? A hook-up. It wouldn't be their typical evening out, but that didn't mean they wouldn't be up for something new. Get Sujata out of his system with some casual sex, the official American way.

But somehow he didn't think that would make him forget a one-of-a-kind woman like Sujata.

4

Around lunchtime, Sujata got up from her desk and stretched her arms behind her back later on Tuesday. She was hungry and planned to eat at her desk and work, which is what she usually did. She had leftovers in the fridge.

She pushed her chic white chair under her matching white desk and stepped into the aisle. InfoQuest was proud of being a successful start-up and flaunted its sensibilities with modern decor. It looked like they'd furnished the place straight out of an Ikea catalog, but Sujata suspected they'd spent way more money than that.

As she approached the kitchen, she could hear the sound of many voices speaking Hindi. Most of the Indians at InfoQuest ate lunch together—it was very much a "We meet at noon" kind of affair. Usually she went earlier to avoid the microwave line, but she was running late today. There were a couple of tables and chairs on the other side of the kitchen, which was quite small, and they were full of Indians.

She was leaning against the side of the fridge, waiting for her food to heat up, when Sanjay, the Apollo project manager, came in, still laughing at something someone had just said.

"Oh, hi, Sujata. How are you?"

"Good." She stepped aside for him so he could open the refrigerator. The sucking sound the door made and the hum of the fridge competed with the microwave noise. "What'd you bring?" She would not think about how much he looked like her ex. At least not again, after that one stupid thought.

"Just some leftover pizza. My kids are into all-American food at the moment." He shrugged and got a plate out of the cabinet and put two slices of pizza in the other microwave.

"I adore pizza."

"It's not bad." He filled his metal bottle up from the water dispenser.

"How are your kids, besides liking American food?" Sujata wondered if she and Rajeev would have had a baby yet if he hadn't left her. Well, not yet, because they would have barely been married a few months by now.

She had to get her mind off this, so she let Sanjay chat about his kids, a star soccer player and a boy obsessed with spelling bees.

"Continuing in the tradition of the Indian takeover of the Scripps Spelling Bee. I love it." Sujata wondered if her and Rajeev's hypothetical kid would have been more sporty or nerdy.

"Exactly. He wants to do it, and we figure there's no harm."

Her mind had a mind of its own, apparently, because now she was wondering what the kids would look like if she and Vivek got together.

Not gonna happen. Get back to the present.

Her microwave dinged so she pulled her dish out and started to head out the door.

"You should eat with us," he said. "Everyone's there."

Sujata stopped. "Oh, I'm not sure. I have a lot to do."

"Come on, you need to take a break."

She never ate with them and that was probably a bit antisocial. "Okay, sure."

"Great."

They both looked at the second microwave. There were eighteen seconds remaining so she set her dish back on the counter.

After his food finished heating, she followed him around the corner of the kitchen to the table—actually two tables pushed together to accommodate the six of them already there. The only two seats left were at the end of the table, one right next to Vivek. Of course.

The man in question looked up and spotted her just as Sanjay sat down diagonally across from him. Vivek's eyes went wide for a second but he gave her his typical smile as she slid into the chair next to him, white like everything else at InfoQuest.

"Hello," he said.

Sanjay had already gotten himself involved in the conversation. Something about the board games they occasionally played in one of the meeting rooms after work. She knew Vivek sometimes joined them, but he obviously felt obligated to talk to her.

"How's your work going today?" she asked.

"Good." He turned back to his food.

She guessed he was annoyed with her.

She wished he didn't have those gorgeous deep brown eyes because they always made her woozy. Listening to a man like Sanjay who clearly enjoyed his family always made her wistful, and having Vivek in front of her was difficult. All the might-have-beens.

It didn't help that they were sitting close enough that she could smell Vivek right now, too, a slightly musky aroma mixed with soap.

Stop that. She'd already told him no. That was that.

She turned toward her still-steaming dish and took a bite of cauliflower.

She breathed in the turmeric. It was still good, though not as good as it had been last night. She glanced over at Vivek's dish. "What did you bring?"

"Pardon?" he said.

She could see out of the corner of her eye that his brow was furrowed. "For lunch."

"Oh. We made chole."

She knew that he and his roommates all cooked together.

They ate in silence for a moment and she couldn't help but notice that even this felt comfortable with him, although it should be awkward.

Had she made a mistake?

No. And soon he was going to be out of her life forever soon.

She wasn't sure how she felt about that, even though she knew it was for the best.

~

VIVEK STOOD in the work kitchen, washing his dish out Friday after lunch, pondering what was happening over the weekend—what picture they were seeing, and the woman who wouldn't be there with them this time—when the woman on his mind walked in with her own plastic container.

"We meet again," Sujata said, leaning against the counter behind him to wait.

"Hi." He scrubbed to get all the oil out, even though it wasn't strictly necessary and concentrated on not thinking about how distressing it was that he wouldn't see her outside of work anymore. And soon, not at all.

David breezed in. "Oof. Traffic jam."

For once, Vivek was glad for the interruption.

Sujata laughed as he came over to dump a cup of water into the sink. "David, have you had a chance to talk to Krishna yet?"

"About?"

"My proposal." She sounded disappointed, but Vivek just stared at his dish as he rinsed it out. He shook his dish dry and turned to see David look at her without saying anything.

Sujata clarified, "Data quality."

"Oh, right. Yes. I meant to talk to you. If you want to put together a presentation on a prototype, he's willing to look at it."

"Okay, great." She sounded happier.

"Oh, I know!" David suddenly said. "Why don't you two work on it together? You'd make a great team."

Vivek stepped back from the sink and turned to look at David, whose eyes were wide with excitement. Sujata looked surprised as she moved to the sink.

"Yes, it's perfect. It will be easier for two than just you alone, Sujata?"

She smiled but it didn't reach her eyes. "Great. Sure. Sounds good."

"Excellent. Let me know when you're ready. Then if there's a true project that comes out of it, you can continue working on it."

After he'd left, Vivek asked, "What's he talking about?"

He wasn't going to kid himself—he was excited to be working with her, even though he shouldn't be. This could be awkward.

Without turning around, she explained that she'd had this idea about a data quality initiative she thought the company should work toward. She thought it would be taking on an entirely new market.

She finished washing her dish and turned around, growing more animated as she continued talking. But as soon as she made eye contact with him, her enthusiasm visibly faded.

"So do you need my help?" He wasn't sure how to take the fact that she obviously didn't want it. Was this about the project, or him personally?

"If he wants a prototype, it would go faster with two of us, I guess." She sounded like she was trying to convince herself. "David wants you involved, so I guess we should sit together and go over the presentation as a starting point. We can modify it as necessary after we create the prototype."

"Have you already finished the presentation?"

She shook her head. "No, not yet. But let me work on it and then I can run through it with you. But you should do some research on the topic first. I can send you some links to get you started."

"Okay, that sounds good."

She headed back to her desk and he fell into step with her, feeling awkward because she wasn't looking at him and was instead fiddling with her container.

When they reached her pod, he said, "Let me know when you want to go over the plan."

"Yeah, I will."

He headed back to his desk and settled in for a long afternoon.

He was looking forward to getting the links from Sujata, but in the meantime, he'd google the topic himself and see what came up.

Who knew—maybe this would help his job search.

~

"It's just terrible," Sujata said, resting her head in her arms. She'd wanted a nice Friday night out with her friends at Clement's, their favorite bar, away from all thoughts of Vivek and their now joint project, but of course now they were talking about him.

"Come on, some wine should help," Theresa said, setting a glass of red in front of her.

Sujata raised her head to watch Casey take a sip of her own wine across the table. She was glad for the relative privacy of their booth, back in the corner, with the seat backs that went almost to the ceiling.

"I think you two will do fine," Casey said. "You're both adults."

"Come on, Casey, it won't be easy," Theresa said. "You know as well as I do that she's into him." She gave Sujata a sympathetic glance.

"Okay," Casey said, swirling her wine. "But think about it. He may not want this assignment any more than you do at this stage. This kind of thing generally adds to your workload, not replaces some of it."

"She's right," Theresa said.

"I know. But it's just so frustrating—it's this huge idea I've being working up for months, and it was supposed to be mine, and now I'm going to constantly have to prove to everybody that it's not his idea. Even though I know he's not going to intentionally undermine me. You know how it is." Now she had to trust both David and Vivek, when she'd avoided letting any man have any real power over her since Rajeev had abandoned her.

Casey and Theresa nodded. The patriarchy was alive and well in corporate America.

Casey raised a finger for emphasis. "But you'll really just need to focus on the work and not what might have been if things had been different."

Sujata bumped her shoulder against Theresa's. "You two are a couple of relationship experts now." They both used to be mostly opposed to men, until they got together with their current boyfriends.

Theresa shrugged. "What can I say?"

"It just seems like the timing is so bad. I mean, we've been hanging out occasionally for a while, and then suddenly we stop and that's when they want us to work together." Sujata sighed.

Theresa faced her. "You haven't told us how he reacted."

"He was fine. He didn't seem overly excited by the prospect, but he also didn't seem as stressed about it as I felt."

"He didn't start hounding you to work on it?" Theresa asked.

"No. I sent him the links and let him do what he wanted. Casey, would you mind taking a look at the presentation before I call it done?"

"Sure, no problem." Casey shrugged. "Just let me know."

"Thanks. I'm going work some more on it this weekend."

"You've got plenty of time," Theresa said. "Oh, wait. Is there plenty of time? Did they give you a deadline?"

Sujata shook her head and swirled her wine. "No, but I want to keep it on David's mind."

"That makes sense," Casey said. "Getting forgotten is always a risk."

Theresa and Sujata both took sips of wine at the same time.

Casey lifted her glass. "But a word of advice, Sujata."

"What's that?"

"You should track all the work you both do so if they try to give him credit, you have everything documented. This was your idea, and you shouldn't let them forget it."

Sujata nodded. Casey was right. Men in the workplace. Ugh.

"How's Liam doing?" Casey asked after setting her glass back down. Liam was Theresa's eight-year-old son.

"Oh, he's great. He's doing so much better with Conall around. It's like he has a real, caring father now, which he never had before." Theresa had an ex-husband, but he was barely involved in Liam's life. The boy had really struggled with a lot of things, including reading, before Conall got involved.

"Have you gotten used to the dog yet?" Sujata asked.

Theresa shook her head. "I like her, but Conall and Liam are in love with her. But she makes such a mess. We have to vacuum every day to keep up with the fur evacuation."

Sujata laughed. "Yeah, I never got that desire to have a pet."

"Dogs I don't get either, but cats are awesome," Casey said. "So irreverent." She had a cat, of course. She started sliding out of the booth. "I'm going for one more glass. Anyone want another?"

"I'll come with you," Theresa said as she stood.

Sujata looked at them. "Another Malbec, please."

"No problem." Theresa followed Casey toward the bar.

Sujata leaned against the side of the booth and brooded. She was going to have to spend time with Vivek, and also try to retain full ownership of her project.

But they were right, really. She could handle this.

Of course, Theresa was right about the other thing, too. The attraction was so distracting. He'd always had a pull on her. Now that they would be working closely, it was going to be that much harder to be around him.

5

Vivek woke with his alarm early Saturday morning for his weekly five a.m. phone call to his parents in Hosur. He hoped that his nieces and nephews would also be around, but they were frequently out playing. His sister Mishti would be busy cooking with his mother and they would take shifts talking to him.

He unplugged his phone from the charger and sat up on the couch that served as his bed. Three guys, a two-bedroom apartment, and he'd drawn the short straw. But his couch assignment was about to end with one of his roommates getting married soon. He'd get the bedroom and they'd find another single Indian guy to take his spot on the couch. There were always guys looking for a place. This was pretty much what all Indian guys did when they came over for grad school. Nobody wanted to waste money paying for an apartment all by themselves.

Vivek threw his blanket to the side and fetched a t-shirt from his suitcase.

The bite of the cold air raised goosebumps on his arms and legs, so he raced back to the couch and threw the blanket around his shoulders. Then he clicked on the number in WhatsApp.

His nine-year-old nephew's face appeared on the computer

screen and his eyes lit up. "Vivek *mama*!" he called, using a term of respect.

"Mohan-*pā*, hi there," he said in Tamil.

"You're late!"

"Only a couple minutes. What have you been up to this week?"

Mohan chattered on about the football he'd played earlier that day and about maths, which he excelled at.

"Good boy. You keep studying hard."

"I will! I want to go to IIT, just like you!"

"It's a lot of work, but I know you will," Vivek said. "Let me talk to Ammaachi."

A crashing sound rattled Vivek's ear—Mohan had dropped the phone on the table—and soon his mother was on the screen.

"Hi, Amma," he said.

"Vivek! Are you eating well? You look thin."

"Yes, Amma, I'm eating fine. We all know how to cook now." This tiresome topic. Like he was at risk of starving. He hadn't told her his bed was a couch, though.

"Are you still saving money?"

"Yes."

"Getting ready for your wife?"

"No, I've told you. Not her." They were on his case to marry a local woman they liked. They didn't know he had other ideas. Of course, he'd never told them about either of the two women he'd dated. Such matters just weren't discussed.

"Vivek, she is perfect for you."

No, Sujata was perfect for him. He couldn't imagine any woman willing to marry a stranger being perfect for him. He wanted a woman with some fire in her.

He'd learned that with his second girlfriend. She'd been so meek that when her aunt got sick with cancer, her family decided his girlfriend would have to drop out of college to be her caretaker. She didn't even try to fight it, even though the family had enough money to hire their own caretaker. She left and moved back to Tamil Nadu, leaving him heartbroken.

He'd been in love with her and thought the feeling was mutual, but her sense of duty to her family surpassed the importance of their relationship. Realistically, he knew many women would have done the same, but that didn't make it hurt any less.

"Vivek!"

He snapped to. "Sorry, Amma. What were you saying?"

"I said you can bring her to America and she will make a wonderful wife for you. She has served us several meals on our visits over there. She went to college and has very good skin."

Very good skin? What—was she otherwise hideous?

Okay, unlikely. They would want beautiful grandchildren. Still, they wouldn't rest until they'd matched him with a perfectly nice Tamil girl. Not a Bengali.

"When are you going to take Nirish's job?" Amma asked.

This again. Every time. "I want to finish these projects at work. I don't want to just abandon them."

But he had finally started applying to local jobs. He'd sent off five applications this week.

His *amma* was especially enthusiastic about the situation because Nirish was her brother and she'd always thought he hung the moon. Vivek found him overbearing.

"Don't let this opportunity pass, *wā-pā*. You can stay in America. You are a smart boy."

"I won't." He looked at the ceiling, not liking lying. The truth was, there was a time limit on the offer. Nirish said he needed to start by mid-April or he'd have to hire somebody else, because they had a big project coming up.

Vivek probably would end up taking the job, which he really didn't want to think about.

Thankfully, Amma moved on to neighborhood gossip. One of his old classmates had gotten married—wasn't he such a good boy, even if it wasn't wedding season. The neighbor's fourteen-year-old daughter was getting more awkward as time went on—you should see her in her braces. But the most exciting news to her was that

Mishti's husband got another promotion at the bank and was really on his way up.

Vivek had never liked his sister's husband. He was a jerk to her and had ruined her chances to have a career. But Vivek had to pretend for his mother.

"That's great, Amma."

"What's the news there?" she asked.

"Kiran bought a new car a few weeks ago. A BMW."

"Oh! Good boy. I always knew he was smart."

Actually, she'd never met his roommate. He filled her in on the rest of his roommates' goings-on.

"When are you going to come for a visit?" she asked.

A visit? More like a bride-meet with Miss Very Good Skin. "I don't know, Amma. I'm very busy here."

"Let me get your father," she said. Soon his *appa* was on the screen, waving at him.

"*Wā-pā*, how are you?"

"Good, Appa."

"When are you going to visit us to meet your bride?"

Not him, too. "I told Amma that they're keeping me really busy here. I don't think I can come any time soon." Not a chance. He wasn't going to meet this woman. And if somehow they tricked him into it, he certainly wasn't going to marry her. He believed in love matches.

~

On the bus ride to her Saturday afternoon dance class, Sujata pondered buying a car. It was something she thought of periodically, but she rejected it the way she always did: the pros did not outweigh the cons—namely, the cost of owning one. Right now she had three thousand going into her retirement and savings each month, which made her feel very adult. More than owning a car would.

Once she had kids, it would be another story.

Not that that was happening any time soon. Hard to get pregnant when you never had sex.

She glanced around for couples, ready to feel jealous, but today there were just solo riders. Most had their headphones on and were in their own worlds.

Why was she in such a mood? She should be looking forward to this class. She loved dancing, after all. And they were working on a new choreography for the performance next month. She should also consider working privately with Nilani, her instructor. There were open spots on Wednesday and Friday evenings.

She got off the bus and walked the block to the studio. It wasn't very impressive from the outside, as it was basically in a strip mall next to a Subway. But once she got inside through the black-framed glass door, she felt happy again. Nilani kept the heat up, a welcome contrast to the cool February temperatures.

Sujata headed back to the changing area, where she could hear chatter in both English and Tamil. The style of dance she did was Bharatanatyam, which originated in the south of India. Specifically, it was believed to have originated in Tamil Nadu, which also happened to be where Vivek was from, by unfortunate chance. Bharatanatyam was an old form. It was a little unusual that Sujata practiced it, given that her family was from Bengal, but her grandmother had been a dancer and taught her when she was young. Sujata missed her so much. Dance was what had tied them together.

"Sujata, hi!" Kaarikaa said. Paree waved. While they and the rest of the students finished changing, the two of them caught Sujata up on their family drama. Paree's sister was going to be marrying Kaarikaa's brother, which still had them both in shock, despite the fact that the arrangement was three months old. The wedding was scheduled for May.

Music burst from the sound system as they headed into the studio and did some very basic warm-up movements, even though the practice itself include warm-ups. The music went off and back on while Nilani tried to get the volume right.

The three of them took their traditional positions mixed in with the four others in the class. Nilani started the music and had them begin with the *namaskar*, when they all bowed down in respect. They also went through all the hand and foot movements that made up the series, starting with hand gestures with their arms spread wide, and then combining them in front of their chests for additional gestures.

Out of nowhere, she wondered if Vivek would like seeing her dance.

Who was she kidding—of course he would.

The bad thing was that she liked the idea of him watching her dance, too.

Next, they started on the first *adavu*—or step—of exercises focusing on *nritta*, or the rhythmic element of the form. This one was called *tatta* and had seven distinct movement sequences, starting with bending the knees with the toes pointed out and slapping the floor with the feet four times, then repeating it while moving the outstretched hands from a vertical to a horizontal position.

With each slap, Sujata felt the tension of the week drain out of her. She imagined each one chipping away at the most annoying event—David assigning Vivek to her project.

They moved through the other *adavus*. Bharatanatyam was a very precise dance form and Sujata had to move her arms and legs into specific positions for each *adavu*, which took a lot of concentration and freed her mind from other annoying thoughts and obsessions.

So she got into a spot of trouble when her mind wandered back to Vivek and whether or not she should invite him to the performance.

"Sujata!" Nilani snapped.

Sujata started and looked over at Paree to get caught up on where they were.

"Pay attention! We only have a month and a half before the performance!"

Sujata gritted her teeth and focused. Nilani had very little patience.

After all the preliminary work, they moved on to practicing the new choreography. For the first part, Nilani had prepared an interpretation of one of the books of the Mahabharata, a classic saga in Hinduism. The Stri Parva book was the story of the grief of women due to the great war the rest of the saga focuses on. People still loved to watch portrayals of it.

They made it through another hour of practice before cooling down and breaking. Sweat was dripping off Sujata's face and arms. This was when she didn't appreciate the warmth of the studio. They chatted about work as they toweled off in the changing area. Sujata slipped back into her jeans, t-shirt, and puffer jacket and said her goodbyes.

Now she was going to go home and work on the presentation she'd started yesterday. And try not to think about Vivek, despite the fact that the near future was going to feature him prominently.

~

SATURDAY EVENING, Vivek sat in the dark theater with all his friends. The picture was funny but it wasn't holding his interest because he couldn't get his mind off Sujata and how they'd been here together just a week ago. He'd held her hand here. Something he'd wanted to do since the day he'd met her. But it hadn't been real.

He blinked slowly, remembering what it had felt like.

So comfortable. Like everything was right in the world. Like he was home.

He tried to pay attention to the picture, a crime black comedy about the coal mafia. It was funny, but the most notable thing about it —and what kept bringing him out of his reverie—was the profanity, which was rare in a Hindi picture, since the censors usually wouldn't approve such language.

It also didn't help that one of the actresses in the picture reminded him of Sujata They shared some features, like Sujata's delicate nose. Not that the actress held a candle to Sujata.

Of course, none of the many women he saw in his daily life did. But Sujata truly was so beautiful that she could be a picture star herself.

On the drive here, they'd talked more about Ishaan's upcoming wedding. Vivek was jealous. Ishaan was marrying a woman he'd known and liked growing up. They'd been corresponding for a while, and she was excited to move to the West Coast. He'd shown them all recent pictures of her and she was gorgeous. She was smart, too, with a Master's in computer science from Johns Hopkins University. She'd fit right in once she moved out here, and have no problem at all getting a job.

This reminded Vivek of the other thing that was occupying his brain space, and that was who the woman his parents wanted him to marry actually was—a bit of a bombshell. Today morning's conversation started off with them still going on about the Atlanta job. They didn't understand why he hadn't already told his uncle he would take it, considering his visa situation.

But then his mom had casually mentioned the last name of the woman they were trying to get him to marry. Up to then, he'd only known her first name—Adya. But now he had her last name, and he'd realized that this was a girl they'd all had crushes on in school. She was nice and outgoing, but she'd had bad acne as a teen and the interest in her had waned. Her acne had cleared up before they graduated. Realistically, she could be beautiful now. Perhaps that was the reason for the "good skin" thing.

But she was not Sujata. How could they not understand? He wasn't even considering marrying Adya, while they seemed to think it was inevitable.

Maybe if he had no luck in the next couple years, maybe then he'd consider an arranged marriage. It surely wouldn't be Adya by then. Even though Sujata was out of the picture now, as long as she was right here in front of him, the idea of some other woman held no appeal whatsoever.

Why did she smell so good? Like freshness itself. Like a field of lavender.

Vivek closed his eyes for a second to clear his head, and opened them to the picture again. He should concentrate on that. It was much more entertaining than thinking about what he couldn't have. He sighed, any good feelings left dripping onto the floor.

He also needed to get his act together and decide what to do about the job situation. He knew his uncle wouldn't wait forever. Basically, he had until mid- or late-March. Just over a month. He just so didn't want to move there. But if he wasn't going to take that job, he'd better get serious about applying for jobs in Portland. He'd send some more applications out tomorrow. He hadn't heard back on the others yet.

Getting something here might make his parents and uncle mad, but it was his life. He already had his friends and his apartment. If he moved to Atlanta, he would have to start all over. He'd probably be able to stay with his uncle for a bit, but then he'd have to find something else.

Vivek shifted his focus back to the movie, letting himself get taken away by the silliness. After it ended, they went back out into the chilly night and got in Kiran's car.

Everyone was quiet and of course his thoughts wandered back to Sujata. He needed to do some research on data quality to prepare for their meeting Monday morning. He wanted to be informed, beyond reading the presentation draft she'd shared Friday afternoon. Some part of him wanted to impress her so she'd change her mind, even though he knew that would never happen.

He didn't know much about data quality, but what he'd read so far had made it clear it was distinct from software quality assurance, so that department wouldn't be handling it. It generally went along with data governance, and InfoQuest didn't have a department for that. They'd have to spin up a new team for it. If he'd been able to stay, he might even have been assigned to the new team if things went well.

But that obviously wasn't happening. Not much would be happening here at all.

If he did end up landing another job in Portland, it could actually be a better situation. He should be able to land a bigger salary. But at the same time, you never knew what you were walking into in a new job. His new coworkers might be hard to get along with, or the projects might be terrible. Or they could be amazing.

The not knowing brewed up some anxiety mixed with excitement.

And any good feeling disappeared when he thought about never seeing Sujata again.

But he needed to move forward, not obsess with what might have been.

The resume would be going out again tomorrow.

6

Sujata pulled her puffy comforter up to her chin and nestled into the bed. It was way too early Monday morning, and she was desperate to get back to sleep. The clock said 3:30 a.m. Who knew what had woken her up, but now she was lying here thinking about her eleven o'clock meeting.

With Vivek.

A not insignificant part of her was looking forward to spending more time with him, but mostly she was dreading it. Why did he have to get assigned to the project with her? It was almost like the universe was conspiring to keep them together.

If it weren't for the fact that they'd never get together, it was the perfect setup for a romance novel with the forced proximity trope, one of her favorites.

She closed her eyes and adjusted the bedspread again to make herself more comfortable and then yawned. Surely she could get back to sleep. It was a simple thing to want to do.

3:42.

Vivek's face—the way he'd looked when he first saw her across the street the last time she'd met them for dinner—filled her mind.

There really was something to be said for someone wanting you. It did wonders for the ego.

She also thought about the hand-holding on account of Rajeev. At the time, she'd been too stressed to think about it. But she could still remember it now, and it still felt nice in her mind. Comfortable. How had it felt to him?

Did he lie in bed pondering her?

A smile broke out on her face at this thought, but then a sense of guilt streaked through her.

3:57.

Sujata had to do something. She threw the comforter off and felt the cool air settle on her body. She clearly wasn't going to fall back to sleep, and thinking about Vivek like that was just not acceptable.

She stretched her legs and put her bare feet on the floor. Thank God for carpet, as cold as the room was. She walked into her closet and changed into her workout clothes before pulling her hair back in a ponytail. She laced up her running shoes, grabbed her keys and phone, and headed over to the gym. Maybe she could pound out thoughts of Vivek with her feet.

Sujata put on an audiobook—a romance involving a secret baby —and started her walk. Five minutes in, she kicked it up to six and got lost in the story and the monotony of the motion.

In the book, the couple was in the good first part of the relationship, where there was lots of great sex. So she should have known her mind wouldn't stay away from the one guy she knew wanted to have sex with her. She thought about his hard-as-steel chest and toned arms. And those hands. He wasn't tall, that was for sure, but he was solid. She imagined feeling very safe in his arms. She still had a hard time picturing him working out—he was such a nerd—but he must. What would it be like with him? Somehow she guessed he'd be different from Rajeev.

Rajeev. God. Why wouldn't he stay out of her head. Normal people got over these things in a year. Almost a year. As much as she was attracted to Vivek, she'd definitively rejected him, so she had to stop thinking about him that way.

She had to do something to distract herself. She turned off the audiobook and switched to music. Some good old-fashioned EDM ought to do the trick.

Okay, any time she thought about Vivek, she would make herself think of something else. A word. But what?

Bananas.

That would do. Because that's what she was for continuing to long for him. Loony.

The low thumping in her earbuds got louder and faster and she was tempted to kick up the speed of the treadmill, but given how early it was she decided not to. No need to wear herself out completely before five a.m.

She'd be done with her run and out of the shower just after five, so she could either start work from home or go in really early. She'd done it a handful of times and it was interesting to see who was there. Several of the directors were early arrivers, and she knew Vivek was usually in before her, but not—

Bananas.

Okay, good catch. She brushed the hair that had come loose from the ponytail out of her eyes and looked at the mileage. She was at 4.2 already. She was going to stop at 4.5.

Then she'd go back and have her shower and go on into work. She could spend the extra time reading some more of the case studies she'd found before meeting with Vivek. He was probably still in bed, the lucky—

Bananas.

Argh.

AT FIVE TO ELEVEN, Vivek unplugged the monitors and closed his laptop so he could take it to the meeting with Sujata. His heart was embarrassingly fluttery in anticipation of seeing her for the first time today. He headed over to the meeting room.

She was sitting at the head of the table facing the screen and already had logged into the room's computer when he got there. The projector was warming up.

"Hi," he said.

"Hey." She didn't look up, focused on getting the presentation on the screen.

She was dressed very casually today, in jeans and a pretty loose blouse, although he would have appreciated a lower neckline.

He sat a couple seats down from her and unlocked his laptop. She looked so serious that he wanted to make her laugh. He opened up the presentation and typed "Hi Sujata" as the subtitle of the title slide.

"What the ...? Hey!" She still looked serious, but her eyes had a lightness that didn't match her mouth.

So he typed the Hindi morning greeting, "*shubh prabhaat.*"

"Stop it," she said, but at least she was looking right at him.

"You know, the corner of your mouth is up—if you do the other corner, it would be called a smile."

Finally she laughed.

Mission accomplished. Vivek grinned at her, feeling puffed up, and then deleted his greeting.

Sujata cocked her head. "I may be too intense about this proposal."

"It's important to you. There's nothing wrong with that. You're always serious about work, anyway."

"I guess that's true. So, did you have a chance to look at the presentation?" Sujata asked.

"Of course."

"Cool." She nodded and put the deck in presentation mode. "Let's just go through it slide by slide and you can tell me if you think anything needs to be added or changed. And this is obviously just a starting point. I want to add a lot more slides with details, and then if we get the go-ahead, we'll still have to develop the prototype, but this should guide us."

"Sounds good." Now she was all business, not looking at him at all. His earlier satisfaction faded. He wanted too much from her. He shifted his chair to better face the screen.

She moved to the next slide, which declared the problem: low data quality is pervasive in business. It costs businesses money, customers, job satisfaction, and more.

"I figure we start here so they have some idea what we're talking about," she said.

Vivek nodded. "Yeah. Not everyone understands how bad it usually is."

"Yeah." She clicked to the next slide and he glanced at her hand as it moved the mouse. She had slender fingers. His eyes shifted to her mouth, which was open, and she was looking at him.

"What?" she asked.

"Nothing." He quickly turned back toward the screen, pushing down the thoughts that had crept into his head when he saw her parted lips. He wanted to feel them between his own. He knew they'd be sweet like sugar.

Brain, stop. He could not continue thinking about her like that. He needed to just be a coworker and be her friend and nothing more in the remaining days they had together. Whatever number of days that was.

This slide gave a formal definition of data quality.

"Good?" she asked.

"Yes. It's a clear definition. Some of the ones I found today morning were less so."

"Okay." She glanced at him quickly.

They went through the next couple of slides, and then she finally got to the part where he had some thoughts.

"So I think we should offer data governance guidance," she said.

Vivek turned back toward her. "I think we could do more than provide guidance. We could easily create our own master data management software."

"That is the long-term plan," she said firmly, emphasizing the last words. "But to start with we'll just be developing a scaled back and simplified prototype to deal with one or two dimensions of data quality."

Maybe he'd said too much. He needed to let her drive this. "Which ones are you thinking?"

"Consistency would be the easiest because it would potentially require less input than the others. Uniqueness might make a good second."

That made sense, but he knew they could do more than two dimensions. He'd already looked into it and thought he could build a prototype without too much difficulty. "You don't think we should try to do all the dimensions on a particular simple case study?"

Sujata narrowed her eyes. "I don't disagree that it would be better to go big, but it's about timing and ensuring success. Let's not get ahead of ourselves. The more we try to do, the more we risk failing. This is supposed to be a small initiative."

She was running it, so he had to back off. Besides, he did see her point. It would be harder to convince them to spin up this initiative if it was huge. But having a bigger long-term plan would make it more appealing, especially if it was something they could grow over time. Get some early adopters and grow the product by developing features according to those customers' needs.

Sujata went to the next slide, one about the specific quality dimensions that could be measured in data

He knew he should keep his mouth shut, but he couldn't stop himself from offering some advice on rephrasing a couple of points that he thought wouldn't be clear to someone who hadn't already dug deep into the topic.

She nodded, and it made some of her hair come loose from behind her ear. He would never stop wanting to run his hand through her hair, even if they were just friends. Of course, he would never do it. And soon the daily temptation would be out of his life.

That was not a happy thought.

She updated the two relevant slides before continuing on to one about the kind of analysis InfoQuest would be able to do for the client.

"Sujata, I had another thought about this. We could do so much more for the client." He started outlining his thoughts. "And then, if we do all of that, we could—"

"Vivek." She said it with finality. "Don't get carried away. Remember this is supposed to be a fairly simple data quality initiative. I don't want to propose too much, or they won't support it."

She was right. He'd even thought about how this kind of approach was best a few minutes earlier. He blushed over his earnestness. "Okay, I will be quiet."

She smiled at him. "You're fine. Just, let's keep it simple."

He nodded and told himself to keep his mouth shut.

She went to the next slide, which talked about some of the software she did think they should develop. Nothing too extravagant, and it would build off what InfoQuest already had.

It was simple, but he had to admit to himself, not too simple. She probably was taking the right approach by creating something that was small—and relatively cheap to implement—but had a tremendous potential for growth.

Sujata went over the final two slides, the first of which summarized the level of involvement for InfoQuest and how it would vary per client. The last one listed potential clients and projected pricing and profit.

She looked over at him again. "What do you think?"

Vivek tapped his fingers on the table and said, "I think it looks good, but just one thought."

"What's that?" Her eyes narrowed.

"I think we should include a couple of detailed case studies."

She laughed. "You read my mind. I actually started doing one already. I intend this to be the foundation of the initiative."

"Would you like me to do the second one myself?"

"Yes, that would be great. But let me show you what I've got so far so we make sure they're different enough." Sujata flipped through tabs to open up another document. "Here we go."

They went through the study of a medium-sized real estate agency and identified some areas to change and others to enhance.

There was also a lot more to add, but she had a handle on it. She closed the doc.

Vivek had an idea for the second case study—he was thinking of something like a grocery chain with memberships—but he thought he'd ask her first. "Do you have thoughts on what the second one should be?"

"I was thinking retail."

He couldn't contain his grin.

"What?" she asked, a tentative smile on her face.

"I was thinking a grocery store." He loved how they were on the same page so often. One more thing he'd miss when he left InfoQuest.

That made her smile official. "Great minds and all that. Let's add some kind of membership, like a rewards program."

"I had that in mind, too."

Their gazes locked and he felt a rush of affection for her.

"Yeah, uh," she started, apparently flustered. She looked away. "We should make things at least somewhat complicated. One thing I just thought of is that we could make it a chain that's been around a while so they have lots of legacy data. Or I could do that with mine."

He wanted that. Like he wanted her. He couldn't have her, but he could do what he wanted on this project. He knew he'd enjoy working on this simply because it would give him a reason to think about Sujata, too. "We could both do it."

"True." She still wasn't looking at him. "It would be very different legacy systems we'd be dealing with, so that would be good. We should both definitely address the differences in how we would deal with the legacy systems versus their newer ones."

"Yes. That would be more realistic, since most of our biggest clients already have many different systems, some old and some new."

"Good point." She watched the screen as she shut the presentation down and unplugged the HDMI cable from her laptop.

They stood up and she looked at him again before turning to the door and heading out. He couldn't read her expression, though it might have been wistful.

That got his mind wondering why. He wasn't her boyfriend so it really wasn't his place to speculate about it, but he so did. He knew they would never be together, but his heart refused to give up entirely.

He needed to work on that.

7

Sujata arrived to her weekly Apollo meeting Monday afternoon and found Conall, her pod mate and Theresa's boyfriend, already there, so they chatted a bit. They had just moved back into their house the previous month, after repairs from a fire several months back. They'd been living in a tiny apartment, along with Theresa's eight-year-old son and a dog. But there were still lots of things to fix up.

Sanjay, the project manager, breezed in. He bore a striking resemblance to Rajeev. It drove her crazy.

He got started right away and went around the room.

"How about you, Sujata?" Sanjay asked when it was her turn.

"Things are going well." She looked at the spreadsheet he had open. "You can update tasks seventy-one, seventy-three, and seventy-four to one hundred percent. I'm about fifty percent on seventy-two."

Why did he have to look so much like Rajeev? She couldn't get past that. Being reminded of Rajeev still made her heart hurt, even though, intellectually, she knew she'd dodged a bullet.

"Vivek, what about your tasks?" Sanjay asked.

Sujata glanced at the man in question, sitting directly across from her. She'd had trouble when it was just the two of them in the meeting this morning. Now, she knew she was the only one in the room imagining how good it felt to hold his hand, even under unpleasant circumstances.

"... is complete and eighty-one is about twenty-five percent done," Vivek finished saying.

"Great." Sanjay continued around the room.

Sujata spaced out on what everyone else was saying because all she could do was think of Vivek and how much she regretted not being able to date him.

Bananas.

Sanjay started on about next stages and other project stuff, but she was only half listening. It was the data quality proposal she most wanted to work on, so she'd have to manage her time pretty well to get everything done. She couldn't let that languish. She'd made some decent progress over the weekend.

As the meeting started to break up, Sanjay said, "Oh, yeah. Vivek and Conall, we've got that meeting next week in preparation for the later meeting with InfoSec. Do you need anything from me for that?"

"I think that may take more preparation than I was originally thinking," Vivek said. "Can we prepone that meeting to some time this week?"

"Sure," Sanjay said. "I'll get something on the calendar for Thursday or Friday."

"Thanks," Vivek said. Then he called Sujata's name as she was almost at the door.

He caught up to her, looking unfairly handsome. "When do you want to meet again about DQ?"

She loved his mouth. Such nice lips.

Bananas. He was off-limits because she couldn't afford the risk. "How about Monday? I've got to spend this week on Apollo. We've got to get everything ready for QA."

He nodded. "That is what I was thinking. But I can still prepare something."

"This is going to have to be our last brainstorming meeting. We'll have to start actually generating data by next week, and the coding soon after that."

"Yes. I already had some ideas about the data generation."

"Great," she said. "Maybe you can work on that while I start coding. I think it might make the most sense for us to split it up that way anyway, to simulate the more realistic scenario of coding for unknown problems."

"Yes, I think that is a good idea." He seemed to be taking this assignment seriously.

She had a good thought. "Though we also need to make sure there are common problems represented in the data. But it would be cool if you could introduce some that I don't know about."

"I like it."

The rest of the afternoon, Sujata worked on more Apollo tasks. Tonight at home she'd start going through the last of the case studies she'd dug up for the DQ project. She intended to summarize a few more, and then they could go deep into her main one and Vivek's.

Sigh, Vivek. She both loved and hated that they were working together on this.

It remained to be seen how this was going to truly play out.

~

VIVEK WALKED into the kitchen Wednesday and immediately saw Sujata pulling her food out of the microwave. He caught her eye and she gave him a funny look that might have been a failed smile, though he wasn't entirely sure. She said, "Gotta run," as she passed him, heading out of the kitchen.

He took his own food out of the fridge, wondering what was up with her. She hadn't seemed unfriendly, just really focused on getting back to her desk.

After heating his dal, Vivek returned to his desk, glancing at Sujata when he passed her pod, but she didn't look up. He took a bite of his spicy lentils before unlocking his computer and starting to read through the code he'd written earlier.

But of course, he was still thinking about Sujata. Was everything okay with her?

Back in the real world, he closed his eyes for a moment, suddenly aware that he'd been staring at a conditional statement in the code for way too long. Maybe he should do some more reading about data quality. He'd thought he'd found a promising company to do a case study on, but he couldn't find enough info about them, so he was still searching. He had the rest of this week to work on it before his meeting with Sujata on Monday, but he wanted to do a good job. He needed to find a better case study.

Vivek scoured the web until he found one that interested him. This one was about a company that instituted a data governance project that resulted in them identifying a security breach that would never have been detected otherwise.

The idea of security pulled him in. Would Sujata like that?

What else might she like?

This errant thought made him smile. He couldn't be asking himself questions like that. He needed to keep his mind on task.

Showing that data quality could help data security would be a great argument for instituting any sort of quality plan. He made a note and kept looking for his main study.

Google and more Google. Vivek was not a fan of research. He knew the info was out there, and it frustrated him that he couldn't just find it. It was hidden from him, just like Sujata's emotional state today was.

Eventually he found a good example. After spending quite a bit of time reading some white papers from the company, he started a slide deck to focus on it, pulling out the most important points.

He might have gotten carried away with bulleted lists, but in a couple of hours, he had a decent draft that he'd be able to share with Sujata. Plus, he'd be able to work on it more tomorrow. He could also look into the data generation.

Thinking about her had Vivek back to wondering if something was wrong, given her odd expression at lunch. She had seemed off today morning, too. He'd passed her in the aisle and she hadn't even acknowledged him. He didn't get the sense that it was personal. It was more that she was that lost in thought. Had something happened in her life? He hoped she was okay.

But Vivek knew he needed to get back to his primary task, the Apollo code. He brought the code editor up again. He noticed that his code was rather spare of comments, so he decided to go back and add some to explain some of the trickier logic he'd been implementing. Commenting code seemed less likely to go wrong than actual coding, given his preoccupied mind.

Because Sujata was still in there. And the more he thought about whether she was okay, the more worried he got. Maybe he should ask her.

He worked some more on the code, but couldn't stop fretting. She was just a few pods over.

Vivek stood up and glanced over to make sure she was there. She was. One of her pod mates was gone and the other had headphones on, so the timing was perfect. As he approached her cube, uncertainty set in, but he forced himself to continue.

He stopped in front of her cube. Her face was a mask of concentration. He started to leave again, but then she looked up.

She blinked a couple times and then gave him a smile that didn't reach her eyes. Something was definitely up. "Vivek. What's up?"

"Hello. I... just wanted to make sure you were okay. You seemed distracted earlier. Is everything all right?"

She blinked again.

Was that hurt that flashed across her face?

"Yeah," she answered, recovering from whatever it had been. "Thank you. I just didn't sleep well and I'm having an off day."

"Okay, I just wanted to make sure," he said, feeling awkward and like he'd possibly crossed a line. Was it his fault she'd looked hurt?

She had a fairly neutral expression, and he knew she didn't want him here, so he said, "Talk to you later," waved awkwardly, and turned.

"Thanks for checking on me, Vivek." She sounded like she meant it, so he glanced back and gave her a quick smile before heading back to his desk.

He felt his phone vibrate and checked it to see an email response to one of his job applications. Perfect.

They wanted to schedule a screen, so he typed a quick response with his availability and then got back to work.

Sujata seemed okay enough that he needed to put her out of his mind and get to work. This code wasn't going to write itself.

But also, he wasn't going to be able to stop worrying about her. How would she be tomorrow?

Sujata had known Valentine's Day would be rough—the first one since Rajeev had left—but it was worse than she'd expected. She simply needed to get through work so she could go home and mope. Alone.

By mid-afternoon, she'd toiled away on her Apollo work enough and needed a break. As luck had it, Gwen chose that moment to stop by.

"Hey, you," Gwen said with her trademark smile. She rested her arms on Sujata's cube wall.

"I'm so glad to see you. My brain's about to explode with everything I'm doing. I need a moment of something other than code."

"Well, I speak plainly, not in code, so you're in luck."

Sujata laughed. "That you do." A thought occurred to her, a perfect diversion. "Hey, do you want to do dinner tonight?"

Gwen grimaced and then grinned. "Can't tonight. Got a hot date with my architect. It's Valentine's Day after all."

That made Sujata grimace this time, though she tried to hide it.

"What, you're not a fan?"

And failed, apparently. "No."

That was an understatement.

Gwen's eyes widened. "Oh, it's your first one since ..."

"Yes," Sujata said. "Anyway, so how's it going with your architect?" No one else was around right now, so they could talk.

Gwen laughed. "Good. I think he might be a keeper."

"That's good. But I can't imagine you with just one guy. Won't you get bored?"

"Maybe," Gwen said. "Maybe not. It's hard to say. I might be tired of the fast lifestyle."

"It does seem draining. Where are you going?"

"El Gaucho."

"Nice." An expensive steakhouse. At least somebody was getting treated well. Not that Sujata was a steak girl—she was a pescatarian, after all.

Gwen picked up Sujata's silk scarf, a paisley in rich burgundy and cream. "This is so pretty. You always have the nicest scarves."

"Yeah, I know. It's my thing. I have a gazillion."

"My favorite is your pale yellow plaid one. It looks so good on you."

"Thanks." The one Vivek had returned to her.

Bananas.

Just then, Conall and their other pod mate returned to the pod, meaning she would be mostly off the hook for anything too personal. Which was good, as she didn't want to talk about tonight and how she wasn't doing anything.

"I'm sorry I can't do dinner, sweetie." Then she whispered, "Maybe you should sign up for OkCupid tonight."

No. "I'll think about it."

"Okay. Or read one of your romances tonight. I'll talk to you later," Gwen said. She came around the side to squeeze Sujata's shoulder and she was off.

Which meant that Sujata had to get back to work. She'd had her little break.

And the rest of the afternoon dragged. She couldn't stop thinking about Rajeev.

He'd always been so sweet to her on Valentine's Day. Even though it wasn't a big deal in India, he'd embraced it. Chocolates, romantic dinners, chocolate-dipped strawberries, pink-dyed white chocolate-covered pretzels. He knew her love of chocolate well. Sometimes, he'd also bring her chocolate to make up for things he'd done that frustrated her. But she still associated it with Valentine's Day. One year he'd even personally made red velvet cupcakes for her.

How could he marry *that woman*?

Her chest ached. The destruction of her heart was complete even as her pulse sped up. She had to stop thinking about him or she might actually start crying, which would be mortifying at work.

She closed her eyes and concentrated on breathing slowly. In, out. In, out. She reminded herself that while he might have been good to her on Valentine's Day, he was bad for her a lot of the other days.

Her heart rate slowed back down and she opened her eyes to a locked computer screen. She unlocked it and stared for a moment at the colored code on a white background.

Then she glanced at the clock. 5:31. She could leave any time. She'd still have to work tonight, but at least she could be home and in her PJs.

She donned her scarf and jacket and grabbed her purse. She glanced in Vivek's direction when she stood up. The top of his head was visible, but she went straight for the front door instead. It had been sweet of him to come by. It was obvious he could tell something was wrong, but he didn't push her. He really was a great guy.

All the way to the bus, she wondered if she was wrong not to date him. Would things be different with him?

But once she was settled on the bus, her stupid mind meandered back to Rajeev.

Bastard.

Then she was tearing up.

Shit, shit, shit. Not on the freakin' bus.

The old man sitting next to her didn't seem to notice, and she managed to regain control with her breathing trick. Though taking the deep breaths let her know just how much her neighbor reeked of cigarette smoke.

Eventually, she got off at her stop and walked to her apartment.

She fell onto the couch and closed her eyes.

Leela. Sujata hated her.

She lay there for a while, seething with anger now. It was clear that she was in no state to deal with anything tonight, so she ordered pizza.

It was only after she'd hung up that she remembered the heart-shaped pizza Rajeev had had delivered to their door on their last Valentine's Day.

Oh, no. And there she went.

She cried and cried. Totally lost it, just like she had when she'd first discovered what he'd done. When she'd gotten that fucking announcement from his horrible mother.

The doorbell rang.

Shit. Oh, no. She was a total mess. She wiped her eyes and discovered they were beyond puffy. It probably looked like she had mini red balloons implanted under her eyes.

She wiped them just as the doorbell rang again.

She had no choice but to face the humiliation. Before she opened the door, she turned off the hall and kitchen light so maybe the driver wouldn't notice.

He was a young white guy, likely in college.

"Whoa," he said as he handed her the receipt to sign. "Are you okay?"

"Fine, thanks," she muttered, knowing that her flaming cheeks now matched her eyes.

She handed the signed receipt back and he got this knowing look on his face and said, "Alone on Valentine's Day, eh?"

She wanted to throw up. God, why did people say such shitty things?

"No." She took the box from him and shut the door.

The smell of cheese and tomatoes leaked out of the box as she set it down on the counter. She opened it and saw the little round sliced tomatoes scattered on top.

Red, of course.

And one of them had been sliced right down the middle by the pizza cutter, pushing the top of the tomato in and the bottom out so it looked like a heart from this angle.

Un-fucking-believable. Sujata couldn't handle this tonight.

She dumped the pizza into the trash, box and all, scrunching it up so it would fit, sauce and grease oozing out.

Then she went back to the couch and opened her computer up to finish what she needed to do for today. Her eyes burned so it was hard to review the code she'd written that afternoon. She was working through it.

But the pizza. She knew it was there.

After another few minutes of obsessing about it, imagining she could still smell the tomatoes, she tossed the computer to the other side of the couch and pulled the trash bag out to tie it off. She slid her shoes back on and took the bag out to the dumpster.

On her way back up the stairs, the middle-aged man who lived in the downstairs unit nodded at her. "How's it going?"

Sujata smiled big—a painful effort—and said, "Great. You?"

He stopped as she passed. "Are you sure? You don't look so great."

This was even more mortifying than the pizza guy. Her neighbor sounded genuinely concerned.

"I'm fine. Have a good night." She raced up the stairs double speed.

As she shut the door, she hoped she hadn't sounded too rude. Then she teared up again. This was worse than she'd expected.

She was not going to follow Gwen's advice and read a novel. Instead she went into the living room, got her yoga mat out, and started going through her favorite asanas. She'd just go to bed after this, and when she woke up, it would no longer be Valentine's Day.

She needed that to happen.

8

"Will you grab the *dal*?" Kiran asked. It was Friday and Vivek and his roommates were shopping. He headed down the aisle with the bags of lentils. He picked up a couple of two pound bags—enough to last them a few weeks—and carried them back to the cart, glancing at the art for sale on the other side of the aisle. Lots of ornate gods and goddesses.

Shopping was still odd for him, despite the fact that he'd been shopping with roommates since he first moved to the U.S. He'd never even been inside a grocery store before coming here. Luckily, he'd moved into an apartment with some older grad students so they knew what to do, or he might have starved.

Ishaan came from another aisle with a giant bag of rice, the other thing they went through really fast. They did sometimes do naan instead of rice, but they generally preferred rice.

"Less than a month left, Ishaan," Kiran said.

Ishaan smiled. He was looking forward to his wedding. Vivek knew he hadn't even seen the bride in months, so he was probably really looking forward to getting the beautiful woman into a bed somewhere. Vivek knew he would be if Sujata was his bride.

Sujata hadn't quite been herself since Wednesday. She'd said she was fine so there was nothing he could do, but it still bothered him.

Ishaan blushed and laughed at something Kiran said, but Vivek had missed it. He followed them down the next aisle, which had a variety of canned goods, oils, and ghee on one side and spices—*garam masala*, cumin, coriander, black pepper—on the other. He grabbed the bag of red chilli he knew they needed.

Maybe Sujata had just been annoyed at him for being brought onto her project, but he thought there was more to it than that.

Kiran was still teasing Ishaan. Vivek breathed in the coriander, turmeric, and cumin that permeated the air in the aisle.

He didn't like to think about it, but he was still jealous of Ishaan. Maybe he should just go back home and meet his parents' pick. He knew she was smart, and she must be pretty, too.

Even though the idea of doing that felt like giving up, some doubt was creeping in. Could he find someone on his own? He already had, and she was perfect, but she didn't want him. Well, she did, but she was unwilling to be with him.

Why did that twist his gut so much? People experienced unrequited love all the time.

But the frustrating point here was that it wasn't technically unrequited.

"Vivek? You there?"

He jerked back to reality. They'd moved on to the next aisle, which held decorative and functional gold pieces, from small candleholders and lamps to water fountains. "Yes?"

"Naan? Get some peas, too."

"Okay." He headed toward the freezer at the back of the store. By this point, they were at the front of the store and Vivek had to pass the displayed saris to get to the freezer. It had never ceased to amuse him that both mannequins were white, and one even had blonde hair. He guessed that they'd gotten them on sale.

He picked up a couple of bags of peas and four bags of naan bread.

He wondered if his heart would end up being as cold as the packs in his hand if he didn't find someone soon.

Would he eventually get desperate enough to consider his parents' plan for him?

Time would tell.

SUJATA BEAT Vivek to the conference room for their Monday meeting about the data quality initiative. She was just getting the presentation up on the screen when he came in.

"Hi." He gave her a smile.

They hadn't seen each other yet today, and he had on a shirt that accentuated his stocky build.

If only she could run her hands up his chest under that shirt. She shivered.

Shit. Stop thinking like that. Bananas.

Plus, there was way more to him than a hot body.

"Hey," she squeaked out, and then cleared her throat. She tried to get the slides into presentation mode, but fumbled and clicked the Share button instead, which got her more flustered.

"So I made some good progress on my case study," he said, sounding completely put together like a normal person, unlike her.

She avoided looking at him. "Great, me too. Should we get started on the main part? We can share our case study stuff after."

"Sure. I did want to mention that I had another idea. If you want to hear it, that is."

She deflated, which was both good and bad—good because now she was finally feeling like a normal person in a work setting, bad because she didn't want him to take this in a different direction. He'd better not try to hijack it. Still, she should listen to him and just make sure it didn't stay only his idea. "Shoot."

"What?" His brow furrowed in confusion.

"Sorry, go ahead."

"Is that what that means?" He laughed. "You Americans and your guns."

Sujata frowned, suddenly ashamed of her country. But then she thought of an out. "I actually don't think that necessarily comes from gun culture. I'm sure it's a sports metaphor. Basketball."

"Oh, okay. Anyway, my idea is nothing fancy, but I thought we could address security in some way."

Dammit. "Security is not traditionally a part of data quality, Vivek." Did she sound snappish? Crap.

He blinked in surprise. "I know, but I think it can be kind of adjacent, or they should be considered together in many cases. But if you don't want to bring it up at all, we don't have to."

Sujata took a deep breath and felt herself start to calm from the inside out. "I see your point, but I really want to de-emphasize it. It can be mentioned, but the focus should be on the quality efforts."

"That's fine. I don't think it should be the focus, either. The data quality perspective is what's really fresh about this idea, anyway. Everybody knows about security."

Okay, he seemed to have toned it down. He wasn't trying to take over. She dropped her hackles. He wasn't really wrong. "Yeah. That's true. It's hard to talk about data and not at least address security."

He smiled at her, and she melted a bit inside again. It was hard to stay mad at him.

Sujata started going through the slide deck. She'd added slides to illustrate the ideas better, and they talked about each, ending up throwing a couple out. It was going mostly well, but she was so distracted by Vivek's appealing presence today.

She stole a glance at him while clicking to the next slide. He was looking at the screen, so he was basically in profile. He had a bit of a five o'clock shadow going on and it was way too sexy for work.

Bananas. She quickly averted her eyes just as he turned toward her.

She looked intently at the screen and tried to reset her brain. What was up with her today, anyway?

This slide was talking about uniqueness, and of course it made her think about how Vivek was a unique guy, even though she wasn't supposed to be thinking about him at all.

She could feel him watching her, but instead of meeting his gaze, she stared at the slide on her laptop screen. Intently, because her mind was desperately trying to go back to him.

What was her deal? It wasn't usually this hard.

Sujata had two quality dimensions left and needed to get through them. She was on the validity slide, and she started to talk about the conformance to business rules, sounding like she'd forgotten what she was talking about.

But she powered on.

She got through the next and last slide and wrapped up. "So that's the core presentation." Breathing a sigh of relief, she felt almost normal.

"I think it's good," Vivek said. "But I did have a thought. I wonder if the section where we go over each dimension might go on a bit long. What do you think about moving it to the appendix?"

She thought back to that section, where she'd been struggling. "I think we need to cover them before we get to the case studies, but you're right that it's too long. I'll just have to figure out a way to get through it quickly. I'll just give the definition of each and not go deeper than that."

"That would be good, so you can decide how much info to give them based on how the meeting is going."

So he could help her with this struggle, but she wouldn't let him help her with her struggles in life. That was off-limits.

But she had to get this going. "Exactly. Then we'll talk through the mini case studies and then for the two big ones, you'll do yours and then I'll do mine last."

"Okay, let me share mine."

She pulled the HDMI cable out and slid it across the table toward him. As he plugged in, she said, "Let's get everything in one slide deck for the actual presentation. I can switch between slides."

"Sure." His deck was on the screen.

She managed to focus on what he was showing her, and he'd

done a good job, so she didn't have much feedback. When it was time for hers, she was also able to maintain focus and things seemed back to normal, even if she did keep stealing glances at his profile while he faced the screen.

They wrapped up with the intention to tweak the presentation a bit—she'd make the changes and he could review them. They'd decide if they needed to meet again this week before the big presentation Monday. David had told them to scale back what they were working on and only do the presentation, not to spend time on the prototype.

For the time being, she just had to keep her head in the game, and away from thoughts of Vivek. She'd rejected him. It was done.

At least in her brain, even if her body wasn't on board. She needed to get everything on the same page.

~

THURSDAY EVENING, Vivek was at home playing a video game when his phone rang. Irrationally, he wondered if it was Sujata, but no, it was his uncle's name splashed across the screen.

Great. More pressure to take the job. He let it ring four times before picking it up. "Hello, Uncle-ji."

"Vivek. How are you?" Nirish had one of those overpowering voices, impossible to miss in a crowd, and almost intolerable one-on-one. Demanding attention.

"Good. How are you?" There was no doubt where this was going to go. Vivek wished he could figure out a way to avoid this. He really didn't want to start over in a new place, especially one where there was no chance he'd see Sujata. And he did have that interview coming up.

"I'm good. Let's talk about the job. I need somebody who can start in the next couple months, so you'll have to give me your answer by next Thursday. If you don't take it—and I don't know why you wouldn't—I'll need to find someone else."

Vivek closed his eyes. He had to face reality. He'd waited too long to find something in Portland, with his visa expiring soon. If the Atlanta job was no longer on the table, he'd have to go back to India. Then it would be even harder to keep his parents from pressuring him to marry their chosen woman. He knew Sujata would never come around, so risking everything to stay in Portland didn't really make sense.

He took a deep breath, and a grimace stretched across his face. "Okay, I will take it."

It was done. He closed his eyes and wiped his sweaty palms on his trousers. His life in Portland was over, he'd officially given up on Sujata, and he couldn't ignore the wave of sadness that washed over him.

"Good boy."

He wondered what the salary would be. He knew better than to ask, however. His uncle would think that was disrespectful, and his parents would never forgive him for shaming them. This would not be a situation where negotiation would come into play.

"I've also got a place for you to live," Uncle said in that booming voice.

Well, at least there was that. Hopefully he'd get his own room, since he was finally about to move into one in his current apartment after doing his time on the couch. If he was on the couch again, he'd be really annoyed. More than annoyed. "You've been working in Python and C, right?" Nirish asked.

"Python is what we work in here. I haven't done C since college, but I'm sure I can pick it up." He genuinely liked coding in Python but was going to hate C.

Nirish asked, "When do you think you can start?"

Vivek closed his eyes again. This was getting realer and realer. He was actually going to quit InfoQuest, leave Portland, move to Atlanta, and work for his overly opinionated uncle for some undisclosed amount.

He'd delay things as much as possible. "There's some stuff I want to get done here." He wanted to see what would happen with Sujata's project, but that wasn't going to keep him here. Still, he wasn't ready to leave her so abruptly. And he really did have some work on the system crawler that he wanted to get done.

"So, when?"

Vivek reluctantly pulled up his calendar on his phone. It was late February, so if he spent another month here, that would put it at late March. He'd love a short break, especially given the move. "How about April ninth?"

"You can't start sooner?"

Well, he could, but he wasn't going to. He was going to be selfish here, and hope his lie was believed. "I just need time to wrap things up."

"You'll have to ramp up pretty quick, then."

Great. His uncle was going to be on him from the moment he got there. The dread in his stomach was solidifying.

But he had to act cool. "If there's any public documentation I can read to get a head start, let me know."

"I'll have one of the guys send you some."

"Okay."

What a disaster. How had things come to this? Why couldn't he have asked about the visa at InfoQuest earlier? Everything was so awful.

"This is great, Vivek. I'm glad you're coming on board."

"Me, too, Uncle-ji."

An era was ending. The one where there was still the tiny chance Sujata would change her mind. Now he wouldn't even be on her radar anymore.

9

Sujata worked all Friday morning on Apollo project tasks. She'd spent extra time on the treadmill this morning and skipped breakfast since she was running late.

So when Theresa showed up, she was glad for a social moment. "Did you bring lunch?" Theresa asked.

"Yes, but did you have something in mind?" Now Sujata realized she was starving.

"Casey wants to hit up the taco truck."

"I could do that. Curries keep." She figured since she'd skipped breakfast, she could justify it.

Theresa rested her arms on the cube wall and threw a quick glance behind Sujata's shoulder, toward where Conall was sitting. She grinned before looking back at Sujata. "Is now good, or do you need a few?"

She glanced at her computer's clock. Just before noon. "I could go now. I have a meeting at one, though."

"That's fine. It's a short walk."

Sujata nodded and stood up to put her jacket on and wrapped her paisley scarf around her neck.

They grabbed Casey on their way out and hit the elevators.

"No lunch with Conall today?" Sujata asked Theresa as they waited for the elevator.

"No, they're going to go out for pizza and to talk video games. This way they don't have to feel bad about leaving me out of the conversation."

"It's too bad you don't play anything anymore," Casey said as Sujata and Theresa followed her into the elevator.

"I'm fine with it. I don't miss it. And actually, Conall doesn't play much either. He never did, but now he plays more with Liam than on his own. So, different kinds of games."

Sujata grinned. "Because once Liam's in bed, you two have other things to do."

Theresa laughed. "Yeah, like work."

"That must be it," Casey said.

They stepped out of the building into a cold day and headed down the busy sidewalk. Casey shielded her eyes from the sun.

The food truck was three blocks down. Most of the trucks in Portland were arranged in clusters called pods, but this was a loner parked just inside an alley. And it was amazing.

Theresa glanced around as they waited at a crosswalk. "So, tell us about Vivek."

"Oh, sure. Everything's fine." She hadn't met with him again since Monday—they'd just chatted over IM and said hi in the kitchen a few times—so she'd mostly kept her thoughts in line. She wouldn't tell them about how she'd been so distracted by him in their last meeting. "We're working together great. It's no problem."

Theresa and Casey laughed.

"How's he been behaving?" Casey asked.

"Oh, totally fine. Professional." Sujata paused. "Almost like he's not interested in me at all, though I've caught him looking at me a few times. But not like before. I think he's finally getting over it."

"That's good." Theresa pressed the Walk button at the corner.

Sujata didn't want this conversation to continue, so she thought she'd bring up what had been on her mind. "So you know how my meeting with David and the others got moved up to next Monday?

They decided they didn't want us to spend time on a prototype before being sure they want to pursue it."

"Are you ready?" Theresa asked.

The Walk sign lit up and they stepped into the street.

"I'm just wondering if you have any advice, especially you, Casey. I'm not exactly nervous, but it is a high stakes meeting."

"Sure," Casey said. "Basically, for an initiative like this, they're going to be looking for something with a small investment and potential big payoff. Like any investor."

"Yeah, and I think this does fit the bill." Sujata stepped onto the sidewalk.

"The trick will be convincing them of it. That's what you want to focus on. The payoff, and how few resources need to be thrown at it."

"Conall says David's a decent guy," Theresa said. "He, at least, should be rooting for you."

"Yeah, I think that is true," Sujata said. "He can be flaky at times, but he does actually want his employees to succeed." It was the truth. She might need to lean on him a bit, make sure he was on her side first. Maybe she should meet with him before the big meeting so he'd have more context.

"You'll do fine," Casey said. "So just make sure to focus on those aspects and ensure they are crystal clear in the presentation. They may look at your slide deck later, but not necessarily, so say everything important out loud. But definitely share the slide deck with them after the meeting. Unless they've given you a hard no already. That's unlikely, however."

They reached the next corner just as the Walk sign lit up.

Sujata wasn't lying when she said she wasn't nervous, but she was feeling uncertain about it all. What would happen if they did give her a hard no? She'd be so bummed.

She could always go out on her own and build it, but it would be so much easier to build off what InfoQuest already had. She wouldn't be leveraging all of the existing code, but she'd be relying on their system crawler. Building that from scratch would just take time. Plus, making a whole company out of thin air wouldn't be easy.

Theresa and Casey were talking about something they were working on, which allowed Sujata's mind to meander back to Vivek. He was being okay about the presentation, not taking over. She did trust him not to claim responsibility. There were plenty of other men she wouldn't have trusted at all, but he was a decent guy.

Their timing was impeccable as they caught the next Walk sign just as they arrived at the intersection and were soon at the truck.

Sujata ordered two fish street tacos and joined the others to wait for their orders. This truck was fast.

"Brr," Theresa said, rubbing her own upper arms.

"I know," Sujata said. "And we've got another month of this."

The guy called Sujata's number and she lathered on the hottest salsa they had.

"Do you want to head back or just eat here?" Casey asked.

Sujata headed to some chairs at a table nearby. "They'll be cold if we go back. Let's just eat here."

But the chairs were aluminum, so the second she sat down, she was ice cold. "Oh, my God. On the other hand, we could just stand."

Theresa laughed and they stood there and munched on their tacos.

"Shit," Casey said.

"What?" Theresa asked through a mouthful of taco.

"I just got sour cream on my shirt." She wiped at the spot and licked her finger.

Sujata nodded sagely. "Those pesky sticky-outy parts'll do it every time."

"Yes."

Just then some of the salsa rolled off her taco and landed on one of her own sticky-outy parts, and Casey and Theresa cracked up.

Sujata wiped it off with her finger. "This is the most action this part of me has seen in a while."

More laughter all around.

Ugh. Was she pitiful? Should she have given Vivek a chance?

It was too late now—changing course would just be messing with him, and he didn't deserve that.

"Ready?" Casey asked. They started the walk back to the office.

Maybe she needed another hobby. Or she should just do more training with Nilani like she'd been thinking about.

Or maybe, if she was lucky, she'd be given the go-ahead on her project and could start devoting all her spare time to that.

She crossed her fingers on both hands, hidden inside her jacket pockets.

~

SUJATA GOT lucky and David had an open slot Friday afternoon. She headed over there, nervous but not overly so. She wanted to exude confidence. She pushed her shoulders back and held her head high.

She waved at Gwen as she passed her before peeking in David's office. He was sitting behind his desk, leaning forward and squinting at the computer screen to the right side of his desk.

He looked up and smiled. "Sujata! Welcome. How are you?"

"Good." She headed in, belatedly remembering to mirror his greeting. "How are you?"

"I'm great. Busy, but we all love that."

"Yeah." She sat in one of the two white wooden chairs across from his desk. "Thanks for being willing to talk to me." That had come out casual yet confident, so she was off to a good start. But then her stomach twisted with the realization that this was a crucial moment in something that could change her life.

"What can I do for you?" he asked.

"I'm basically just wanting to give you an overview of the presentation for Monday, in case you have any tips on anything I should change or highlight. I'm uncertain about this presentation, since I don't know all the leaders who will be there."

He nodded. "I'm happy to help. But don't worry, they are all good guys."

All guys was one of the issues, with all the stupid sexism that was still rampant in the tech world. But she'd have to trust the process. Sometimes women still broke through.

She relaxed her face. "Great. The slide deck isn't finished, but I'll just go over the talking points."

Her stomach glitched again. This was so damn important.

"You'll be busy this weekend, huh?" he said teasingly.

Was he teasing her because he thought she looked nervous? She hated that idea, but managed a wry smile. "Such is the life of a programmer."

He laughed. "We don't expect that every weekend here."

"I know. And we appreciate that." This was getting off track.

David leaned back in his chair and tented his hands. "So tell me about your proposal. Oh, and does Vivek need to be here?"

Of course he'd ask. Why was everybody trying to take away her project? "No, I'm just going over the material. He'll be presenting some of it."

He nodded.

"Okay." She clicked on the first slide. Her plan was to run through the slides herself rather than show David. She started off with the definition of data quality, going reasonably slow to make sure to give David time to absorb and react, especially since he wasn't seeing the slides.

He nodded at the definition and said, "That makes sense to me."

"Great." She relaxed a bit. He was following and seemed to be grasping everything.

Then she started going through the different data quality dimensions and David nodded along.

He glanced at his screen while she was talking about uniqueness, and she panicked a tiny bit. Was she losing him?

He was looking at her again, but now she was worried. "Are these making sense to you?"

"Yes, they seem clear."

She made a mental note to make the uniqueness slide more interesting, and moved on.

"Currency?" David asked when he saw what was on the slide. "What does money have to do with this?"

"Not that kind of currency. It means 'recent-ness,' basically. Is it as up-to-date as it should be, that sort of thing."

"Ah." David laughed.

Even though he seemed engaged, she was doubting herself and didn't really know how this was going. He wasn't saying much, which could be good or bad. Her stomach twitched again. When she got through the last dimension, she decided to do a quick check.

"Do you think it's clear so far?" she asked, quelling the tremor that tried to creep into her voice.

He cocked his head to the side. "I feel like I'm following, but I think what's missing is why. It's all very abstract at this point."

"Oh," she said, stretching it out a bit as a chill coursed through her at the realization. "You're right. We actually have some small case studies we thought we'd run through, plus a couple of bigger ones. Maybe we should start with one."

He nodded. "I think that's a great idea."

She debated whether to let Vivek do his, or to do hers. She decided on hers. "Let me run though it really quick, if you don't mind. I'd love to hear if it's easy to follow."

She covered her mini case study quickly. "That's one of them," she concluded.

"Yeah, that was more interesting. It makes it clear why these things matter."

He checked his computer again. "I've got another meeting in five. Did you have anything else you wanted to talk about?"

"No, I think that's enough. You've helped me. I'm going to rearrange some things and have a more interesting beginning." She stood up. "Thanks so much."

"No problem. You really do need to nail this presentation to get support for the initiative. But I believe in you. Monday will be great, Sujata."

"Thanks." She ducked out of his office. Gwen was on the phone, so she'd just head over to Vivek's cube so they could coordinate, and she needed to tell him about the shift of the mini case study to the beginning. It might mean they'd throw out his and instead end on the two big ones.

Her heart did that irritating little skip as she turned the corner and could see the top of his head at his cube.

Get a grip. Also, the top of his head was not a particularly sexy part of him.

But other parts surely were.

Bananas. She needed to be all business now.

When she was almost at his cube, he noticed her approaching so he was smiling when she finally stopped on the other side of his wall.

Stomach flutters distracted her.

"Sujata."

"Hey." His hair was looking particularly good today, shiny and windswept or something. Bananas. "So, I just went through some of the slides with David. He made a very good point that will help us fix the beginning of the presentation. I'm so glad I talked to him."

"Are you nervous?" Vivek asked.

"I'm just not great when there are high stakes," she said.

"This idea is great and you've got a strong presentation. Just try to be confident."

"Okay. Thanks for the pep talk." They both laughed.

"So did you need me to do anything?" Vivek asked.

She mentally regrouped. "So, I want to change the presentation a bit." She explained, and he agreed that starting with a mini case study made sense.

She switched her laptop to her other hand. "I'm going to be working on this over the weekend. Let's meet Monday morning to finalize it before the actual presentation."

"I'm still working on my case study. It's mostly done, but I'm trying to make it as clear and interesting as possible."

"Yeah, same here. So I'll set something up for the morning, and we can see where we're at." She nodded to herself, then added, "Hopefully basically done."

Vivek laughed. "I'm sure we will be. It's going to be fine, Sujata."

She loved how he said her name, with that South Indian *t* so different from how English speakers said it.

"Okay." She needed to get out of here. "See you Monday."

They gave each other an awkward wave, and she turned to leave.

Why was it so hard to be around him? She had made her final call on things weeks ago. Sliding back into her seat, she re-docked her computer and opened the top.

The presentation was still calling her name.

10

Sunday morning, Vivek sat on his bed/couch with his laptop. This couch was saggy in the middle. One day, when he was married, he'd have a house with a comfortable couch that would not be used for sleeping, and multiple beds that were, including one that he would share with his wife.

Who would not be Sujata. He sighed.

He got back to the data quality project in preparation for the meeting tomorrow. He was adding depth to his case study.

He knew Sujata wasn't very interested in the security aspects of the project, but he was still including references to it. Emphasizing security would differentiate their offerings from those of their competitors.

"Vivek, you want to go out to lunch?" Kiran asked. He and Ishaan sat in the kitchen, talking about something. Vivek was trying not to listen.

Vivek didn't look up from his computer. "No, I've got too much work to do."

"So do I, but there's plenty of hours in the rest of the day."

"Maybe I don't want to go, either," Ishaan said thoughtfully.

Vivek tuned them out.

Focusing on security in data governance just made sense. What was the point of managing data if it wasn't secure? How could that be considered effective? At least Sujata wasn't opposed to this idea—he wasn't going to try to outdo her or anything, so he had to be careful how he talked about it.

He didn't know why she wasn't more interested, anyway. Maybe it was just because it wasn't her idea? This whole initiative was hers, after all. But it wasn't like he was trying to take credit for anything. She could continue to own it. He just wanted to help her succeed. It would be his last thing before he left InfoQuest and Sujata forever.

Kiran and Ishaan were in the kitchen, still debating going to lunch. Vivek could not tune them out. He was trying to do some more research. He'd been updating his own set of slides, which they'd incorporate into Sujata's deck tomorrow morning.

The guys went back to their rooms and it was quiet again.

Vivek found something really interesting for his case study and was typing that up when Kiran came back out and asked, "What are you doing this afternoon, V?"

Vivek finished typing out his thought and said, "I thought you were going out to lunch."

"We decided not to," Kiran said. "Ishaan's making lunch."

Ishaan looked back. "I am?"

"You are." Kiran gave him his winning smile.

"Fine." Ishaan got up and headed into their tiny kitchen and opened the fridge.

"Let's play poker after lunch," Kiran said.

Vivek sighed. This is when he missed having his own room the most. There was no escape. They'd want him to play. And he just wanted to work today. If he wanted real peace and quiet, he'd have to go into the office.

~

SUNDAY AFTERNOON, Sujata tucked her feet under herself on her couch and positioned her laptop on the arm of the sofa so she could work. She had to get this presentation done. When she pulled the slide deck up, she immediately realized she'd forgotten to take a picture of her whiteboard Friday after she'd worked up several important points.

What were they? She closed her eyes and pressed her fingers to her forehead trying to remember.

Nope. Wasn't going to happen.

Dammit.

She'd have to go into the office, which was deeply irritating.

She wasn't going to change out of her yoga pants, though. Nobody else would be there. She packed up her laptop, threw on her jacket, and headed out.

Forty-five cold minutes later, Sujata was settled into her desk. She figured she might as well just work here. It was warm and she could avoid going back outside for a bit.

The whiteboard had all the answers she needed. She pulled up the presentation and added two more slides, between completeness and currency. She would focus on uniqueness now.

This was actually one of the things she was most excited about. She had some good ideas for how to detect and manage uniqueness. She dug in and cranked out the other two slides before staring at the uniqueness slide and trying to absorb it and brainstorm what she should actually add.

The elevator dinged in the distance and she went on alert. Was somebody here? She looked toward the elevator bay and saw—of all freaking people—Vivek.

His eyes widened when he spotted her, but it turned into a smile as he got close. Her stupid heart was doing a telltale fluttery thing.

Bananas.

"What are you doing here?" he asked.

His voice just made the fluttering more intense. She had no control.

"Hey," she said, inwardly cursing her ridiculous heart. "I had some stuff on my whiteboard I forgot to record."

He nodded.

"What are you doing here?"

"My roommates were driving me mad today morning. Chattering away." His gaze felt intense.

She felt that look, and forced a chuckle, which came out all weird. "Gotta love roommates." She couldn't be happier with her choice to live alone. She liked other people fine, but it was nice to have the bathroom all to herself. And the fridge.

"Are you working on the presentation?" he asked.

"Yeah."

"I am, as well."

Of course he was. But to be fair, this might actually be a good thing. She could get his opinion on her changes today instead of last-minute tomorrow. "You could sit here so we can work together." She motioned at the space next to her desk, where they kept an extra chair.

After a pause, Vivek shrugged and said, "Sure." He sat down after peeling off his coat, pulled his laptop out of his bag, and scooted up under the desk before asking, "What are you working on right now?"

"I just finished up a slide on uniqueness. I decided to add more info in the appendix in case they ask me to share the presentation. But I'd really like to go through the whole thing with you again in a bit. I think it just needs some fine-tuning."

His closeness had her mind and body imagining what might have happened between them if things had been different.

"Sure," Vivek said.

"But not quite yet," she clarified. "What are you working on?"

"The case study."

He smelled fresh, like soap.

"Yeah, I worked on mine this morning. I'm happy with it. But we can go over both of them today and put the final presentation together so it's ready." Was she stretching out this time together? What was wrong with her? She should suggest they both go home and collaborate over Zoom.

"That would be perfect," he said, his eyes looking soft and inviting.

They both got to work. Sujata added to the uniqueness section, happy with what she had. She decided to read through the whole thing once more, including the case study, before asking Vivek to look.

She scrolled back to the beginning of the slide deck and started reading. But Vivek's presence beside her was a huge distraction. She kept having to rein in the desire to roll her chair ever-so-slightly to the right. They were already close enough that she could feel the heat coming off of him.

Focus. She'd rejected him and needed to stop letting her body get carried away. She forced herself to roll her chair a bit to the left, putting more space between them.

Then Sujata steeled her mind for more focused work and started going through the deck slide by slide.

Once she made it to her case study, she was feeling good about the main presentation. She stole a glance at Vivek, who must have felt it and caught her eye, and she immediately flushed. She could have sworn his eyes twinkled, so she quickly looked back at her screen.

Bananas.

Sujata managed to get through the case study with only a few more tweaks. This thing was definitely ready for a second opinion.

"I think I'm ready for you to look at this whenever," she said.

Vivek nodded and they made charged eye contact again.

He cleared his throat. "I need about ten more minutes and I'll be ready, too."

"I'll just run to the ladies' and be back in a few."

"Great." He turned back to his computer and she pushed back her chair and stood up.

In the bathroom, Sujata looked at herself in the mirror as she washed her hands. She hadn't even put on her usual eyeliner today, so she thought she looked tired. She didn't feel tired, however. She felt energized and alive, all because she was cozied up with a guy she couldn't have.

She dried her hands and looked in the mirror again. Her hair looked especially good today. Shiny and straight thanks to her hairdresser.

Shaking her head, she sighed. Her appearance didn't matter. She was not out to impress anyone.

Sujata headed back to her desk, tension in her belly mounting the closer she got to Vivek. She sat down and rolled up to the desk, avoiding looking at him, though she felt his gaze on her.

"Five more minutes," he said.

"Sure, no problem."

She pulled out her phone and checked her personal email. Nothing exciting, but Kavya had played in Words with Friends, so Sujata needed to make her own play now. She went in and managed to make a 62-point play, very pleased with herself.

"Why are you smiling?" Vivek asked.

"Oh." She hadn't realized he was looking at her, and she felt exposed. "Just this game my sister and I are playing. Are you ready?"

"Yes. Should we go over everything?"

"Definitely." Sujata pulled her laptop off the dock so she could put it between them and clicked back to the first slide, which stated the problem. She let Vivek read it and said, "To get their minds in the right place, I was going to put my mini case study after this slide." She carefully avoided looking at him and tried not to breath in his scent. Something clean.

"What's the next slide?"

"A definition of data quality."

Out of the corner of her eye, she saw him nod. "That sounds like a good idea. We give an example before defining it."

"Not much to say here," she said to the definition slide. "I'll read this and answer their questions about it. There are always questions."

"They'll want to understand how it's different from quality assurance."

She nodded and continued to stare at the screen. It was soap. Vivek's soap was a brand she'd smelled before, but couldn't pin down. It was nice. A very inappropriate image of him in the shower applying said soap popped into her head and she had to fight it.

Sujata hit the right arrow harder than necessary. "Here I'll talk about the ideas behind data governance and stewardship before introducing the improvement cycle on the next slide." She clicked to it.

They studied the slide, neither saying anything. She wanted to scoot over so they could be shoulder to shoulder. She resisted. He was holding his hands under the table, which was probably a good thing.

She flipped to the next one, which contained the actual proposition for the InfoQuest initiative. "So before this, we'll do our case studies, first you, then me."

"This is good," Vivek said. "But if you bold the key words it would be better."

Sujata looked at him, bemused. "You care about design?"

He shrugged and half smiled at her. "Sure. I have some other thoughts, too, but we can talk about those at the end."

"Really?" Her mind went somewhere totally inappropriate about what kind of thoughts those might be. She mentally checked herself. "Okay."

Even his partial smile lit up his eyes. She so wanted to touch him.

And if she wasn't wrong, he was staring at her mouth now. Her neck was instantly warm.

She quickly looked back at her screen and hit the right arrow. "Okay, um." She had to get ahold of herself. "This one talks about what the software needs are."

She could see him turn back to the screen and nod to himself.

"You think we could really finish a prototype in four weeks?" he asked.

She'd estimated that length of time for the two of them focused on a proof of concept of the software needed for the initiative. "You don't think that's enough?"

"You've said we'd do it in Python. But if we want to reuse some of Apollo's code—which we should—some of it's in Java. We'd have to create the interfaces first."

"We wouldn't have to start from scratch. I know where some Python versions of the original Apollo code exist, so we could use that to build off of. Just for the PoC." Then she lost her train of thought because she felt his eyes on her.

Bananas, bananas, bananas.

"Oh, that's good." His voice just drove her crazy, the good kind of crazy, which was very bad for her.

"But really, we'd be working with the outputs primarily, so we might not need it. We maybe could get an API created so it wouldn't have to be on flat files." She couldn't even glance at him because she was remembering that hot look he'd given her. "We could start with that. Plus, the Apollo documentation is up-to-date and very good."

"Okay. Four weeks then." He surprised her by touching her forearm when he said it.

That made her turn, and she could see that he was staring at her mouth again, his eyes dark and intense. So she wasn't the only one feeling it.

Before she could think better of it, she leaned toward him and he met her halfway.

His lips were soft and yielding. But then he gripped her shoulders and pulled her closer, her chair rolling with her until her knee bumped the seat of his, and the kiss quickly grew more urgent. His tongue began exploring, encouraging her to open for him, and she did.

She gripped the front of his shirt and held on for dear life while every nerve in her body was firing. Vivek's hands slid down to cup her bottom and then her heart lurched as he lifted her and pulled her forward until she was sitting on his thigh, with teasing pressure on her hot center, all the while his tongue slid against hers and his hands were in her hair.

There was nothing Sujata wanted more than this. Her breasts were crushed against his chest and she ran a hand along the back of his neck, the short hairs on his nape pushing against her fingers. How could she have put this off for so long? What had she been afraid of?

Abruptly, Vivek pulled back, his eyes wide. She leaned forward to close the distance again and Vivek picked her up and put her back in her chair. That's when she heard it.

"I'll just be here for an hour or so," a distant male voice said.

She spun her chair back to face the desk and stared at the white surface next to the laptop.

"David," Vivek whispered.

"Oh, my God. Holy shit." She panicked, her heart going bonkers for two completely exciting-but-in-completely-different-ways reasons. "Do I look okay?"

He turned and patted her hair a few places, putting some strands behind her ear, the simple touch of his hand on her ear reigniting the fire in her belly.

"Now you do." He smiled.

"I'll pick up dinner on the way home," David said, much closer.

Sujata's heart was still pounding like crazy, and she worried David would know what they'd been up to if he noticed them.

David continued talking to his girlfriend as he turned the corner to his office.

"Phew," she said. "Dodged a bullet there."

Vivek laughed and looked at her sideways.

She glanced at him and back at the screen.

"I have a feeling you're going to tell me that was a mistake," he said quietly.

"Let's just finish the presentation, Vivek."

But he was right. It had been a mistake. A wonderful mistake, never to be repeated.

"Okay, so the next slide lists all the data quality dimensions," Vivek said.

"Yeah." She pulled it up and they stared at it. She kept thinking about his hands in her hair and all her other parts touching him and how good he'd felt. How could that be so wrong?

But it was. It was too much of a risk. She might really fall for him, too fast.

She moved to the next slide, the appendix, and slowly flipped through them. Each dimension was shown in greater detail, but there was a lot crammed on each slide.

"This looks good," he said after she'd gotten to the third dimension, "but I think it might be better to split up some of the info on each dimension rather than having it all on one slide."

His voice was husky, and she was glad she wasn't the only one still trying to recover.

But he was reading her mind. "We did talk about this before, and I just got carried away adding stuff."

"I think the information is great, it's just overwhelming to look at."

He was totally right. "I see what you mean. This isn't for us to go over at the presentation. They'll just flip through it later, possibly."

"Correct."

Why did she like the way he said that word? She shouldn't like his voice so much. She nodded. "I'll work on that this evening. I'm not going to change much."

Sujata saw him nod in agreement out of the corner of her eye. She clicked to the next slide and they stared for a moment.

"Looks good," Vivek said.

Then she ran through the rest of the dimensions, actively forcing herself to not think of his sexy voice. She got to the final part of the appendix, a deeper exploration of each potential client's needs.

"I think this one looks good, too," he said.

"Cool." She moved to the last slide, trying not to feel feelings because his gaze was on her.

Vivek shrugged. "It's great."

Sujata heard footsteps, and she and Vivek turned to see David standing at the entrance to her pod.

"What are you guys doing? Deadline looming?"

"We're working on the data quality presentation," Sujata said.

"Oh, of course! How's it going?"

"Good. I think we've fixed the issues you helped me identify." Sujata hoped that she wasn't still flushed enough that he'd wonder what else they'd been up to.

His eyes widened in understanding and he said, "Great. I'm looking forward to seeing it tomorrow."

She smiled. "Yep. I'm looking forward to it, too." This was not remotely true.

David patted his thigh and said, “Okay, excellent. I’m headed home now.”

Once he was gone, they went through the case study slides and strengthened some of the descriptions in the appendix before calling it a day.

They put their jackets on in silent unison and headed toward the elevator.

The kiss was heavy on her mind again as Vivek pushed the front door of the building open.

“Vivek,” she said.

“Yes?” He turned to look at her.

She opened her mouth to speak, but nothing came out.

“Oh, no. I was right,” he said.

“You were. It was a mistake.”

“Why?” Vivek asked. He sounded a tiny bit desperate and she felt bad about messing with him.

“I just can’t. I don’t know how to get over him. A year hasn’t done it.”

“Maybe a relationship would actually help you move on.” He sounded exasperated.

She looked at the desk. He might be right, but she was too afraid to try. As good as holding his hand had felt, kissing him was even better. She’d fall fast.

She just couldn’t imagine how she could handle it.

11

Sujata glanced at the clock on the computer screen as she clicked to the next slide. Seven minutes into their big presentation Monday afternoon, and she'd already lost the leaders.

"Data quality pervades everything a company does," she said.

The three directors—Sandeep, Aarav, and Chang—looked bored, judging from their posture in their chairs, despite the fact that they were facing the screen. The VP, Krishna, was on his phone. Vivek was sitting next to her and gave her foot a subtle tap with his own, which made her feel a bit better.

How could she get them back? This was so important to her—if this didn't get supported, she'd have to go back to just being a regular software engineer with nothing interesting going on. She'd feel like she had no future here, except as a grunt. How had she gotten so tied into this?

David glanced over at her and nodded, his rugged good looks hard to deny. He'd told her she had to nail this, and she knew that Krishna was famously hard to please.

Sujata took a deep breath. "To wrap this case study up, I'll talk about the success of the data quality initiative."

Now two of the men were looking at their phones.

Great. It was so annoying. Was this because she was a woman, or were they just like this? And they said teenagers had no attention span.

Her stomach roiling, she was summarizing the impacts of both the bad data quality and the initiative that fixed it when Krishna interrupted her.

"So I need to understand the actual financial ramifications," he said, somehow sounding impressed with himself.

She was not nailing this.

But she could. All was not lost yet. She smiled and said, "I was about to get to that. They didn't release the exact numbers, but they lost ten percent of their customers, including their first one. So in the millions, for sure."

But now Krishna was looking at his computer, open on the table in front of him. He nodded as an afterthought.

Sandeep was thumbing something on his phone.

Shit. This was bad. How could she get them back?

Vivek tapped her foot again, and she shifted in her chair. She'd never realized how uncomfortable these chairs were. But she had to keep going, so she finished that case study and started on the next, which she got through without interruption, but also with minimal attention from the men.

This was never going to work.

Sujata's stomach was definitely queasy now, with dread creeping up her spine. All this work and emotional energy she'd put into it, for nothing. She was glad for Vivek's supportive presence so she wasn't all alone.

She couldn't let it get to her.

Steeling herself, she wrapped up the case study, shifting in the chair again. And gave herself a damn wedgie through her thin pants.

Shit. Now she was going to have to figure out how to get to the bathroom after the meeting without anyone noticing.

They were still not engaged. There was just this vibe of boredom pervading the air. But she could sense attention coming off of Vivek.

She had to keep trying. "For our purposes, the definition of data quality is the degree to which the data represents reality to the consumers of the data, based on how they intend to use that data."

She tried to focus on the content and not think about how pointless this all felt now. She started talking about governance and stewardship and then dove into the data quality improvement cycle, realizing only after she finished that she was speaking way too fast. She just wanted to get this train wreck over with.

Krishna said, "So—Sujata, right?"

She blinked. How could he not even remember her damn name? "Yes."

"Great. So you're saying that it never ends?"

"That's basically right." Was this a good sign? Never ending would mean more involvement from InfoQuest. She kept going.

Now, it was Vivek's turn to present his case study. She flipped to the next slide and gave Vivek a nod so he would start. Getting a break should be good for her.

"Thanks, everyone. I'm going to talk about a farm, which seems like an odd company to consider data quality on." He paused to give everyone a chance to laugh, which they did. Then he explained that they tracked all of their animals and all the food and other supplies and machinery they had at two different locations.

It was weirdly comforting to hear his voice, even though he was talking about pigs and cows. At least he believed in her.

The other men in the room were all looking intently at the screen as Vivek talked through the points.

Maybe he'd finally found the audience and they'd be interested after all.

She should have started with humor, too.

But anything she'd tried would have landed flat, since she was so nervous. That would have been worse than skipping the joke.

Vivek had gone through much of the case study, and it was obvious that everyone was engaged, which was frustrating. But maybe they'd still be engaged when she got to her final case study, which was also interesting.

"Next slide, please," Vivek said. She flipped to the next one and he continued. He was doing well, which made her feel both pleased for him and worried for herself. She didn't want to be outshone. Even though he was shy, he just had this natural charm that came out when he was comfortable. He was obviously more confident when talking about work than personal things. "There's one other area that isn't strictly related to data quality, but is part of the overall picture of data management, and that's security."

Aarav and Krishna both seemed to perk up at this.

Great. She'd known he was going to bring it up, but now it made her even more nervous. It deviated from data quality too much. It was fine as a tangential thing, but otherwise it could be a problem. She hoped they didn't latch onto it. She needed to come up with a plan in case they did.

She'd just remind everyone that it was more of an adjacent thing, not the focus.

Vivek continued and she watched the men. Okay, they were interested in what he was talking about, but they weren't *that* interested.

She shouldn't worry, anyway. It looked like this whole thing would be a flop and they'd get no support. She couldn't help but frown.

"So that's that case study," Vivek said.

Sujata was caught off guard since she'd been so deep in her head, so she was glad when he continued.

"Were there any questions?"

Sandeep wanted more detail on the various data systems they had used and Vivek talked about most of them being modern, but one was a legacy system they were looking to replace.

They kept going a bit and switched to some questions about security, which made Sujata's stomach get queasier. And that freaking wedgie.

It was so obvious that they responded better to Vivek than to her, and that was almost definitely a gender thing. All men, and then her. Sometimes, being the only woman was more than annoying.

Still, she organized her thoughts in preparation for her case study.

They weren't addressing the slides, so she moved to the one that started her part.

Once they had quieted down, Krishna and Chang looked at her, so she smiled and said, "Well, I'll be bringing us back to the city, away from the farm. Mine's with a tech company. A gaming company."

Vivek smiled, but clearly she needed better presentation humor. Despite feeling flustered, she flipped to her first content slide and got started.

It seemed to be going well and she relaxed a bit, but then Chang started messing on his phone and Krishna on his computer and her heart sank.

Why was this so damn hard? Why did they find her so boring? She was usually such a strong presenter, sure of herself and knowing what she was talking about. This sucked. It meant way too much to her.

She wrapped up her case study and Krishna did ask a few questions—apparently he was a gamer, or at least had been.

His apparent interest gave her a sudden burst of confidence. She knew this was a good idea, she just needed to convince them. Sound confident and like an expert. "To start, our solution will focus on six data quality metrics, which can be tweaked if the client chooses."

They were getting close to the part that Sujata believed might convince them. She started talking about potential clients, actually resorting to crossing the fingers of her left hand in her lap. But this took them down a rabbit hole for a few minutes. She was losing hope—at this rate they were going to run out of time. She crossed her legs, which made the wedgie worse.

After things quieted down, she clicked to the next slide, where she covered pricing and projected profit. This was somewhat made up, but she knew she had to add it in there, so she hoped it seemed feasible to them.

Chang said, "This looks very promising."

Great, maybe they were more receptive than she'd thought.

Sandeep nodded. "I agree. I'm especially interested in some of the security options. It seemed relevant to SOX and HIPAA compliance."

Sujata deflated. The room suddenly was freezing. She rubbed her bare arms and wished she was wearing long sleeves.

"Can you talk a little more about that?" Sandeep finished.

"We haven't really developed anything for that. Maybe Vivek can address it. But I should mention first that security is not considered a part of data quality, even though the two often work in harmony." She looked at Vivek, willing him to not be too fascinating. She needed them steered away from security.

Vivek grimaced ever so slightly, like he felt bad. Which was thoughtful, but didn't help. Why did Vivek's primary contribution have to get so much of the attention?

He discussed various aspects and the others seemed engaged. Even David seemed rapt, despite having been silent during the whole meeting. She was disappointed about that—she'd thought he might support her more.

When Vivek wrapped up, Sujata explained again how security wasn't generally handled as a part of data quality. Nobody seemed to care, and she wallowed in her disheartenment for a moment.

Vivek tapped her foot again, which made her heart melt a smidgen even though she didn't know what he was trying to convey, and she was irritated at him for his theft of her thunder. Which wasn't entirely fair, since she'd invited him to answer.

The awkward silence continued until David said, "Five more minutes. What do we want to do about this? Should we proceed? I can't free them up for the next two weeks, but I can give them quarter-time on this project if we think it's worth pursuing."

"It's your call, Krishna," Aarav said.

Krishna was Sandeep's boss, and Sandeep was David's. David had invited Aarav and Chang to the meeting just because he thought they'd be interested, which Sujata appreciated. Even though it turned out not to be true.

"Sandeep and I need to discuss it," Krishna said. "Can you send us the slides, Sujata?"

"Sure." This was at least promising. She glanced at Vivek and saw his expression turned pained for a second.

Oh, right. If this was approved, it would mean that they'd have to spend more time working closely together.

Krishna and Sandeep stood up.

Sandeep said, "Thanks again, that was great, guys. Good job, Vivek." He paused the tiniest moment. "Sujata."

Was he freaking kidding? Her mind was about to explode. Suddenly she was no longer quietly sad and disappointed. Yet again chauvinism reared its ugly head. Of course this would happen to her.

Vivek immediately said, "This whole thing was Sujata's idea. It's her project. I just helped with the presentation."

She was thankful that he'd said all that, but would he really be able to resist the attention and benefits of getting the credit if this effort actually went somewhere? She wasn't sure. Regardless, her dismay had turned to flaming anger, her belly on fire in the bad way.

The other leaders all left, and David gave them a winning smile and said, "Good job, guys. How do you feel?"

Sujata closed down the presentation. She didn't trust herself at the moment. Did David really not see Sandeep's dis? He probably was just being nice by pretending all was not lost.

She could feel Vivek's eyes on her, but then he said, "I thought it was good. I'm anxious to hear what they say."

Closing her computer, she said, "Yeah, I'm curious, too." And still seething mad.

"I thought you presented everything very clearly," David said.

She nodded, knowing how this was going to go, even though she hoped to be wrong.

Was that possible? This was definitely one of those situations when being wrong would be awesome.

Plus, how was she going to get out of here with this damn wedgie?

"See you guys later," David said as he exited the meeting room.

Vivek was nervous. Sujata looked so good today—she had on a delicate yellow satin blouse and black trousers—but she was standing with her computer under one arm, staring at the now-blank projector screen, a lost expression on her face. He was between her and the door, but he felt weird just leaving. What if she wanted to talk about it?

But maybe she didn't. He did not have a good feeling about Sujata's prospects here. The guys had really fixated on the wrong thing, and he hated the way Krishna wasn't certain of her name, and how Sandeep only thanked her as an afterthought at the end. This did not look good. He shifted on his feet.

Sujata seemed to come out of it and made eye contact with him, her mouth in a subtle frown.

"They aren't going to support the initiative, are they?" she asked.

He gave her an encouraging smile he did not feel. "They might. They'll go back and talk about it. I hope they make the right decision. You have to have faith."

"They liked your security idea more than anything else." She had a flat expression on her face.

So it wasn't just his perception. "It was supposed to be an afterthought, like this is just something you could add on for more money."

She was still staring at the screen, looking defeated, mouth turned down and shoulders slumped.

"I still have hope they will make the right decision." Vivek really wanted her to feel better, but he didn't know what to do. "This is a great idea and it fits into our portfolio so well. They'd be stupid to pass it up."

She sighed. "Could you give me a minute?"

He nodded and left the room, heading to the kitchen for tea.

As he was pouring the hot water, Sujata came in and pulled a paper cup out of the cabinet and filled it with coffee.

"That looks old," Vivek said.

"Yeah. Crappy coffee to round out a crappy afternoon." She put enough sugar and cream in there to make it palatable to a six-year-old. She looked at his surprised face and gave a weak laugh. "I know. I'm hoping it makes it tolerable."

"At least you'll get your daily intake of sugar."

She smiled and took a sip, her face contorting. "Blehk!"

Vivek laughed.

"Oh, my God, this is horrific." She dumped it in the sink.

"Well, at least you gave it a chance." He flipped the switch on the coffee maker and dumped the dregs in the sink.

"I give up," Sujata said, leaning against the counter. "I just wish you hadn't brought up the security stuff. I think it took them down a path, away from what I was really proposing."

He didn't think it was a bad thing to mention, but she was right that it distorted their view. "We should have saved it for the very end."

"Or not included it in the proposal at all." From the look on her tense face, she was pissed at him. He wanted to defend himself—it wasn't his fault they were all idiots—but he kept quiet.

He put the rinsed-out pot back on the burner, wanting to pat her on the shoulder. He figured he shouldn't, especially now that she was mad at him. There was really nothing he could do to make her feel better. They both read the room basically the same way.

She shook her head and pushed off the counter. "I guess I have crap to do."

"Yeah, me too." He wanted to undo all of his security ideas. Or better, make the leaders focus on the right things.

They walked back to their desks, getting to hers first. As she got settled, he said, "Don't give up yet."

She rolled her eyes. "Okay, sure. It's fine for you to say. This doesn't matter to you at all."

That stung, but he got it. "It's not about me. I want them to greenlight it. I know it's a good idea." And her presentation had been good, too—she had done a great job of laying things out. He really hoped that adding the security thing in hadn't ruined everything. Only time would tell.

12

By Friday, Sujata was vacillating between believing that they liked her idea and were trying to figure out how to support it, and that they hated it so much they didn't even bother talking about it.

She was working on some code when she realized she was hungry, so she locked her screen and headed into the kitchen. She had a fish curry in the fridge, leftovers from one of her better concoctions lately. She'd made it last night to distract herself.

Once she had it in the microwave, she looked around. The Indians were at their favorite table. Vivek was on the end. He waved at her so she smiled back, but she had a ton to do, so she didn't plan to join them.

The microwave dinged, so she grabbed a paper plate and put the container on it. She pulled a plastic spoon out of a drawer, set it on her plate and turned around to find David walking in. He had on what looked like an expensive suit, which was unusual. He must have a meeting with financial types. Everyone else on the West Coast was casual.

"Oh, hey," David said with a slight smile. "Great, I'm glad I found you."

Sujata's stomach was instantly tight. He looked like he had purpose in his eyes. Maybe it was good news.

He glanced over at the table for a moment, but then turned back toward Sujata and walked over. "I was thinking Vivek should hear this too, but it doesn't really impact him since he's just put his notice in. Listen. I heard from Krishna and they've decided not to go with your idea right now."

Her heart sank like a dead submarine. She wanted to close her eyes and let the feelings disappear into the darkness, but David was still standing there, looking at her. She had to say something.

"Did, uh, they say anything about why?" she asked.

He nodded. "There already is a security initiative in play with another team, and they thought they would be too similar."

Was he freaking kidding? "But the project didn't inherently have anything to do with security. It was just a possible thing that could be added on, not even required."

He nodded sympathetically. "Yes, I argued that. He didn't budge. I'm sorry—I know you worked hard on this."

Sujata was frozen, feeling the burning behind her eyes. She focused on keeping it together. "Okay. Thanks for letting me know."

"You do good work, Sujata. There may be another time you could present this proposal again, or maybe you'll come up with something even better."

"Thanks." She scrambled out of there, avoiding looking in Vivek's direction.

When she got to her desk, she realized she had left her damn curry on the counter. She sat for a moment, trying to regain her composure.

"Hey." Vivek was looking at her from the other side of her pod wall. "You forgot your lunch."

"Yeah." She was on the verge of angry tears. Why had he brought up security? Would it have been any different otherwise? Why had David even assigned him to work with her on this?

He moved over so he could hand the container to her, also handing over a plastic fork.

She took it, and then the other thing David had mentioned so casually, that Vivek had put his notice in, finally registered. "David said you put your notice in."

"Oh. Yeah." He looked surprised. "My last day is in four weeks."

"Wow, I can't believe you're going to leave." She was disappointed, but the anger was still there. "Krishna turned the proposal down because they already have another security initiative going on right now."

Vivek closed his eyes for a moment, then opened them again. "I'm sorry, Sujata. I really don't understand why they fixated on that part. I never claimed it was supposed to be a huge part of the work, either. It seems like moving up in the corporate world really does rely on who likes you rather than what kind of brain power you have."

At least he understood that it was partially his fault. But he wasn't wrong about the other stuff, either. "Yeah. That's true."

He stood there staring at her, chagrined, and she looked back. They said nothing. Vivek finally turned toward his desk. "I'd better get back. You need to eat your lunch, anyway. I'll see you later."

"Thanks for bringing my lunch." She appreciated his thoughtfulness. This wasn't all his fault. The directors and VP were all just morons.

But before she could even get the lid off the curry, Theresa showed up, looking concerned.

"They said no," Sujata muttered.

"Oh, no. I'm sorry." She came around and gave Sujata a side hug, while Sujata twisted to hug her back. The awkward contortions made them laugh, and Sujata felt marginally better.

But then she pressed her fingers to her forehead. "I'm so bummed."

"Yeah." Theresa went back to the outside of the cube. "It sucks. Was there any hope for future consideration?"

"Not really. But the worst part?" She looked pointedly at Theresa.

"What?"

"They rejected it because they already have another security initiative going." Sujata couldn't get the frown off her face.

Theresa's eyes widened. "Are you kidding? Vivek's add-on thing? So stupid."

Sujata had told her and Casey about the meeting, so they already knew it was a potential issue.

"They fixated on that. It totally pisses me off."

"It should. It's stupid." She shook her head. "I'm just so sorry."

"Thanks."

"Are you still able to come out tonight?" Theresa asked. "Maybe it would be good for you to distract yourself and try to loosen up." It was their regular Friday night out.

Sujata nodded. It would be a good idea to drink some wine. Maybe even enough to need to take an Uber home.

"Let's brainstorm with Casey and see if there's anything that can be done. You never know—there might be something else you can do."

"I doubt it." She knew she wasn't usually this beaten down. She sighed. "I guess I'll live. I don't know why I let myself get so invested in this."

"It's because you care. Let's talk more tonight."

"Yeah. Thanks for the hug."

Theresa headed off. Sujata had just opened her lunch container and unlocked her screen when she saw Vivek headed her way again.

But he just nodded and smiled as he walked past her cube.

She watched him walk away, now feeling guilty about being so mad at him. He hadn't meant any harm.

She would have to get over it, pretend it never happened, and just do her job. Assuming she could get her mental shit in order.

That thought, that she needed to get back to feeling okay, somehow instead triggered thoughts of Rajeev and his rejection of her. Just like with him, she'd been thinking she was valued and appreciated here. Then he'd just dropped her like a dirty rag. And these leaders couldn't even be bothered to remember her name for an hour, and then they just cast her hard work aside like it was nothing.

She closed her eyes and allowed herself to feel the feelings for a moment, but she just had to move on. She took a deep breath and opened her eyes to look at her computer. She unlocked it again to reveal the code she'd been working on before lunch.

She could always find a new job that would respect her ideas. Or even develop this on her own outside of work.

That last thought was interesting, even though it would be a while before her confidence would build back up again and she would be brave enough to try something like that.

FRIDAY NIGHT KIRAN was driving Ishaan to the airport, Vivek tagging along because they were going to a game night afterward. They chatted about the wedding plans while Vivek went over the conversation with Sujata in his head for the millionth time. It was so stupid that they'd rejected her proposal because of the security addition. They'd obviously paid no attention to anything Sujata had said—instead they'd just heard his contribution. He'd seen it in the meeting, and now he knew he hadn't been misinterpreting things.

The hum of the tires had replaced the voices in the car. Vivek knew Ishaan well enough to know that he was nervous and dreading the next thirty-plus hours, which is what it would take him to get home. Who knew what Kiran was thinking about.

Kiran interrupted Vivek's reverie. "So why'd you end up taking your uncle's job instead of finding something here, Vivek?"

He closed his eyes as his heart sank just thinking about it. "It was a timing problem. He didn't give me much time to decide. I might be able to find something here, but if I didn't get something in time, his job would no longer be available." He didn't want to think about it, but it would be the big topic tomorrow when he called his family. "I didn't want to have to go back to India."

"But what's with you and Sujata?" Kiran asked. "I never did understand that."

The first thing that popped into Vivek's head was the memory of her on his lap less than a week ago, and he had to close his eyes for a second to compose himself. How could they fit together so perfectly like that, yet she could just throw it all away? Then, that image was replaced by her pinched face this afternoon. She was really upset about this, although she was trying to cover it up. But she was mad at him, and he understood. He was mad at himself. He should have just kept his mouth shut.

"Her proposal got rejected, and it's partially my fault, so she's really angry with me." He explained what had happened.

"I guess she really doesn't want to date you now," Kiran teased.

"Correct," Vivek said. He didn't know why he felt so despondent right now. He was leaving, anyway.

No, he knew why. Now he'd be leaving with their friendship broken, all because of one little idea he had. She would be forever mad at him, and that felt terrible.

"It's such a shame," Ishaan said. "She seems into you."

Vivek said nothing and silence descended on the car again.

Ishaan was lucky. He was happy about where things were going in his life.

Soon enough, Kiran was pulling up to the curb in departures. Ishaan got his suitcases out of the trunk and they waved at him as he turned to head inside. Vivek moved up to the front seat and they took off.

PART II

SPRING

13

It was this Saturday afternoon bus ride to her Bharatanatyam practice that made Sujata most seriously consider buying a car, since it was her longest commute. And here she was again, struggling with what she should get.

She was leaning toward an Audi, but felt guilty about not going with something more practical—i.e., less expensive—like a Toyota. Toyotas were good cars, too.

She rolled her eyes at her decidedly first-world quandary and pulled the stop request cord.

Besides, thinking about cars always had her remembering the drives back to Vivek's apartment after movie nights. His roommates rather transparently arranged it so it was the two of them in the back.

She tried to put the whole car question out of her head. If she was going to be struggling with something, it should be how shitty she still felt about the failure of her proposal.

And how she was still mad at Vivek, even though she knew it wasn't *really* his fault.

Whatever. For now, she was bussing it. Starting next week, she would be coming in to the studio on Tuesdays, Thursdays, and Saturdays through March in preparation for their performance at the end of the month.

Would Vivek still be here on the thirty-first? She'd wondered before if she should invite him to the performance, guessing he'd enjoy it. Even though he was modern. Bharatanatyam was from his own state, after all.

It still felt weird that he was leaving. But that was that.

The bus slowed and she hopped off and walked briskly down the sidewalk to the studio, hugging herself against the chill, even though it was getting warmer every day now. Just before she reached the door, that slightly pungent bread smell coming out of the Subway next door hit her. She pulled open the glass door and relished the warmth inside as she climbed the stairs to the studio.

She heard the other women chatting in Tamil before she got into the changing room, but they greeted her in English as she walked in. Hearing Tamil always reminded her of Vivek, since it was his first language. She mentally sighed. She needed him off her mind.

Everyone talked while they finished changing, but cut the chatter the second they got into the studio proper, as Nilani was particular.

"Welcome, please warm up," Nilani said as she fiddled with the music. Things were tense right now because of the recital prep.

Soon Nilani had them going through the various movements following the *namaskar* opening. Although she had always loved it, Sujata had been self-conscious as a teenager doing this form of dance, knowing that it would look bizarre to most Americans, even Indian-Americans if they'd grown up here. The foot slaps especially had embarrassed her. But now she found the deliberate movements and positioning meditative, similar to yoga, especially once they moved on to the *nritta*, which focused on rhythm.

She was finding it good today. Even though her mind kept slipping to the big rejection yesterday, she was doing reasonably well. She imagined the foot slaps as hand slaps across the faces of all those idiots.

Okay, so maybe she wasn't doing so great.

The group continued going through the *adavus* together, and

Sujata did her best to focus. But soon they got to the actual performance prep.

The first part of it was from the traditional Bharatanatyam repertoire and involved everyone—the seven dancers, with Paree as the soloist. After this, there was some original choreography that Nilani had developed for the entire group, based on scenes from the Mahabharata. Sujata, Kaarikaa, and one other dancer also had short solos afterward. Today they were going through everything but the latter solos. Sujata was always so impressed with what Nilani came up with. She was strict, but very creative.

Once they were through the preparatory exercises, Nilani got everyone in position for the first part, leaving Paree watching since she would learn her part separately at first.

The movements were familiar, as this segment was relatively formulaic, so no one struggled too much, and Sujata could already feel the rhythm and essence of the dance steps imprinting on her brain. Remembering physical things was different from remembering purely mental things, and she loved the way developing muscle memory felt, almost primal.

Like her freaking lust for Vivek. Bananas. She forced herself to focus back on the physicality of what she was doing and tried to forget Vivek for the moment.

Once they'd gone through it once, Nilani asked them to go through it again while she worked with Paree.

Sujata and the others went through the steps, only getting mixed up at one point. But they self-corrected and got through it well enough, although she was glad Nilani hadn't caught their slip-up. They started it a second time, but now Sujata's mind wandered again to the fact that Vivek really was leaving.

She moved her arms in rhythm with everyone else and decided she would invite him to the performance.

Then her mind slipped to the Monday presentation again. There went a foot slap, this one dedicated to Krishna. And another, that one to Chang. Slap, Aarav's smug face. She withheld the next one from

David, because she believed he'd tried his best. There was only so much he could do.

But the next two were reserved for Vivek and his stupid security idea.

Okay, this was soothing. She kept going, working out her frustrations with one gesture at a time.

Soon enough, Nilani was back and they started working on the next part of the performance. This was the part Sujata was excited to learn, and Nilani's choreography did not disappoint this time, just as it never had before.

They went through this one twice, then did their cool-down movements, and Sujata realized that she really did feel better than she had before coming. As disappointed as she was, there was something so fortifying about physical action.

But it didn't change the fact that being covered in sweat in the hot studio was gross once they stopped moving.

She went with everyone back to the changing area and they talked for a bit, Paree and Kaarikaa chatting about their siblings getting married soon. Once Sujata was back in her comfortable jeans, she was out the door, heading for the bus.

Maybe she *should* buy a car. It wouldn't be pretentious to drive an Audi, would it? She was single and made good money. Why not?

Was that who she was, though? She honestly didn't know. For some reason, Vivek leaving had her shaken. Even though she was kind of mad at him. And then not. She knew it wasn't really his fault. Her mental state was all over the place right now. She just hoped she could get herself back in order, and start liking her job again.

She should be able to get herself there. But one thing was clear, which she had no control over—Vivek would no longer be there with her.

VIVEK SAT in the dark theater Saturday night, Kiran to his left. It was weird with it just being the two of them, but everyone else had some kind of conflict.

This was a thief caper and it was hilarious, but his mood didn't quite match the feeling laughter is supposed to give. He could not stop the increasing regret he felt about bringing security up in the presentation with Sujata.

She had told him she didn't want to include it, but she was too nice to completely forbid it. He knew she must regret that, so he felt doubly bad—first for contributing to the reasons for them to reject the proposal, which obviously upset Sujata, but also for making her regret not standing her ground enough.

He should have paid attention and respected her wishes. He closed his eyes at the discomfort from the memory. He hadn't realized he was being overbearing, but he kind of had been. He knew she didn't want to include the topic, but he did. And he chose to do something he wanted even though it specifically went against what she wanted. What a rubbish friend he was. He felt vaguely ill.

He was really obsessing about this. But that was because, in a lot of ways, it was a bigger deal than it might seem at face value. Basically, he hadn't respected her expertise and had ruined her chances.

Dammit.

On the screen, a man was wearing a yellow dress as a disguise, but the big revolver he was carrying in his hand undid the efficacy of the outfit. And he'd had to hike up the skirt over his knees, so the overall effect was pretty funny.

Vivek made himself laugh with everyone else, and it did make him feel marginally better.

Still, he wondered what Sujata was up to tonight. He knew she had her dance practice in the afternoon, and he knew that she often went out with Theresa and Casey Friday nights, and hung out with Gwen sometimes, but he had no other ideas about how she spent her weekends.

He hoped she was keeping herself busy and her mind away from the rejection. If not, it would be partially his fault, and that made him feel rubbish.

Also, the fact that he was leaving was weird. He'd always held this hope that he and Sujata would somehow stay friends even if he left. But with this incident, it seemed unlikely.

The whole thing was a shame. He'd really believed that her idea was great, and not too difficult to develop.

But the thing was, she could totally do it on her own. Maybe he should suggest that.

If she did try to create this on her own, however, she would have to rewrite the crawler, however. That was what made it so easy to implement at InfoQuest. The crawler was already done. And it was a complex beast. Vivek would know, since it had been his to maintain since he'd been here.

Who would take over on that? No one knew it better than he did. There was definitely some knowledge transfer in his future.

If Sujata did decide to go out on her own, he could totally help her with the crawler. Not all of his knowledge was proprietary—he had a solid understanding of a crawler all the way from a high-level abstract concept down to the InfoQuest-specific implementations. But he didn't need to use the InfoQuest knowledge to develop one she could use.

He had to think about this. He might not be the right person to suggest this to her. Maybe he could give her some strong hints? Build her up and then nudge her in the right direction? This seemed like the best path.

Whatever ended up happening, she was within her rights to be mad at him. He just hoped that faded before he left, so that at least their friendship wouldn't end on bad terms.

~

Sunday evening, Sujata was finishing up her yoga routine when her phone rang with Kavya's ringtone. She held the Natarajasana pose for another thirty seconds while the phone kept ringing. It would be nice to vent to Kavya, but she needed to get into a better mental space first. She'd focus on her yoga and once she was done, she'd call Kavya back. She put her left foot on the floor and lifted her right leg up before doing a few other manipulations. She reached her left arm straight out and held the pose for a minute.

This should help her relax. But of course nothing except three hours of dance yesterday had helped, and the frustration had crept right back up to Friday levels by tonight.

She forced her muscles to unwind and went through a final sun salutation before lying down in corpse pose. She was supposed to be unwinding, but her body and thoughts were still tied up in knots.

Still, she was curious about why Kavya had called. It wasn't like they never talked, but usually there was an initial reason for the call, and then they would end up talking for an hour about everything and nothing.

What would be really nice would be to see Kavya in person. Maybe she should plan a trip. Maybe over the summer. She had the vacation days available.

After several minutes, Sujata got up and went over to the bed where she'd tossed the phone.

She'd just text Kavya.

—Can I call you back after a quick shower?—

Maybe she'd feel better after one. It hadn't helped yesterday, but maybe today would be different. Who knew.

Kavya replied right away that that was fine, and Sujata had her shower and then sat at her desk. She dialed and Kavya answered on the first ring.

"Hi, *didi*." Sujata started combing her wet hair. "What's up? Everything alright?"

"Sure, fine. I just hadn't talked to you in a while."

That sounded fishy. Should she be worried? "We talked Tuesday."

"Oh, well, that's true." Kavya was quiet for a moment. "So, tell me about the proposal. Have you heard anything yet?"

"It was rejected." She closed her eyes, reliving the pain of David telling her.

"Oh, man. I'm sorry, *shona*. I was worried when you hadn't texted me an update."

Sujata had told her about the presentation on Tuesday, but she couldn't bear to type out the words Friday. She launched into a more detailed recounting while she continued combing her hair. This was another of those things that was usually soothing, but not tonight. The comb kept getting caught because she was going too fast.

"So how's Vivek been since then?" Kavya asked.

Sujata dropped her hand. "It's partially his fault they said no." The sense of injustice filled her stomach with heaviness. She explained what David had said.

"That sucks." Kavya sounded genuinely mad for her.

"But also, it was just a bunch of men with power being men with power on Monday." She explained how they had dismissed her but built Vivek up. She continued to comb.

Kavya scoffed. "Sometimes I hate this world. It didn't matter that you knew way more than he did, did it? I hate that so much."

"Yeah." Sujata frowned. "I also found out that Vivek's leaving. His last day is the thirtieth. Which is weird. He'll actually be completely out of my life. I doubt he'd want to stay in contact once he's left Portland."

Kavya laughed. "Oh, I doubt your doubt, *shona*. He's so hung up on you."

Sujata exhaled. "Maybe. I don't know how that will go. Will we just be Facebook friends? What would that mean?"

"It would mean you'll question yourself when he marries somebody else," Kavya teased.

"Ha. This is probably accurate." She set the comb down and started braiding. The idea of Vivek no longer being around did make her feel unhappy. Which made no sense. She had no control of her emotions right now.

"Hey!" Kavya said suddenly. "How have I never seen a picture of this hunk? Do you have one?"

"Of course not." She pulled the progressing braid tight and crossed over the next strand of hair.

"Oh, come on. You take selfies. You must have a group photo or something. I want to see what he looks like. Please?"

She really didn't have any pictures of him on her phone, which was weird. But she could grab one off LinkedIn. "Fine, but you'll have to wait because I'm braiding my hair." Time to reroute the conversation. "But *didi*, I know you didn't call to talk about Vivek. You're stalling."

"No." She stretched it out.

"Is everything okay?"

"I'm sort of freaking out. Ankur came up to see me yesterday."

"No way!" This was a genuine surprise. He was such a shy guy. But Sujata loved it. She knew those two were perfect for each other, but she didn't think either would have the gumption to do anything about it. She figured it would be entirely arranged by their parents.

"I know." From Kavya's voice, she was obviously smiling.

"So, what happened?" She couldn't imagine how it went down. Ankur was even shyer than Vivek, who at least had been brave enough to ask her out, even though he was obviously nervous.

"Sujata! Nothing *happened*."

Sujata laughed. "That's really not what I meant. But now you sound guilty."

"I'm not," Kavya said. But she totally did sound guilty.

"So, really, what happened? Did you guys talk?"

"I think we're going to agree to it."

"Oh, my God! Really? That's awesome, Kavya!" Sujata's mouth had stretched into its biggest smile in a week.

"I know. I'm in shock."

"My big sister's getting married!"

"Calm down. It's not going to be for a while. Not until after first year of grad school."

"Definitely. Still, it's exciting. Maa and Baba are going to be so happy." Of course, this also meant they'd be on Sujata's case to get married soon enough.

But she wasn't going to think about that. No reason to rain on Kavya's parade.

"You'll find someone, too, Sujata," Kavya said quietly.

Trust her sister to read her mind. She'd say what she was supposed to say. "I know."

"They're not all like that."

"I know." Sujata knew that was technically true. She really ought to think about doing something to meet men, but her heart just wasn't in it.

It didn't help that that particular body part was already spoken for, even if she'd never admit it, which she never would. Bananas.

Sujata finished the braid and pulled up Vivek's LinkedIn to get his headshot—and, wow, did he look good in this shot, with a grin that exuded confidence. She had to send a mental message to her lady bits to calm down. She sent the screenshot to Kavya. "There. That's Vivek."

"Aw, he *is* cute."

Sujata sighed. "I'm aware."

And he was even more appealing in person. His voice, his body, his usual thoughtfulness. Bananas bananas bananas.

14

Sujata worked away on one of her coding projects Monday, her mind only going to the rejection occasionally. Programming was a good way to keep mentally busy. It could be satisfying, especially when you figured out something tricky, which she'd done this morning. It definitely had put her in a better mood.

She wasn't a loser, after all.

Her brain wasn't totally doing what it was supposed to, though. She still found herself going back to the proposal, wondering if she might be able to change it and submit again. Obviously not right away, but eventually. A twist of hope flitted through her stomach at the thought.

She'd have to wait a while, that was for sure.

Maybe she could continue working on the proposal, make it even stronger. She'd have to be judicious with her time and prioritize everything else, but she did have slower times occasionally, and she could always work on it at home. She could get so much done if she really put her mind to it.

It was probably pointless, but at least she could have a tiny bit of hope.

She continued working on her code, trying to figure out how to identify the language in a particular set of text data. She'd learned this wasn't an entirely solved problem, but what she'd figured out this morning was that she could look at the frequency of letters to get a sense of it. There were always little things about projects that made them understandable or solvable. The same was true of people.

"Hey, Sujata," someone said.

She'd been rather focused, so it jarred her, and she glanced up to see Vivek on the other side of her pod wall. A surge of confused irritation and desire went through her.

She made sure her face was neutral, relaxing her lips and eyes. "Hi." The guilt he felt was plastered on his face.

"I just wanted to see how you were doing. I'm still frustrated at Sandeep and everyone." He looked guilty.

"I'm good," she said automatically. Irritation spread through her chest. She'd been doing such a good job of not dwelling on it *too* much this morning. She absentmindedly picked up a Bic pen. Why hadn't she stood her ground when he suggested including security? It was likely a gender thing. Even though she was pretty confident, she was still conflict-averse and often found herself agreeing with men even when she didn't actually agree. It just seemed expedient in the moment.

"They are idiots."

"Well. Thank you." She tapped the pen on the desk a couple times.

"I'm going to stay mad at them for not listening to you. You did a good job presenting everything clearly." He spread his hands to emphasize his feelings. "They just didn't pay attention."

That seemed right.

He continued, "It would have been something really valuable to InfoQuest, and you're the perfect person to lead the project."

"Thanks."

She felt something in her chest, an idea she could only feel. Was there something she could do about this? Other than just try again later? There was no reason to expect it would go any differently next time, especially if it was the same small-minded men judging her.

"Other companies would be smarter than they were and would jump at the chance," Vivek said.

Sujata really could just do it. She was skilled enough. Although she'd thought of that before, she hadn't seriously considered it. Now she was going to do it. Realization burst inside her, spreading joy everywhere. On her own, outside of work. There wasn't anything proprietary in the basic idea. Yes, there were parts of the software they would have been able to leverage here, but she could build that on her own.

"I could just do it on my own," she said, sounding surprised even to herself.

Vivek smiled, eyes lighting up. "I was thinking that, but I didn't want to tell you what to do. But you absolutely could. You should do it."

"I should do it." A giant grin stretched across her face.

That made Vivek look even happier.

She knew it wasn't his fault. He believed in her and the project. Her heart swelled with affection.

But that feeling burst when she remembered he was leaving. "Where are you moving to?"

His smile disappeared and he exhaled. "Atlanta. My uncle has a transportation company there, and everyone's been pestering me to take the job he offered me months ago. I just caved. It seemed inevitable."

"You're not looking forward to it." She would miss him, as weird as that was. She'd spent the last year rejecting him, and now she was bummed he was leaving. She had such confused feelings around him. If things had been different, if Rajeev hadn't been quite so awful—like if he'd just broken up with her like a normal person—it might have been different. She and Vivek might have been perfect together.

"My uncle is rather overbearing. But I guess it could be worse. He will sponsor my green card, so I won't have to worry about my visa again." He nodded thoughtfully, looking off to the side.

"Well, at least there's that." She might have been ready to date him eventually, but obviously it was unreasonable to expect him to wait indefinitely, and he was practically gone, anyway.

"Yeah, at least there's that." He looked at her again. "I'd better get back to work."

"Me, too. Thanks for inspiring me to come up with a new plan. I'm actually excited." She totally was.

"I'm excited to see what you can make of it. It's a great idea. See you later."

Sujata said bye, and he headed back to his desk, leaving her distracted and stewing on thoughts about how she would develop the idea on her own.

She was excited for the future now. She had something worthwhile to keep her busy.

Maybe it was unusual for someone her age to be only looking forward to a future filled with work, but she was excited about the project, and it was all that her heart could handle right now. She couldn't wait to see what came of it.

~

ON FRIDAY, Vivek went into the kitchen and was pleasantly surprised to see Sujata sitting at the table with everyone else. She looked up at him when he sat next to her while his food was heating, and gave him her friendly smile. Sanjay was on his other side but the others were deep in a conversation in Hindi about pictures.

"Hi," he said, unable to keep from grinning.

"Hi." Her gaze fell to his mouth for a quick moment before she looked straight ahead.

She still wanted him. In spite of what had happened with the proposal. His body reacted to that.

Calm down, Vivek.

"Did you bring something?" she asked, motioning to the empty space in front of him.

"It's in the microwave."

"Ah." She took a bite of her curry, still watching him. It looked like chole, one of his favorites. Rather like the woman with the spoon in her hand.

He sincerely hoped that being away from her would free him from her spell. That would be the only good thing about Atlanta. He was going to have to start over in terms of friendships—he'd have to find some guys to play cricket with—and he'd have to revisit looking for a potential wife, even though he'd still be hung up on Sujata.

He should have tried harder to stay here. But he knew that if he did, it would really be for Sujata, and that was a bad reason to stay here since she'd made it very clear that nothing would happen between them.

The microwave beeped three times so he went over to grab his food. He pulled the top off his plastic container and flipped it upside down and under the container so he could carry it without burning himself. The steam shot up to waft past his chin. He breathed in the smell of the *sambar*, a vegetable and lentil stew.

He sat down next to Sujata again and stirred the sambar to let it cool a bit. It occurred to him that he wouldn't sit next to her very many more times in his life. He pushed down the melancholy. "Did you decide to go ahead with your independent project?"

She nodded. "I started figuring out the components. There really are two high-level ones—the system crawler and the data analyzer. But I was also thinking that adding a data catalog as a presentation layer would make it all more appealing."

"That's a great idea." He had a good feeling about this for her. She was smart and always got things done even to her own high standards. He knew she could do this. But the crawler would take her a lot less time if he helped her, since he knew InfoQuest's so well, and they'd be very similar. But he wasn't offering. He'd help if she asked.

She swallowed her bite of curry. "I thought so. It's extra work, but this need isn't going away. There aren't that many companies out there doing work in this area, especially combining these things."

Vivek couldn't keep himself from saying, "You could get funding for this. Venture capitalists love tech companies."

She frowned thoughtfully. "I wasn't even thinking that far ahead. But you're right. Pretty intimidating, though."

"Yeah, I can see that." He guessed that she had imposter syndrome, like so many perfectly smart and accomplished women he'd met. It made him sad, because he didn't know how to build someone up in that situation.

"I'm also not sure at what point to reach out. I feel like I have to write much of the code first, so that I'm entirely sure I can do this. And I know very little about the crawler. Unlike you." Sujata bumped his arm with her elbow, the point of contact lighting up.

That was an invitation, if ever there was one. He smiled. "I'm happy to help you with it."

"Oh, I wouldn't ask you to do that." She waved her hand dismissively and wiped her mouth with a napkin, dropping it into her lunch container.

"I don't mean writing it or anything," he clarified, absentmindedly rubbing the spot on his arm that was still on fire. "But I could help you with the design. I know you're entirely capable of developing it yourself, but you could avoid some stumbles this way."

Her eyes glowed, looking touched by his offer. "I just might take you up on that."

Was she happy because she'd be getting help, or because it meant talking to him some more? He hoped it was the latter.

"Did you see Gaurav's photos yet, Vivek?" Sanjay asked from Vivek's other side, jarring him out of his thoughts. Gaurav was one of their coworkers who'd gone back to India to get married.

"No." He didn't really want to look because he was jealous.

Sanjay had them up on his phone and started flipping through them.

Gaurav's bride was pretty, though she had a lot of makeup on for the wedding. That was pretty normal, to be fair. Vivek imagined Sujata made up for her own wedding. He could picture it.

"Gaurav got married?" she asked, leaning in toward Vivek to see the photos better. "I'm so out of the loop."

"Yeah, he left a couple weeks ago," Vivek said, unable to avoid breathing in that lavender scent of hers as she got closer.

"He looks happy," she said.

"That's his nervous smile," Sanjay said with a chuckle, which made the others laugh, too.

"You're right," Vivek said. "But I know he's also happy."

Kiran nodded. "True. He was looking forward to this for months."

Sujata had a faraway look in her eyes. He wondered if she was thinking about a wedding that never was. He didn't know how far along they'd gotten with their plans.

But then their eyes met and she smiled awkwardly. He returned it and wondered when she'd get in touch about the crawler. Maybe this weekend. He could hope, or maybe nudge her in the right direction.

15

Sunday morning, Sujata got situated on her couch, computer on her lap, ready to talk to Vivek on Google Meet. She had her tea on the side table. She'd splurged on some sugar today, hoping it would give her the burst of energy she needed after a late night coding.

It might not have been the best choice, since she was already excited about talking to Vivek. She felt like a seventh grader about to talk to her crush the first time, which made no sense, since this was going to be an all-business conversation.

She connected to the meeting and found a large, green, cartoon-style dragon head instead of Vivek's face, which made her laugh out loud. Then she heard him laugh right back, which made the sides of the dragon's head stretch out, which in turn made her crack up even more.

"Oh, my God, Vivek. You totally caught me off guard. You're usually so reserved." She started scanning through the filters.

The dragon's eyebrows furrowed. "I'm not really reserved."

She clicked on the cowboy hat, which gave her a brown leather hat, a scruffy gray mustache, and a blue necktie.

Vivek snorted and the dragon's eyes narrowed as he laughed.

Suddenly the dragon head was gone and there was Vivek, still smiling.

God, he looked good. He rocked the rugged jawline, and she loved his dark eyes. You could swim in the depths of them.

She turned off the cowboy hat, unreasonably sad that they had to be serious. She really did need to get this info from him. “So, thanks for talking to me.”

“No worries. I’m glad to help. I’m just really excited that you’re doing this. I hope you are a huge success and they regret not taking you more seriously.”

That made her heart swell. He sounded so earnest. She hoped the same thing, but it was so sweet that he was so on her side.

And it didn’t hurt that he had this sexy five o’clock shadow and just-got-out-of-bed hair.

Bananas. She couldn’t think like that. “Did you get your own room? It looks like you’re in a bedroom.”

He smiled. “Yes, when Ishaan left.”

They stared at each other for a moment. She hadn’t really thought about it before, but she knew that Vivek liked her not only because of her looks, but also for her mind. It hadn’t been that way with Rajeev. He didn’t understand what she did and didn’t really care. His doctor work was so much more important to him.

Yet for her, his intelligence was part of the attraction. And it was the same with Vivek. She couldn’t imagine ever dating someone who wasn’t smart. What would they talk about?

“So,” Vivek finally said, his voice deep with some kind of emotion. “What do you have so far?”

“Yeah, we should get started.” She actually just wanted to chat—that was the mood she was in. She’d gotten sentimental now that he was leaving. But he was right. “So now there are four primary components, two of which are similar to what we have at work. Those two are the crawler, which is obviously what we’re talking about today, and the analyzer, which I’ve got experience with.” That was the part she worked on at InfoQuest. “Then there’s the data catalog, which is the least interesting piece. And the last piece is the advisor, which is the part that will make recommendations. These last two are totally new."

He nodded. "That makes sense. I was also thinking you could potentially take the output from InfoQuest if they are a customer."

It was like he could read her mind. "Yeah, I was planning on it. That would make the crawler unnecessary, but not all customers will have it. But let's start with the crawler."

"That's true. How do you want me to do this? Should I talk high level? I need to know how much detail you want. I may draw some things. I borrowed Kiran's whiteboard."

Sujata laughed. "A whiteboarding session? Nice." It was also nice that he was taking this so seriously. He obviously really did want to help.

He started in on the design of InfoQuest's crawler, saying they could discuss logical modifications once he was done explaining it.

She listened, taking notes and asking questions along the way, all while feeling almost giddy with excitement about the project and the fact that he was helping her for absolutely nothing in return. It was going to be so weird when he was gone. Horrible really. She was only now realizing how much she'd always depended on him. He made it seem possible that she was lovable. Rajeev had killed that, making her feel not good enough for anyone, but Vivek had just always been there, admiring her, even before Rajeev had left her. Or disappeared. Whatever.

"So that's the high level," Vivek said. "But I want to draw some of the components a bit further down."

"Whiteboard time."

He smiled at her and picked it up off the floor. "Of course."

It was a large one that was meant for a wall, and he held it in his lap while he wrote, obscuring all of his body except his face. She studied that part of him because he was looking down and wouldn't know she was staring. His hair was thick and glossy. She wondered if he used coconut oil on his hair, like a lot of Indians.

Sujata really was excited about this project. She'd worked late last night, full of energy. She knew she could do this, and it was going to be awesome when she made it and could finally quit InfoQuest.

Vivek looked up. "Okay, here we go." He awkwardly tried to turn the whiteboard around, but hit the wall.

"One minute," he said. He held it off to the side and managed to get it, but then the laptop was too close and it was zoomed in too far, which made them both laugh.

"We should do this in person," Sujata said. For some reason, she really wanted to see him in person again, even though tomorrow was Monday and she'd see him then.

"What, at a Starbucks?" he joked.

"You could come over." As soon as she said it, she panicked. What was she doing?

Wanting to see him was no excuse for this. He'd never been to her apartment before. What would happen with the two of them in an entirely personal space with no one else around?

His raised eyebrows gave away his own surprise. "That might actually not be a bad idea. Do you have a whiteboard?"

She shook her head, still freaked out. But he was right about it being easier. "If you don't mind the bus ride over, you could. But you don't have to if you have other stuff to do today."

"No, it's fine. I can bring the board."

"Cool." She gave him her address and they figured out the buses.

Now she had to clean her apartment—it was not ready for visitors. But it would take him at least forty-five minutes to get here, so she could get some cleaning done. She launched herself off the couch, almost tripping on the blanket that had been across her lap. She caught herself against the wall and scrambled into the kitchen.

In less than an hour, Vivek would be *in her apartment*. She was in shock. And it was all her own doing. This wasn't normal bananas, this was bananas Foster or something else on fire.

~

VIVEK STEPPED ABOARD HIS BUS, the whiteboard tucked under his arm.

The bus was fuller than he'd expected and there were no completely empty seats. Everybody in the sea of faces looked grumpy and disinterested. One woman narrowed her eyes at him, possibly trying to figure what he was carrying. There was a mix of people and he spotted an open seat next to a white man in a baseball cap who seemed inoffensive. Should be no problem.

Vivek turned sideways and held the board close so he could get down the aisle. He sat down next to the man, who glanced over and did a double-take at the sight of the board, which Vivek had to keep in the aisle, propped up vertically so it wouldn't block access to the seat in front of him or behind him.

He felt very self-conscious.

Then, as he was slipping off the straps of his backpack, the board fell sideways and hit the seat on the other side of the aisle.

"Sorry," he muttered, but the young woman in the seat said nothing.

He felt himself blushing and decided he'd be taking an Uber home from Sujata's apartment.

Sujata. He would see her in a few minutes. A thrill ran through his chest. He was going to her actual apartment.

Had she meant anything more by inviting him? He didn't think so. But it had to mean *something* that she'd invited him over.

He sat there, holding onto the whiteboard through numerous stops with people getting off and on, and a few more curious looks. When a guy behind him got off, he kicked the board, which jerked in Vivek's arm. It was likely an accident, but who knew for sure? The guy had said nothing, just continued down the aisle.

Seriously, was Vivek the first person in world history to bring a whiteboard on a bus?

But who cared? He was going to be in Sujata's apartment in a short time. It was worth the hassle with the whiteboard.

What would she be wearing? He'd never seen her at home. Would she be dressed up nice, or in pyjamas?

Well, to be fair, he already knew what she'd been wearing on her top half—a simple red t-shirt. It was rather close-fitting, though, which would be even nicer in person.

Finally, the man next to him got off and Vivek only hit the board against one seat trying to get out of the way. Then he scooted over next to the window, the board finally contained within the seat. All the hubbub had rubbed off the writing on the board. He'd have to redo it all. No big deal, it just meant more time with her.

But then he looked down at his stomach; his white shirt had a bunch of blue marker ink on it, some in the shape of words dragged a couple of inches.

He sighed and rolled his eyes. What a mess.

Things went fine for the rest of the journey, and he got off near Sujata's apartment without hitting anyone or anything else with the board. It was a couple of blocks before he reached her place, and now that he was close, his pulse quickened in anticipation.

By the time he knocked on her door, his whole body was buzzing. Why was the mere idea of her doing this to him? He saw her all the time at work without being so affected.

But this was her home.

She opened the door, and for a millisecond there was a look of confusion on her face, but then a smile broke out and her eyes flashed.

That was desire if he'd ever seen it.

"You brought the whiteboard!" she said. She had on jeans and the thin red t-shirt did nicely show off her breasts. Her beautiful hair was pulled back.

The sight of her made his whole body reverberate. He would never have full control of his body around her. But he needed to answer.

"Of course. Although, I nearly beheaded several people on the bus trying to sit down."

That made her laugh. She moved to the side. "Come on in."

As he stepped in, a fresh scent he couldn't identify enveloped him. To the right was the kitchen, and the den was straight ahead. He felt her behind him, and he wanted to turn around and take her in his arms. Instead, he kept moving forward, toward a navy sofa.

"We can sit on the couch," Sujata said. "I don't have a big enough table."

The couch faced a balcony, a small glass-topped coffee table in front of it. A red brick fireplace filled the corner of the room. On the left wall was a large abstract painting in reds and yellows. Even though this was just a simple apartment with basic decoration, it still felt like Sujata—bold and vibrant.

He squeezed between the couch and coffee table, which was empty except for a laptop and notebook, and sat down. He rested the whiteboard against the table. His pulse was still going strong. Of course it was. He was actually in *Sujata's* apartment with her now.

She sat down at the other end of the couch, an unfortunate kilometer between them.

But that was reasonable, since they were together to work, not do anything else.

So why was she looking at him like that? The desire was back in her eyes and he was frozen in his spot because he shouldn't do the thing his cock wanted him to do, which was to crawl over there and start kissing her and see where that went.

But it didn't matter what he thought she was feeling—he had to honor what she said, which was No.

"So," Vivek started, clearing his throat, which felt thick. "Let me redraw the architecture of the crawler. It got all over my shirt, but I doubt you can read it there."

She looked at his shirt. "That's hilarious. I recognize a database icon."

"Yes."

"Oh, shit. I didn't offer you a drink," Sujata said, her cheeks flushing pink. She hopped up and faced him.

He smiled, amused at her flustered state. "A water would be nice."

She nodded and disappeared into the kitchen.

He picked up the board and held it awkwardly in his lap, the top part resting on the coffee table, and sketched out the system as it was designed at InfoQuest, which was standard for this kind of system.

She returned with two glasses and set them on the table, carefully avoiding the whiteboard.

She sat close to him while he was labeling the components, and he again smelled her enticing lavender scent, which made him want her so much that he had to grip the whiteboard and marker hard to keep his hands in place.

He took a surreptitious deep breath. "So here it is. Did you have questions?"

"Why don't you walk me through everything? I know we talked about it already, but it will help to hear it a second time. If you don't mind." She glanced at him, but leaned back and away from him.

Was she as affected by him as he was by her?

"Sure." Vivek walked through the various components, explaining what each did, why it was needed, and how it was related to the other components. He only mixed up three components, calling them by the wrong names, because he couldn't stop thinking about being here with Sujata.

While he was going through everything, she scooted closer, most likely to see better, but he relished her scent and the warmth of her shoulder against his.

They continued talking about the system, whiling away the time with talk of code and inputs and outputs.

Out of nowhere, his stomach growled loudly.

He immediately flushed, but Sujata cracked up. "Hungry?" she asked.

"I think so. I hadn't really noticed. What time is it?"

She looked at her phone. "Five thirty. Do you need to go?" She paused. "I can make something for dinner if you want to stay."

This was just getting better and better. Of course he wanted to stay. "I don't want to inconvenience you."

"It's no inconvenience. I was going to have to make something anyway. But I've been craving a quintessentially American thing. Have you ever had mac and cheese?"

He furrowed his brow and tried to think what that was. "Pasta?"

She laughed, which lit up her face. "Technically, but it's so much more. And less. If you're up for something different, I will share with you the joy of my childhood when I visited my friends' houses." She narrowed her eyes in thought. "But if you hate it, I do have some left-over chole."

"I'm sure it will be fine." He had no idea what to expect. Either with the mac and cheese, or with Sujata this day. He knew what he really wanted, and it had nothing to do with pasta.

"Let's go, then." They got up and he followed her to the kitchen. She got a blue box out of the cabinet and got a pot of water heating on the stove. She grinned at him. "You're in for a treat. Or at least a surprise."

Should he be worried? He didn't care, since he was standing in Sujata's kitchen with her. He just smiled back at her, wishing things were different and this situation was a regular occurrence. He loved how domestic this moment was, like they were just hanging out together making dinner. He leaned against the counter next to the stove while she was standing in front of the heating pot.

Sujata's pupils had gotten big, making her eyes darker and more intense.

His whole body wanted to kiss her. But he didn't think he should go down that route, even if she did look like she wanted it. It would just lead to another painful rejection. He watched her watching the pot, his mind swirling with desire.

Without meaning to, he leaned forward just as she stepped toward him, and they were kissing again.

She was so soft everywhere—her lips, her breasts, her hand on his stomach, exploring. Her lips were delectable, and she sucked on his lower one, which felt so good that he let her do it for a while, but then he kissed her jaw until her breath hitched. The lavender scent he so loved was strong here.

He returned to her mouth and plunged his tongue in and she immediately yielded, sliding hers against his. He wrapped his arm around her to pull her closer, and her hand moved to run up his back. A shiver ran down his spine and into his legs and toes.

Her other hand slid to his back, while their mouths were locked in a pleasurable battle. He brought his hands up to run his fingers through her thick hair. Right now, he didn't care if she rejected him after—in this moment, everything was worth it.

He moved away from her mouth and started kissing her neck. She tilted her head back to give him better access, and he kissed his way up her jawline to her earlobe. An earring was in the way, so he made his way down and kissed the delicate part of her neck, thinking that maybe this wouldn't end in a rejection. How could it? It was so perfect.

Her hands were hot on his back, her fingers spread possessively. She tasted like sunshine, lighting up his soul. He shifted back to her mouth and a desperate sound came from the back of her throat, setting him on fire. They went in deep together, heads angled for better access, and their tongues tangled in the best way.

And then, a sizzling sound.

Sujata noticed it at the same time, because she pulled away and they both looked at the pot, which was spilling boiling water over the sides.

"Crap," Sujata said, moving the pot to the side, sloshing even more water out.

Vivek leaned against the counter again, breathing heavily.

Her cheeks were flushed, and now she was avoiding his gaze. She opened the blue box and pulled out a large white packet before dumping the pasta into the pot. She turned the burner down and slid the pot back in place.

Dammit. Again. His heart was still about to burst out of his chest. That had been so, so right—why couldn't she see it? Or, he knew she saw it—why was she denying it again?

This was such rubbish, the way she toyed with him, even if it wasn't her intention. She was weak in one moment, and stubborn in the next.

"Vivek," she said after stirring the pot, staring at it. "I am so attracted to you. You know this. I like kissing you way too much. But I am just not ready to have another relationship. I was so hurt by my ex-fiancé's betrayal. I want to, but I can't."

He was so annoyed. At least she didn't deny the connection they had, as strong as steel. He pushed off the counter and faced her again. He shouldn't ask. He shouldn't hold on to hope. It wasn't rational. But he was going to, anyway. "When do you think you'll be ready?"

At that, she turned to him, looking almost forlorn. "I don't know. But now you're moving."

"That would not be a real deterrent. We could deal with a long-distance relationship if it meant we could be together." He made sure to keep his voice level to not reveal how desperate this whole thing made him feel.

But he wasn't weak. He was so right, and it was just a matter of her seeing it, too.

Still facing him, Sujata closed her eyes and frowned. When she reopened them, she took a deep breath. "Why don't we say this. You get on with your life in Atlanta. If you meet someone, great. When I feel ready, I'll get in touch, and if you're still free, let's give it a shot."

Vivek's heart had slowed, but now it nearly burst with joy.

She turned away from him, looking afraid at what she'd just said. She stirred the pasta.

"I can wait for you," he said. He felt emboldened. "And what's stopping us from enjoying my last few weeks here?"

"I don't think you should wait. But if it so happens that it works out, great." She was being practical, but he could tell she meant it. "But I'm not sleeping with you before you leave for Atlanta. I'm not like that."

"That's fine. But you don't think I'm going to give up on you and go back to India and marry some random woman my parents pick, do you? No. This isn't like picking a shirt. 'This one or that one? Today I feel like blue.'"

She grimaced. "I get it. But Vivek, what if I never get over it? Some people never recover from heartbreak. You know what a mess I am about this."

"You just need to learn to trust again." The earnestness in his voice was embarrassing.

"Like it's easy, Vivek—like I can just snap my fingers and be like, Bam! I'm better."

He had a sudden desire to find the jerk ex-fiancé and punch his slender nose. He cupped her elbow. "Maybe you could try it."

"No. Stop trying to pressure me." She put her fingers to her forehead and stirred the pot with her other hand.

That stung. He thought he was being really patient here. Most men would have applied much more pressure than he had. But he said nothing because he didn't want to be a jerk.

Sujata nodded once. "Let's table this and revisit in six months if you're still single."

Six months. That was definitely possible. Something concrete. In six months, he would just be getting his stride in the new job and would be working and hanging out with whatever friend group he ended up with. But what if her choice was still no? He would really have to move on then. There would be no more waiting and hoping. That would be it. But it was a reasonable thing to do. "That works."

She slid the pan to the side, the soft skin inside her arm visible. "Can you grab the colander from that cabinet?" She pointed to the one by his shoulder.

Guessing, he pulled out a green thing with holes in it. "This?"

She nodded, not taking the opportunity to tease him for not knowing this word. She was looking serious, but she put the colander in the sink and dumped the pot's contents in it. "Can you get the big bowl that's in there, too?"

After he handed it to her, she opened the packet and dumped a bright orange powder out of it into the bowl.

"Um," he started. The color was very surprising.

She laughed and measured and poured some milk into it before stirring it. Then she dumped the pasta in and put a dollop of butter on top and stirred the butter in until it melted, and then she stirred everything together.

She looked over at him with raised eyebrows. "Surprised?"

"Yes. I am afraid of tasting this." His stomach was genuinely active with trepidation. The meal was apparently ready, all bright orange and staring at him from the bowl.

She smiled. "If you don't like it, I won't be offended. My *maa* thinks this is an abomination and refused to ever make it. When I was eight, I begged her to make it and she bought a box. She boiled the macaroni, but when she opened the packet and saw the color, she refused to mix it up, and I ended up having macaroni with butter on it."

Vivek laughed. "Were you sad?"

"I cried for an hour. To get so close only to be turned away. I was devastated." She scooped a few pieces of the pasta up and held it out for him to taste.

He smelled it. It smelled ... not horrible. So he wrapped his lips around the spoon and pulled off and ate what was there. It tasted like it smelled. He figured he could stomach this for Sujata. "Okay, I will try this. A small bowl, though."

"Great." She gave him another of her smiles. "I will warn you that if you end up not liking it, you'll need to wait for a bit to eat Indian food. The flavors do not mix well."

He nodded and took the bowl she offered him. This felt like the beginning of a new adventure.

Six months. He wasn't going to think about the amount of time he'd already waited. This would be the last six months, and then they'd be together, or he'd absolutely have to move on.

16

Tuesday evening a couple weeks after she had Vivek in her house—something Sujata had still not recovered from, with that incredible kiss and her promise to give him serious consideration and a final, definitive answer—she and her fellow dancers were working their way through the middle piece for their recital coming up Saturday. They had one more practice and a dress rehearsal on Friday. This piece was fun because Nilani had dreamed it up, and she could be so creative. She was a traditionalist when necessary, but then she let loose with stuff like this.

Sujata and Paree were on the left of the stage with another pair on the right and the other three in the back. The dancers in the back were doing some relatively simple moves, while Sujata and Paree and their counterparts across the stage approached each other with simple rhythmic moves, mostly hand movements with powerful sideways steps, which was difficult to do, but looked very cool.

It took a lot of concentration, but she was practically an expert now in thinking about Vivek while doing other things. Even though it had been over two weeks, that kiss was still on her mind constantly. Those hot looks he'd given her before they'd kissed made her belly tingle. She still wondered if she'd made a mistake in not dating him.

On top of those doubts, Friday was his last day. The fact that he was leaving had been getting increasingly unbelievable with each passing day. His flight was Monday, and that would be that.

Except not really. She would have to give him an answer eventually—she would not be ghosting him like Rajeev had done to her—and meanwhile, she could always contact him for more help on the system. It was hard to know what the right thing to do was. She moved her arms around, fingers spread wide, palms toward the hypothetical audience, and started sliding with Paree back to the left.

Nilani was watching all them closely, though she seemed fixated on Kaarikaa and one of the other dancers today. Sujata was glad it wasn't her—she was too raw right now to take more criticism. She and Paree and the other pair shifted toward the back, while the others moved forward. This part was easier because the focus was on the front three dancers. They would wrap up the second story of this piece, segueing into the next, where Sujata had a role where she had to pretend to die. It was very dramatic and kind of fun, even though it also did weirdly make her think seriously about her mortality, which was the not fun part.

She wondered if she was wrong to give Vivek hope. She honestly didn't know where she was going to land. Maybe she would finally be willing to try. If it was a long-distance relationship, it would be less demanding so maybe simpler to ease into.

Sujata shifted on the stage to get into position for the next moves, checking her spot against Kaarikaa. She seemed good, and now it was just some waiting.

The data quality project had actually been going well, and she had written up the overall architecture and some of the high- and medium-level design of the four components. Everything was flowing really well, and she felt good about starting the coding, although she was fighting the urge to call Vivek with questions. She moved her arms from her left side, then over her head to the right. As repetitive as this part was, it was also emotionally soothing. Thinking about him leaving wasn't quite so disconcerting.

Sujata had already gotten decently into coding the analyzer, but she wasn't going to start the crawler until she had a first pass done on the analyzer, and the data catalog would come last, after the advisor. So it would be a while. Now she had to move diagonally across the stage with Kaarikaa, while Paree went with Kaarikaa's partner.

Soon, they were all moving around to partially surround Paree while she had her solo, which ended the segment.

The final piece was the one where Sujata and two others each had short solos. Kaarikaa's was first, then Sujata's. Although there was also some trepidation, she loved doing solos. Everything was focused on her, rather like how it would be to run her own business.

They were all standing around, taking a short breather. While Sujata went through her solo in her head, Nilani was talking to Kaarikaa, who was nodding, head down. She was getting a talking to. Sujata knew she'd had a rough couple of days with insomnia, which hit her sometimes, but Nilani had no patience for any kind of weakness.

For some reason, Sujata wondered what Nilani would have thought of Vivek in the early days when he was so shy around her, but obviously interested. So many people mistook shyness for lack of confidence, which she supposed it sort of was, but Sujata had a hard time believing that not being an arrogant prick was in any way bad.

The fewer people who were around, the braver Vivek got. He really was a good guy. She knew that and had always felt a connection with him.

Not dating him had probably been a mistake. Even if he'd still ended up moving away, she could have dated him while he was here. That might have helped her get over Rajeev, and then he also wouldn't be moving away.

Or maybe the six-month promise was the mistake. She felt like a confused middle schooler.

Nilani rounded them up, their small break over.

They all had background roles during the solos, so Sujata got into position and started her dance, watching Kaarikaa and sending positive vibes her way. She got through her solo, and now Sujata was up. Her stomach flipped in concern—Nilani was a major taskmaster today. Sujata moved toward the front and started her routine, which involved some of the more powerful leg movements she loved. But she had to be perfect, perfect, perfect. She danced, sweat rolling down her forehead and into her eyes, but there was nothing to be done for it.

This was nothing like dancing with her *nanī* in the kitchen when she was a little girl, but the love for the form was still there.

She kept going, deciding mid-solo that she really would invite Vivek to the performance Saturday. She wanted him to see her doing something she loved so much, something that made her feel so much, in both her body and her mind. She'd really intended to invite him before, but never asked. She'd do that tomorrow.

How would he accept it? Would he even want to come?

Who was she kidding—of course he would. But at least now he wouldn't read anything more into it, since he was leaving a day and a half later.

Sujata finished up her solo with a dramatic body shift, then sank into the background for the final dancer's solo.

She finished out the piece with her background role, a relief after the intensity of the solo. She wondered if she'd be able to cope with being the solo person in her business. Maybe she could bring Vivek in.

No, that wasn't worth it. She didn't want him stealing her thunder again. She might never really get over that, even though she had technically forgiven him.

A short while later, they all headed back to the changing room, beat and ready to get home. They all changed in silence and soon enough they were heading out. Sujata wasn't in a hurry because she'd have to wait for her bus—one more thing she had to endure tonight, before getting home and taking a warm shower and getting into bed, where she could dream about whatever she wanted. Maybe do some thinking about Vivek and the six months.

Even though she was tired, thinking about the project had her energized. There was no telling what the future held—it could be amazing, or it could be a big flop that left her at InfoQuest. But she had a good feeling. She started down the stairs, excited again for where this project was going to take her.

Even if it was without Vivek.

~

On his last Wednesday at InfoQuest, Vivek was wrapping everything up. He closed the drawer in his file cabinet and set the two programming books that he'd put inside it months ago on his desk. He'd see if anyone wanted them. Otherwise, his desk was empty. He wasn't one of those people who had really moved into his cube like some of his coworkers.

Today, he'd done a lot of documentation and had another knowledge transfer meeting with Xin, the engineer taking over as the primary maintainer and developer of the crawler, in an hour. He'd eaten lunch with the Indians as normal, and everyone was wishing him well. Sujata hadn't eaten with them this week, and he wished he'd seen her more.

Soon he'd be gone and might never see her again. He leaned back in his chair, feeling glum. There was that six months thing she'd promised, but if she didn't decide to give him a chance, he really wouldn't hold on any longer.

He had to not get his hopes up. And he wondered if it was wrong to hold out for someone who wasn't sure. It kind of looked bad from that perspective, but it wasn't that she wasn't sure. They both knew she wanted him. There was just this constraint she'd put on herself. She'd wrapped her heart in chains. He wasn't foolish for waiting, but beyond the six months he would be. He would have to take his future into his hands again.

He closed his eyes against the wave of sadness that rolled through him. Then he opened them again, rubbed them, and looked at the paragraph he was writing. He hated writing. It was just not his thing. He had a lot more to get down today, though, so he needed to focus.

He was documenting the recovery process the system had when certain failures happened, and it required a bit of looking into the actual code to write up, because it wasn't something he had dealt with very often—the software was well-written and rarely failed.

He'd made it through two more paragraphs when the image of Sujata just before they'd kissed at her apartment came into his head, and he relived all the sensations that came right after that.

Then he remembered the mac and cheese, and that broke the spell. This was not an American thing he was going to pick up. That color was not natural for food that wasn't a fruit.

He shook his head and got back to work, opening up the code so he could check on one condition. There was a weird calculation in there and he didn't immediately understand it, so he was focusing on the code.

"Vivek. How are you?"

His head jerked up, and it was Sujata, standing right there.

"Sorry, did I surprise you?" she asked.

"No, I'm fine." What an idiot. "I was just looking at some tricky code. Just finishing all this stuff up. I'm glad you came by. I was needing a break from all this documentation."

He moved the books he'd put on the desk, and they hit the whiteboard leaning against his pod wall so that it slid forward and he had to catch the books and the whiteboard.

Sujata laughed. "You're not very good with the whiteboards, are you?"

He couldn't prevent a goofy grin from spreading across his face as he repositioned everything. He loved a good inside joke. "What can I say?" But now he was thinking about the kiss at her apartment, and that needed to stop. He was getting worked up.

Sujata was still smiling. "I actually wondered something." She looked off to the side, suddenly appearing nervous, then turned back again. "Would you be interested in coming to my recital Saturday?"

That surprised him. He knew she practiced Bharatanatyam, but he didn't know she did performances. He wasn't leaving until Sunday, so obviously he would go. "I would love that."

Sujata's smile grew bigger. He wondered if she'd been afraid he'd say no. That was funny. Like he'd pass up a chance to see her dance.

"I'll text you the info."

"Great."

She still stood there, and he didn't know what to say. All he could think was that this might be one of the last times he'd see her. He might never kiss those soft lips again.

From her intense eyes, she might be thinking the same thing. After the silence had gotten awkward, she said, "Uh, so who's taking over for you?"

Just then, Vivek spotted Xin walking toward him and he realized they were meeting any second now. His heart sank. What terrible timing with Sujata right here.

Xin popped over and said, "I'm going to be a couple minutes late."

Vivek nodded. "Be there shortly."

"You have a meeting?" Sujata asked.

He stood, even though he could totally be late with no consequences. But it would be rude to just sit and chat with Sujata, however much he wanted to. "Yes. Xin is taking over. Another KT meeting."

"Ugh. Those are the worst. You're always trying to remember what exactly are the important things to tell them, and then they never remember it, anyway."

He laughed, walking around his cube wall. "We're in room one-sixteen."

"Cool. I'll walk that way with you. I need to go to the break room, anyway."

They walked in comfortable silence until they reached the break room.

"Okay, I'll see you later," Sujata said.

Vivek nodded and they shared a look. She was as sad as he was. He couldn't decide if that was good or bad for the six-month cutoff.

He continued on around the corner toward the meeting room. All he could do was hope she'd miss him enough to be willing to give a relationship a real chance.

Friday, Sujata went with Theresa and Casey to an Italian place for lunch.

"Are you going to miss Vivek?" Theresa asked Sujata.

"It's his last day, right?" Casey asked.

"Yes to both." She nodded absentmindedly and paused for a last-minute mental check before she said her next thing. "I never told you two, but we actually kissed on two separate occasions."

"Really?" Theresa's eyes were wide. Casey looked just as surprised.

"Yep. Oh, my God—the first time was when we were both in the office on a Sunday, and David almost caught us." Just thinking about that day had her heart going bonkers, half hot and bothered and half mortified.

Theresa and Casey were both staring at her with wide eyes now.

"I know, I know," Sujata said, looking down in embarrassment. "It was so intense I didn't even hear the elevator ding, or at least it didn't register. We'd started in two separate chairs, but I ended up basically in his lap."

Casey and Theresa were both laughing so hard they were practically crying.

Sujata was grimacing, reliving it all.

"I'm glad David didn't catch you. That would have been the height of awkward. And the next time?" Theresa asked.

Sujata took a sip of her water. Not the best liquid courage, but it would have to do. "So we were on a Meet call about the crawler."

They were both watching her with amused and expectant looks on their faces.

"So, he had this whiteboard he was drawing on." She could totally go down a rabbit hole here and should get to the point. "Basically, he was struggling to write on it and show it to me on the screen, so I randomly told him we should meet in person. And I invited him over. Even then, I didn't know why."

"And ...?" Theresa said.

"Yeah, he came and we worked on the system design for a while, and then I told him he needed to try box mac and cheese, and then we kissed. So, yeah."

Casey laughed. "Interesting summary."

"I don't know why you didn't just date him, Sujata," Theresa said, also smiling. "You like him."

"I know. I have some regrets." She wasn't going to tell them about the six months.

"I'm curious about the mac and cheese," Casey said. "Kraft?"

"Is there any other kind?" Sujata asked.

"I loved that stuff as a kid," Casey said.

Theresa smiled. "Same here. I've never made it as an adult, not even for Liam. What did Vivek think?"

Sujata laughed, picturing his concerned face, still flushed from the kissing, when he first saw the color. "Well, he tried to be nice about it."

They thought that was funny. Then Casey asked if his help had actually been helpful, and Sujata explained what she'd been able to accomplish in terms of system design. "But it would definitely be easier if I just had him write the thing."

Casey tapped her chin. "You know, have you considered bringing him in? It might be nice to have a second person to get more eyes on your code and such."

Sujata frowned. Just then their food arrived. The server put their plates down, steam rising off each plate of pasta.

"The thought had crossed my mind," Sujata said. "But this is my idea, and Vivek getting involved already screwed everything up once."

"Yeah, I see that," Casey said, spinning her fork in her spaghetti to collect some. "But you should think of this differently. This has nothing to do with work and other people making decisions for you. You could bring him on as a partner. Or you could hire him as a contractor, but you'd have to pay him in some fashion. Either way, you'll want to draw up an agreement with a lawyer that defines your roles and ownership."

Sujata hadn't thought about it that deeply. She stirred her

spaghetti, a rare carb splurge. She'd been dancing so much more lately that she could afford it. In the project, she wanted ownership. But Casey wasn't wrong about having a second person around. Who would do code reviews for her?

Theresa looked thoughtful as she cut her chicken. "This would definitely complicate things. Maybe you should consult with a lawyer before even asking Vivek, to find out how things can be structured and so on."

"That would be a good idea," Casey said. "Lawyers aren't cheap, but you wouldn't need many hours with them. A couple would be plenty for the pre-conversation."

This had Sujata's brain cranking away. If they did this, what would happen after the six-month mark? Maybe she should wait until then. But that would delay everything.

"I think you are right about consulting a lawyer. I need to understand what the possibilities even are." She had to think about both business and personal possibilities.

"Do it," Theresa said.

"I think I will."

"If you do, also ask about how investors can be handled." She waggled her eyebrows, which made Theresa laugh, but Sujata just stared at her for a second.

Was Casey saying she might invest in her business?

"I might be able to partially fund some of the work, for a stake," Casey said.

Okay, then. Things were getting real.

Sujata recovered and said, "Well, thank you. That would be amazing. Though I have to get a lot more organized. But I should reach out to someone. Who knows what I'll find out. But I'm not committing to anything yet." She needed more information before she could make any kind of decision. The future seemed complicated, but it was welcome complication. She just had to be smart about it.

17

Sujata's performance wasn't in a very big venue. There were not more than three hundred seats, so it felt cozy. Vivek and his friends had managed to get third row seats right in the middle. He'd been unsure about bringing them with him, but they'd seemed interested, so here they were.

They were waiting for things to start. The tension in his belly was building at the mere thought of seeing her on the stage. There was all the talking and hubbub around them from more people coming in and sitting down. Vivek turned around and saw that the place was fairly full, which surprised him. He'd assumed it would just be friends and family since this wasn't a professional group.

Kiran was talking to one of their friends, which left Vivek to listen and look around more.

The stage was empty, with simple lighting directed at it. He thought about how in a short time, Sujata would be up there and he'd have every right to stare at her body as much as he wanted. His stomach twitched at the thought. He needed to keep his own body in check, with nothing going on below his belt.

His friends were still talking and he was free to look around. The place really was pretty packed. Not every seat was taken, but it was just empties here and there.

Suddenly everything went dark, so Kiran stopped whatever he was in the middle of saying.

When the stage lights came on, a woman in a bright red sari with gold accents that were sparkling in the light strode to the center of the stage. She gave an intro about herself and her studio, and then explained that there would be three distinct pieces tonight performed by her advanced class. She talked a bit about each, but he didn't pay much attention because he thought he knew what to expect.

Once the dancers were on the stage, his eyes instinctively sought Sujata, and he found her on the right side, completely still and looking down, like everyone else. She was wearing a classic Bharatanatyam outfit in deep orange with gold down the front. Her feet were together so the skirt appeared almost fitted, but he could see the compressed accordion-style folds that would allow it to expand when her feet were farther apart.

Vivek felt odd. He was proud to know her and that she cared enough about her roots to practice an old dance form, even though she was so American in so many ways. It just further solidified how perfect she was for him.

The music started up, the traditional stuff, and movement started in the center of the stage, with a woman in a darker costume doing some of the preliminary movements. Vivek glanced at everyone and dutifully watched the only woman moving, but soon enough they were all shifting so he looked back at Sujata.

She was doing the hand motions that were the hallmark of this style of dance. He wasn't really a fan, but his sister had practiced it so he'd seen plenty of her performances.

All the dancers began working their way toward the center, and the traditional part continued. Honestly, it was a little boring since he'd seen this so many times, so he just watched Sujata. She had stopped, and her feet were spread and pointing out to the sides, her knees bent. She was doing the hand movements.

Even though this type of dance wasn't as physically demanding as some, requiring precision more than vigor, Sujata's athleticism was still clear. He'd actually forgotten that dancers were always so fit.

He felt a surge of something he'd expressly told his body to avoid. He would have to pay more attention and control himself.

This part continued for another quarter hour or so, with the dancers moving around and carrying out their parts together and separately.

Then they finished and moved off the stage. Vivek expected more of the same from the second part, so he was surprised when upbeat music began playing and the dancers all walked purposefully onto the stage, again getting into position. He of course zeroed in on Sujata again. She and the other dancers moved much more than was typical in this type of dance, but their positioning and hand and feet movements still gave it the right feel, even though it was flouting tradition.

Soon he recognized that this was one of the old Indian stories. Sujata wasn't one of the primary dancers in this piece, but he was still surprised when she and three other dancers threw themselves on the floor in death, before rising again and exiting the stage to allow the other three to finish the piece. His heart was racing at watching her die, even though he knew that was stupid and she was actually fine. He shook his head to reset.

The next piece was another story but also modernized, and he really enjoyed it and Sujata's gorgeous body moving around the stage. They'd donned new costumes, a sari-like wrap in light blue that left her midriff visible. The best part was near the end when she had a true solo, defying the traditional style yet again. She did an impressive spin without losing the impact of her feet planted at the beginning and end, all while including the traditional hand motions.

His whole body was energized while she moved around the stage, looking like a woman a man could only dream up. She was it, she was the dream.

Five months and one week. This was the last chance, and he hoped she'd make the right decision. But it was one she had to make on her own, no matter what he thought. He just had to wait, and come up with a backup plan in case the answer was no.

AFTER THE SHOW, Vivek wanted to see Sujata, so he convinced his friends to wait a bit. Surely she'd come out to talk to him.

He would be leaving Monday, and he did not want to go without speaking to her again. It had been two weeks since they'd kissed. It would be many more before they ever kissed again—if they did.

Sujata emerged from the side of the stage and started down the steps, and his heart lit up again. She was still in the last costume and just looked so beautiful, the pale blue fabric making her skin look smooth and radiant.

A big smile stretched across her face as soon as she spotted him, which lit his heart up. He slowed his feet so he walked normally rather than running to meet her halfway. Her face was still flushed from the dancing. Her eyes glowed with happiness, which set his entire body on fire.

"Did you like it?" she asked when she reached him.

"Of course, you were amazing," he said, not having to lie.

She stepped forward and surprised him with a hug. The press of her breasts against him was so nice. She smelled of a floral perfume she didn't normally wear, and he was convinced he could feel the heat coming off her body. That made him picture her solo again, with its spins and those deliberate foot placements.

Sujata ended the long hug, something he wasn't ready for. It was like how their whole friendship might be ending.

"Thanks for coming, Vivek," she said, stepping back, eyes glowing.

"I loved it. I grew up watching my sister's Bharatanatyam performances, but this was different." His first crush was one of Mishti's fellow dancers. And here he'd gone and fallen for another skilled dancer.

"You never told me your sister was a dancer. What did you think of all the newfangled stuff Nilani does?"

"I liked it. I didn't even know there were people doing anything that wasn't totally traditional. It was really interesting."

He felt like he needed to yell so she could hear. It was loud from all the conversations all around, so he stepped a tiny bit closer so they could hear each other better. He wanted to hug her again, but that part of this interaction was over, at least for now. He wanted to caress her hair.

She swept her hand across her forehead and wiped it on her costume top. "She has a group she tours with over the summer. She's quite well-known."

"That's interesting. I was surprised at how many people were here."

Sujata laughed. "Yeah, they're here for her, not me."

"Well, I was here for you. And I'm glad I came. You really are great at this."

"Thanks, and I'm glad you came, too." She was still smiling, and a light kept reflecting off her eyes, making them sparkle. "So your flight leaves Monday?"

Vivek nodded. "I'll be packing up tomorrow."

"I hope you have a good flight, free of crappy weather." Her smile had mostly faded and she looked more subdued. Was talking about him leaving making her sad?

He wasn't happy she was sad, except he kind of was because it meant she cared about him.

"So are you all packed?" She rolled her eyes at herself. "I guess no, since you just told me you're packing tomorrow."

He laughed. "Yeah, and I have to go buy a couple new suitcases because the ones I have are in bad shape."

"Ah."

Why were they talking about this stupid stuff? Everything was coming to an end. Was this the last thing they would ever talk about?

"Nice job, Sujata," Kiran said, coming up behind Vivek.

"Thanks." They exchanged a few more pleasantries and then they all stared at each other for a moment. Vivek wished Kiran would go away.

Someone called Sujata's name from the stage. They all turned to look, seeing another of the dancers, still in costume. "We need you for a second."

"Okay," Sujata said to her, then turned back to Vivek and Kiran. "Well, I'll let you guys go. I'd better get back there."

No. He wasn't ready. He nodded and turned to leave, but then he realized this really might be the last time he'd see her. He turned back around and called her name. She'd already made it to the stairs, but she rushed back and they hugged again. Neither said anything, and he squeezed her like his life depended on it.

They broke apart and stared at each other, his heart racing at the intensity of his feelings. Were those tears forming in the corners of her eyes?

"I'm glad I met you, Vivek," she said, a quaver in her voice that shot straight to the heart.

"I feel the same." It was hard to say, since it meant the end.

They were quiet, but their locked gazes felt so intense.

Sujata looked down. "I'll let you know."

"Okay."

It was probably time.

They stepped farther apart and gave each other an awkward wave, then she turned and started quickly up the steps, and Vivek caught up with his friends, his heart breaking with each step.

This was excruciating. The six months couldn't be up soon enough. He glanced back, but she was out of sight.

Once they were outside, the fresh air cleared his mind a bit, but he wasn't going to be worth anything the rest of the night.

Tomorrow he'd be packing, and then he'd be flying to Atlanta the next day. And then he'd be starting his new life. The one he didn't really want. Why did his uncle have to be there, with his stupid job offer? Why didn't he just look harder for a job here, even though his family would have been mad?

Things weren't officially impossible with Sujata, but with him out of sight, he would be out of her mind, too.

He would just have to start over in every way. But not until he had her final answer.

SUNDAY NIGHT, Sujata closed her computer and leaned back against the couch. She was feeling antsy. Vivek's face after her performance last night popped into her head. She'd felt so good after the dancing that she'd been overexcited to see him—she'd hugged him without really thinking. Twice. It had felt bittersweet, full of regret, even though nothing was decided permanently yet. Kiran had looked amused at their interaction.

But she'd been happy to see him, and was giddy from being energized and exhausted at the time, and she couldn't stop thinking about him leaving. He'd seemed happy enough to hug her, and they'd talked more after that, before she'd had to leave. What if being away from her made him lose interest, but being away from him convinced her she'd made a mistake?

His flight was tomorrow so he was probably all packed and ready to go. It seemed weird that he would really be gone. She'd almost made a fool of herself last night when she'd nearly started crying.

She knew she shouldn't, but she picked up her phone and typed a message.

—What time is your flight tomorrow?—

She hesitated. But what would it hurt? She hit send.

Then she regretted it, her stomach dropping. She shouldn't be doing this. It wasn't nice to him. Or maybe it was? She was a mess.

Why was this so confusing? She'd rejected him, but then given him a timeframe in which she would either reject him again or start dating him, and now he was moving away. If she did reject him again, that would be final, wouldn't it? They would likely never see each other again.

She felt restless. Even though she should still be beat after the performance last night, she had all this energy in her legs. She needed to do her yoga.

Her phone dinged, making her jump. It was just Vivek responding. —*Noon*—

What did he think of her contacting him? They didn't normally text. And their goodbye yesterday had been so intense. His leaving had her more confused than it should. And she still had to decide if she should try dating him. She should give that real thought, even though it terrified her.

—*Safe travels!*— she texted back. It would be better for him if she didn't just randomly text him.

She really needed to be honest with herself about what she wanted and could handle.

But for now, she'd do some yoga and take a shower. Avoidance, her oldest best friend.

Sujata headed into her bedroom and dropped her phone on the desk before rolling out the yoga mat on the floor. She calmed down just thinking about the next few minutes, because yoga always made everything better. She tossed her socks in the laundry hamper and stepped onto the mat in mountain pose, feet together and hands to the side, palms facing forward.

She dropped her arms, feeling some stress seep out of her, and started on the sun salutation series. Although the calmness stayed with her, it didn't keep her from thinking about Vivek and what he could possibly be doing right now. He wouldn't be doing InfoQuest work, obviously, so she couldn't imagine what it would be.

Sujata continued moving through the sequence, arms in the air. She kept going, moving into the second series.

She would really need to think about what she wanted after he was gone. She couldn't keep flip-flopping. She owed him an honest and final answer.

And perhaps herself, as well.

She dropped her arms slowly to finish the second sun salutation. She leaned forward and pinched her toes before sliding her hands under the fronts of her feet.

As Sujata moved her leg back for extended triangle pose, she wondered if Vivek did yoga. She should know more about him, given how long they'd known each other. She realized he knew much more about her than she did him, and that made her feel really guilty. She hadn't always been good to him. She closed her eyes to clear her brain and continued on through the sequence.

She didn't always do it, but she decided to add the headstand, so from downward dog, she put her head on the floor and bent her arms so the forearms were flat next to her head, interlacing her fingers behind her head. Then she slowly lifted her right leg until it was perfectly vertical, and started the process with her left leg.

Then her strength abruptly failed her and she totally lost her balance, falling sideways so that her left ankle hit the edge of the desk, hard, before she collapsed in a heap.

Her left ankle was screaming in pain. She hadn't felt anything like it in a long time, despite countless dancing injuries. Her heart was racing in panic; she needed to calm down and take stock. She hadn't moved and she was lying mostly on her left side, her right leg out and her left leg back. Her left ankle was throbbing and giving sharp, shooting pains—had she broken it? She tried to move it and the pain shot straight to her stomach, making her nearly throw up. Nothing else hurt in her legs or back, although her neck was a little sore—but nothing like that damn ankle.

Sujata needed to sit up. She should stop panicking and just deal with the situation. She used her right foot and arms to shift herself until she was sitting up, treating the left foot gingerly, until her legs were out straight in front of her. She was breathing heavily from the effort. She pulled her left pant leg up, afraid of what she might see. She couldn't see anything wrong, though.

No, wait. There was a distinctly red area that actually looked swollen. Shit. How was she going to handle this? This required medical attention, and here she was, all by herself in her apartment. Her stomach clenched and her pulse quickened again with fresh panic. How long was she going to be unable to dance?

She closed her eyes and concentrated on breathing. She had to calm down.

There was no way she could walk with this injury, with how much it hurt just sitting there. But she was going to have to go to the ER, somehow. No bone was sticking out and she couldn't really see anything wrong with her ankle, so if it was a break, it wasn't a terrible one. But she just had a bad feeling.

She'd have to call someone for help. She felt around the top of the desk but couldn't find the phone. She was going to have to stand up to reach it.

On her knees, she held her left foot off the ground, which made it throb even more. Then she grabbed the desk and pushed off the floor with her right foot until she was up. She grabbed the phone and hopped over to the desk chair, every hop jarring her ankle and generating excruciating pain.

Having the phone in her hand was great, but who was she going to call?

What would Vivek think if she texted him for help?

No, that was too much to ask of him.

Or was it?

Argh. Why had she done this to herself? She cursed herself for pushing too hard. She should have skipped the headstand, given how hard she'd worked last night. She was such an idiot.

Okay, who else? Gwen might be good. Definitely not Theresa because she had Liam, although she guessed that Conall would be able to help. She could also ask Casey.

But what she needed was support for walking, and that would be much easier for a guy than a woman. But not just any guy. A guy like Vivek, who she obviously wanted in her life but was too afraid to give her heart to.

Whatever was going on in her heart, asking him felt like the most natural thing. His flight wasn't leaving until noon tomorrow, so he could help her tonight and still make his flight.

She stared at her phone, still pleased with her choice of a purple case. But she knew she was stalling. Why was asking for help so hard for her? She made up her mind. Time to take action.

—*Um, I might need some help*— she texted.

—*What happened???*—

She explained the basics. God, it was so stupid. Who injured themselves doing yoga?

—*I'll be right over!!!*—

She sat in the chair, trying to figure out how to get to the front door. Her room was in the back, so she had to get out the bedroom door, down the hall past the bathroom, make a right turn to the entryway, and get the front door open. Hopping would be excruciating.

She almost hit herself on the forehead when she realized she was sitting in a chair on rollers. Duh.

So she pushed herself out the bedroom door, down the hall, and onto the linoleum by the front door, right next to the kitchen. And she waited.

Her entire foot was hurting now and the pain was moving up her leg. She realized she had some Advil in the bathroom and rolled all the way back there. She pushed herself out of the chair, the pain in her foot flaring. She got the Advil and rolled back to the kitchen for a glass of water and took two of the pills. She sat and pulled out a plastic baggie from a drawer before rolling over to the fridge and pulling herself up to fill it with ice. She grabbed the dishtowel and sat back down, brought her foot up to rest her calf on her thigh, and applied the ice pack. Then she rolled back to the entryway.

The ice helped a bit. But she could also see the redness spreading from the outside of the ankle. She'd hit that desk really freaking hard.

She closed her eyes and tried to will the throbbing in her ankle away.

—*Tell me what happened. I'm in the Uber*— Vivek texted.

She explained in more detail this time.

—*I'm so sorry this happened to you. But don't worry, I'll help you*—

—*I think I just need some help getting to the emergency room. I can't walk. But I should be able to handle it from there—* What if she did need more help? Who else could help her? Theresa or Casey would, or Gwen, but they all had busy lives and she hated to inconvenience anyone.

—I can stay with you at hospital—

—I'd hate for you to have to do that—

He didn't respond right away, but then texted, *—I'm coming up your stairs—*

She rolled forward and opened the door, having to roll back to make room for it.

Then Vivek was standing there. His mouth fell open when he saw her and worry etched across his brow. "Are you okay?"

Her remaining panic wafted away. Everything was going to be okay now. She smiled ruefully. "I know it's stupid, but it was the only way I could get around."

"So it's this ankle?" he asked.

She moved the ice pack. "Yeah."

"Oh, it's so swollen. That looks painful."

"It surely is," she said, trying to sound chipper.

Vivek looked confused for a second. Apparently he was taking this very seriously.

"Let's get you in a car," Vivek said. "I told the driver to stick around because we'd probably be needing him right away, but I don't know if he's still there. Let me request a ride. What's the name of the hospital?"

She named the one that Rajeev did not work at and he fiddled with his phone. "Yes, he's down there. Where are your keys?"

She pointed to the hook on the wall where she hung them. "Could you get my purse, too? It's on the coffee table."

He grabbed it and handed it to her. She dropped the keys in and zipped it up.

He looked down at her for a moment. "Why don't you roll out in your chair so I can get the door locked, and we can leave it here." Hers was the only apartment on this floor, so no one would even see it.

She let him push her out, the threshold causing a bit of trouble, but eventually she was out. He locked the door and put the keys in his pocket.

"Ready?" he asked. "Can you stand on your good foot?"

She responded by standing up, careful to be gentle with the injured foot.

"Okay. I think I'm going to carry you over my shoulder. Otherwise the hop down each step will be jarring."

Her face flushed with embarrassment. What a mess.

He crouched and wrapped his arms around her and lifted her by the butt, which was also embarrassing, but what else could she do?

She kept her injured foot away from his body and took in his familiar earthy scent, some clean shampoo aroma breaking through. And the fact that he could pick her up like it was nothing was hot, even though her mind should not be registering that right now.

He made it down the stairs reasonably quickly and got her into the car, which was a bit of a production, but they managed it.

"What did you do to yourself, sweetheart?" the driver asked. He was wearing a Sikh turban but sounded totally American.

"Ugh. Something stupid. Who injures themself doing yoga? That would be me."

The driver laughed as Vivek got in on the opposite side.

He squeezed her hand quickly, which she loved, and then as soon as he had his door shut they were off.

Sujata was a bundle of feelings—pain, for one, and then anxiety about what they'd say at the ER about how bad it really was. But she also felt a great affection for Vivek. Of course he came through for her. He always did. Would she ever return the favor?

18

Vivek woke up abruptly, immediately disoriented. The lights were still on, the TV was going, he was lying at an awkward angle. Sujata's head was resting on his shoulder. She was out, breathing nice and evenly. Her eyelids fluttered slightly and he wanted to kiss them.

He looked away to kill the urge. He carefully slid out from under her, moving a pillow to replace his shoulder. He walked around the bed and adjusted the comforter so he could cover her with it. Her crutches were leaning against her side of the bed.

They had gotten back from the hospital just after one, but she didn't want to go to sleep right away, so they watched some TV—a show about flipping a house in Atlanta, of all places—then obviously both fell asleep. It was just after three now.

The fact that he was the one she'd called when she needed help did seem like a very good sign for them as a possible future couple. But he couldn't let himself read too much into it. He didn't know if she'd reached out to anyone else first.

He should not let himself get his hopes up.

He headed toward the kitchen. Sujata's computer was closed and sitting on the coffee table, and a throw was strewn across the couch.

In the kitchen, the pantry door was open and a rubbish bin inside was nearly full.

It was nice to see what her place looked like lived-in. She obviously hadn't cleaned her apartment before texting him. He felt like he was seeing a part of her he'd never seen before. She could be so guarded, but here he was the in one place where she must feel comfortable.

It also was the place he'd kissed her for the second time.

Vivek searched the cabinets until he found a glass and poured himself a water from the tap. He leaned against the counter, suddenly overwhelmed with the memory of the kiss they'd shared in here.

What a kiss. Only to be followed by that infernal rejection.

But then she had opened up, making herself more vulnerable with him than she ever had. He believed that she really was trying to convince herself to stop being afraid.

Vivek headed back to the bedroom and took a sip from the glass of water he had brought in. What happened a few months down the road was irrelevant here. Now, he was helping a friend in need. She was asleep now, but he wasn't sure what condition she'd be in when she woke up. She had a simple fracture and they gave her just a brace because they wanted the swelling down before putting on a cast. She had an appointment Tuesday morning for the cast. He had already moved his flight to tomorrow, although he might have to move it again.

They'd given her some pain medicine, but also told her ibuprofen would help if she didn't want to take the prescription pain meds, so he went looking for that.

There was nothing of use in the kitchen cabinets or drawers. It was more likely to be in the bathroom, but going through somebody's bathroom business felt more invasive. Still, he headed into the bathroom and found that she had open shelves and he could see a bottle of ibuprofen. When she woke, she could take it or the prescription.

Vivek took a glass of water and both bottles into the bedroom.

He was wide awake, so he headed into the den and looked around. There was a small bookshelf between the fireplace and the balcony door that he hadn't noticed before. It was full of paperbacks, obviously fiction.

There were mostly man chests—some covered, some not—on the books he pulled off the shelves. He replaced all but one, which he carried to the couch. This one had three people on it—two men and a woman.

He would never have guessed Sujata was a romance reader. Given how opposed she was to a relationship, it didn't entirely make sense. But it probably was a really good sign for him—she obviously wanted to believe in love, she just had that one jerk holding her back.

Maybe if he read some of this, he'd understand her better. This one was called *Charmed by a Duke*. So he leaned back and opened the book, relishing how quiet the place was, so he was sure he'd hear Sujata if she moved.

After he recovered from reading the first chapter, which had two men and a woman and it was all very shocking, his curiosity was piqued. Why would Sujata be reading something like this? He'd gotten a few more chapters in when suddenly Sujata called, "Vivek, are you here?"

"Yes!" He jumped up and raced in there, finding her looking uncomfortable but still safely in the bed.

"Do you have the medicine? My foot is really hurting."

Vivek pointed to the nightstand.

"Oh, thanks, I didn't even look."

He stepped in. "Which one do you want?"

"Let's try the prescription to see how it makes me feel. I sometimes have strong reactions to medicine, so it would be good to try it with someone here."

He opened the bottle and got a single pill out. She was already mostly sitting up, so he handed her the glass and pill.

Sujata got it down and said, "Thanks." She looked at him and smiled, a gesture that went straight to his heart. She was being her real self here.

"Thanks for helping me," she continued. "I will call my *maa* because she, I think, can come and stay with me for a few days, until I get used to everything. Then you can head down to Atlanta. I want you to have at least a few days to get settled before you have to start your job."

Vivek nodded, happy he'd been able to help her. "I already moved the flight to Tuesday at three, so we have time to figure things out."

"Thank you for being so accommodating. You don't know how much I appreciate you."

"It was no big deal." Of course he'd adjusted things.

She grimaced. "I really need to go to the bathroom. I'm sure I can get there on my own, but I wouldn't mind if you would be around in case I need help. I'm not used to the crutches yet."

"Sure."

She lifted the comforter and turned sideways so her feet were hanging off the bed. He handed her the crutches and took her hand to help her stand on her good leg. He followed her as she crutched to the bathroom, shut the door, and turned the fan on, and then he waited.

Soon she was out. She smiled again. "Managed it."

"Great. I had faith in you." He suspected she didn't like to be dependent on anyone else.

After she was back in bed again, she closed her eyes.

She was obviously still in pain, but she looked mostly okay. Still beautiful, of course, if disheveled.

"I can't believe I did this to myself doing the most gentle exercise on the planet," she said.

"Maybe you should have tried tai chi instead?" he joked. "I think it's considered even gentler."

She laughed and looked at him, smiling. "Thanks for coming over. I don't know what I would have done if you hadn't. This is one of the few times living alone is a real problem."

He resisted the urge to point out that she didn't have to live alone, if only she'd make the leap. "I'm happy to help. I'm just glad you asked me."

She pressed her fingers to her forehead.

He would never admit it to her, but he absolutely loved that he was the one she'd called. She knew he was trustworthy. Maybe this would even make it so clear that she would go all the way and trust him with her heart.

"Can you bring me my computer? I want to email David that I'll be out at least the next couple days."

Vivek brought her the laptop and they said goodnight. She reached out to him and they hugged awkwardly, which he enjoyed more than he should have. Then she waved at him as he backed out of the room. He returned to the couch to try to get some sleep.

Instead, his mind was roiling with possibilities, and he found himself getting back into the novel he'd started, against his better judgment. He assumed the three people in the book would end up together, but they were having all sorts of problems along the way. But it was kind of funny, because the woman was a writer and very naive, as she was supposed to be in Victorian England, and she was getting roped into writing a certain type of novel that she hadn't even known existed before.

He could relate to having his eyes opened to different things. Though not really to the three people thing, which was definitely weird. Did this sort of thing happen in real life? And did it really happen in England in the 1800s? He really had no idea.

He wanted to be a good friend to Sujata for now, but he couldn't help but hope that in doing so, she would notice that he really was a good guy, and start to trust him completely.

This leg injury was obviously a bad thing for Sujata, but maybe something good could come out of it. Something good for both of them.

They'd figure out next steps tomorrow after she talked to her *maa*. Would there be problems for her if her family found out he'd helped her? Some might assume they were a couple and not approve. He didn't know how conservative her family was. He hoped there weren't problems. He'd know tomorrow.

TUESDAY AFTERNOON SUJATA sat on the couch, Vivek a few feet away from her at the other end. There was a nice, domestic feel. He was in what looked like old jeans and a polo shirt, ready to travel, his shoes on the floor by the door. He was doing something on his computer.

She was housebound for the week, so she was theoretically working on her business idea at the moment. But mostly she was having fond feelings about Vivek. She was so unhappy that he was moving.

In fact, she was thinking about telling him she wanted to try dating. But she didn't know how to bring it up. And the timing was weird.

They had gone to the doctor this morning and she now had a bright pink cast, because why not? She had crutches and instructions to be careful. It was incredibly annoying to be laid up. Nilani was very ticked off with her.

Vivek had made a trip back home and picked up all of his stuff. His suitcases were parked in the kitchen since he was heading to the airport today. Sujata's *maa* was arriving soon to help her deal with everything. She was kind of looking forward to Maa coming, but it would also be distracting.

It felt totally natural for Sujata and Vivek to be sitting here, working companionably. It might have been nicer if they were both in loungewear, but she'd had to get properly dressed for the doctor this morning—well, if you count yoga pants as proper, but she did have a nice shirt on.

Out of the corner of her eye, she noticed a book on the floor under the coffee table. It was one of her romances, and she felt a twinge of embarrassment that Vivek had seen it. And holy crap, it was one of the ménage books.

But why was it out here? They were all on the shelf, across the room.

"Did you read one of my books?" she asked Vivek, who was head down on his computer.

"Oh," he said, a sheepish look on his face.

"You did!" She cracked up.

"Well, I was curious and I didn't have anything to do and I couldn't sleep."

"And what did you think?" She really was curious, given the three protagonists and extra risqué subject matter, which starts off right in the beginning in this one. "I should point out that lots of women read books that are outside their actual … proclivities."

"Uh … I wasn't sure about the three people. And the duke is kind of a jerk. But I like the woman and the other man." His face was red.

"Oh, the duke's not that bad. Did you finish it, or figure out where it was going? And what did you think of that scene where Lillian drops the papers?" She raised her eyebrows.

"It was kind of shocking. I was confused that you were reading a book like that."

"Did you disapprove?"

"No, not that. Just … surprised."

He looked like he meant it. There was no badly hidden expression of disgust or anything.

"What are you working on?" she asked.

"Just flipping through pictures one of my cousin's friends posted from his wedding."

She laughed. "Show me some."

He scooted over and turned the computer so she could see. She could smell his earthy scent, but tried to focus on the pictures. The bride was in a pretty sea green sari with purple highlights, the requisite large gold earrings hanging from her ears.

Sujata wondered what she would wear if she ever got married.

That was an odd thought. What if she never got married? It was hard to imagine ever getting beyond her fears. But maybe she should just be brave and talk to Vivek.

"Is your cousin the groom?" she asked.

"Yes."

"On the horse?" she asked, laughing.

"Hey, it's part of one of the ceremonies. His father is from the north."

There were some of the groom on the horse, wearing his fancy embroidered kurta. Vivek flipped to the next photo, showing the bride and her family dancing, then loads of the bride and groom together.

Sujata suddenly felt jealous of these people who were allowed to be happy, and never had their fiancé abandon them. But she needed to get a grip. Was this why she was thinking of telling him she wanted to try?

She didn't think so.

"Are you a hopeless romantic?" she teased.

He side-eyed her. "Hopeless might be the right word."

Oof. Good call on his part. But it might not be true. "Maybe not."

He looked at her, eyebrows raised.

The intensity of his gaze made her turn away, but out of the corner of her eye, she could see him frown.

She was being an asshole again. Giving him hope but not following through.

But it wasn't going to be the same this time. She'd really give it a shot. And maybe it would work. Her stomach flipped at what she was about to do. Maybe a few years down the road, she and Vivek would be starring in a wedding ceremony. That thought warmed her.

It was time. Her pulse immediately kicked up. She took a deep breath.

"I think maybe yes, maybe I am ready to try." This was possibly the hardest thing she'd ever said. What a leap. She was going to risk her heart again. It was terrifying and exciting, and her heart raced just thinking about how things had just changed.

"Really?" he asked, then laughed. It wasn't his normal, warm laugh.

"Are you mad?" she asked. Oh, God, had she messed everything up?

"Do you mean crazy or angry?" He looked miffed.

"Angry."

"No. I'm happy. But Sujata, the day I'm leaving?" He held his hands wide, rightfully exasperated.

"I know, it's bad. I'm so sorry I was an idiot for so long." She felt stupid. But she also was desperate for him to agree. "Please, let's try."

"Is this because I just showed you all those wedding photos?" His brow was raised, his face otherwise neutral.

She couldn't tell if he was serious or teasing, but she was leaning toward serious. "No, I've been trying to work up the nerve to say something since well before I knew you were looking at wedding pictures. It's not spontaneous."

"Okay. You know I'm happy. Obviously I'm happy." His eyes glowed over the huge smile that now stretched across his face. "More than happy. I really don't even know what to say." But then doubt crossed his face. "You're not going to change your mind again, are you?"

She grimaced, morphing awkwardly from a smile. "It's completely fair for you to ask that. No. I want to try a real long-distance relationship. For real. I mean, we can't know if it will last forever, but that's my intention."

He studied her for a moment, then moved even closer, until she could smell his soap—her soap, actually, since he'd showered here. He'd been naked in her apartment. She had thought about it at the time and tried to push her imagination down, but it was back. Her core warmed.

They were hip to hip now.

He was going to kiss her, and for a moment she was terrified because it would make it real. This was the official start of them dating.

She leaned in and their lips met, that now-familiar fire spreading throughout her body. His arm slid around her back and she twisted more toward him.

He cupped her face in his hand and she felt like he was looking into her soul.

"Are you sure about this, Sujata?"

"Yes, please kiss me. I need this." Her heart was about to burst from her chest.

Vivek leaned in and gave her a tentative kiss on the lips, maybe still worried she'd get spooked.

She was not going to get spooked.

She ran her hand up the back of his neck and head, pulling him in. Her cast might make this awkward, but they would manage.

"Not so fast," he teased.

He started kissing her next to the bottom of her ear, then repeated it on the other side. She felt her breath hitch. How could this feel so good?

Because it was Vivek doing it.

He came back to her mouth and sucked on her bottom lip before he parted her lips and their tongues were tangling. She was so deep in desire that she was dizzy.

One of Vivek's hands was spread across her lower back, under her shirt, and the other held her shoulder, but he was being so gentle that she wondered why she hadn't trusted him from the beginning. Vivek was a rare man, and she'd wasted so much of her recent life avoiding him.

But screw regret. She pushed her hand up under the front of his shirt until she could feel the hard muscle there.

He angled his head to the other side. She was still totally caught up in this kiss.

She turned her body to face him, her left foot resting on the floor. Then she ran her hands across his pecs. God, she wanted to see him.

He started kissing her jawline, working his way to her earlobe, which he bit gently.

"Take your shirt off," she ordered.

He immediately obliged, so fast it made her laugh, despite her pounding heart.

"Your shirt, too," he said through ragged breath.

She pulled hers over her head, not even self-conscious about being half-naked in front of a man for the first time in more than a year. Without him even asking, she unhooked her bra and slowly removed it, Vivek staring intently at her chest. His eyes flashed with desire.

He shifted to be closer and palmed her breasts. It felt so good to be touched like this again that she was cursing her cast, even though it was the only reason he was here, the only reason they were now a couple. Or, not the only reason, but they never would have gotten to here if he hadn't had to come rescue her. He would have just boarded his plane Monday, and been gone.

She reached around to touch his back, feeling the hard muscles there.

He thumbed her nipples.

Her body was begging for more, but she wasn't sure if it was too soon. They had known each other a long time, however. She heard herself moan as he continued to work her breasts. She reached for his cock, which felt promisingly substantial.

She opened the top of his jeans and he leaned forward to kiss her again, hungry.

Out of nowhere, a knock on the door shocked them both and they jerked apart.

"Oh, my God, that's my *maa*," she whisper-yelled, out of breath.

"Already?" Vivek said, reaching down to hand her her bra and shirt. Then he buttoned his jeans and grabbed his own shirt, quickly putting it on, smoothing it down with his palms.

Sujata had her bra on and was trying to get the shirt over her head when another knock came and she hear someone call her name. Yes, her *maa*.

"Coming!" God, they'd almost been in an even more compromising position. Sujata would have died. She was possibly already dying, from the jumpy stomach that was threatening to take over.

Vivek's face was tense. "Should I get the door?"

"I'll go," she answered, then called, "Coming, Maa!" She grabbed the crutches and scooted forward, grimacing with the movement. Vivek helped her up and she crutched to the door, holding her toes just off the floor to keep from putting weight on the bad leg. She was also willing the extra color out of her face and telling her heart to chill out. Vivek stood back and Sujata shifted to the side and opened the door.

The first thing Sujata saw was her *maa*'s shocked face.

"*Beta*! Oh, no, you're hurt!"

"Maa, you know that, that's why you're here."

"Of course, of course, but I'm *seeing* you on crutches. It's different." Maa had on black jeans and a simple white blouse. She was usually pretty casual, and it was so nice to see her. She reminded Sujata of Kavya, who she also wanted to see. They had the same eyes and nose.

Maa pushed the door farther open and came in to give Sujata a hug that was awkward with the crutches.

"I'm glad you could come, Maa." Sujata suddenly felt an urge to cry. She missed her family. She should go home more often.

They stepped far enough inside that Sujata could shut the door.

Her *maa* stepped back and spotted Vivek standing a few feet away. "Who's this?"

He waved, shy again. And probably freaked out from almost getting caught. His shirt was not tucked in and he look disheveled, but at least the state of what was in his pants wasn't visible.

"This is Vivek. He helped me get to the hospital and doctor and everything."

"Thank you for helping my Sujata, *beta*."

"I was glad to help. I should get going. My flight leaves in a few hours."

"Come on in, Maa. Go sit on the couch."

"You come sit down, too, *beta*."

Sujata crutched back to the couch and gingerly sat down at the end. She would need the arm for help getting up. There weren't going to be strong arms to pull her up anymore. Those were on the way to the airport any second now. It was frustrating that she couldn't kiss Vivek goodbye, but there was no way with her *maa* there. She couldn't even let her know that they were together. Her *maa* was pretty progressive, but there were definite limits for a woman who'd grown up in India.

Vivek brought Maa's pink suitcase in and put it in the living room, quickly packing his laptop in his bag. "It was nice to meet you, *Shreemati* Das."

She gave him a big smile. "It was lovely to meet you, too. Thank you again for helping her."

He grabbed his own suitcases and waved at Sujata before heading out.

It was horrible not kissing him goodbye. And they hadn't even talked about how this was going to work.

"Who's this boy, *beta*?" Maa asked.

Sujata could not be remotely honest. For one thing, she worried that he might change his mind before he landed in Atlanta.

Unlikely, but she wasn't ready for this. "A friend from work. He just got a new job in Atlanta and that's where he's going today. He was supposed to leave Monday, but he delayed his flight for me. I was really thankful he was able to help. He's a really nice guy."

Man, she was going on.

"He would look good in a kurta, wouldn't he?" Maa winked.

"Yes, Maa." She wanted this topic to wrap up.

Everything was crazy right now. She was excited about where things might go, but it was so uncertain. In a few years, maybe she'd be running a successful company, or maybe she'd be married to Vivek, or both. Or neither. The future was unknown.

19

"Maa, I'm okay on the crutches." Sujata made her way down the hall after a not-quick bathroom break, surprised at how much crutching used her core muscles. Even with how fit she was, they were sore. "You're just going to get in the way."

"Sujata," she chided.

"Sorry." She had sounded more snappish than she'd intended. "I'm just stressed. And sore." It was true. Her ankle just constantly ached, and any wrong movement amped it up to eleven on one to ten.

"Okay, *beta*." Maa stepped back and Sujata got to the couch, where she carefully sat at the left end. The arm would be helpful for getting back up.

"Do you want a drink?" Maa called from the kitchen.

"I'll take a bubly." She could hear Maa pulling a glass out and filling it with water, and then the fridge open and close, then the pop of a can being opened. She really did need to work on her system, but it was going to be difficult with Maa here. The woman was chatty, and they hadn't seen each other in a long time. And of course she was worried about Sujata and excited about Kavya's wedding that they were already planning. Also, they genuinely liked each other, so it was going to be hard to focus on work. Kavya and Sujata were lucky, growing up with a fun *maa*.

So yeah, no work was getting done for a while. Also, she was going to have to minimize the amount of thought she gave Vivek even though there was a ton to process. They were dating now! And they'd almost gotten it on in this very spot. She was very glad Maa assumed she was still an innocent. She had never learned the truth about Rajeev, either.

Maa returned bearing the drinks. She handed Sujata her can and sat down at the other end, cross-legged and sideways so she was facing Sujata.

"Maa, I do have to work. We can catch up first, but I need to work this afternoon."

"Okay, *beta*."

Maa looked around the room, her gaze landing on the painting Sujata had over the fireplace. "That's new."

"Yeah. Casey was involved with this organization that had a charity auction, and I won this. I love it."

"It's impressive. How much did you spend?"

Of course she'd ask that. "I think about two thousand dollars. It was for a good cause." She said the last bit defensively.

"*Theek ache*, *beta*, I was just asking. No judgment." Her palms were out and her face was open, so Sujata knew she was not actually being judgmental. Maa continued, "I've never bought original art before. It's very ... what do the kids say now? Bougie."

Sujata laughed. "I'm so offended."

Maa reached over and patted Sujata's hand. "It's okay, *beta*, you're the best kind of bougie."

Sujata was glad Maa was here. "I think you're just jealous, Maa."

They laughed some more and Sujata took a sip of her bubly.

"What is this?" Maa asked, holding up the bubly can, which is when Sujata finally noticed Maa had had her nails done, which she had literally never seen before.

"It's just carbonated water with a tiny bit of flavor, but no sugar or artificial sweetener."

Maa tried it. "Mmm, that's good. I bet your *baba* would like this. So tell me again exactly how you injured yourself. I had trouble picturing it from what you said before."

Sujata described the mishap.

Maa shook her head. "You're not supposed to injure yourself doing yoga, *beta*."

"I'm aware." She couldn't keep the snark out of her voice.

"Maybe don't do any more headstands," Maa said, taking another sip.

"It's only because I was so worn out from the recital. I've done them a bunch of other times."

"You just need to be careful."

"Since when do you get manicures?" Sujata asked.

"What, a middle-aged lady can't do this?" She waggled her fingers at Sujata.

Sujata smiled. "No, I have just never seen you with painted nails."

"Some of us from work had a girls' night out. Except it was more afternoon."

"You and a bunch of professors raided a nail salon?"

"Yes, it was my first time. And then a happy hour. And then we all went home and made dinner for our husbands."

"I'm so glad you're my *maa*, Maa. You crack me up."

Maa looked very happy. "Thanks, *beta*. I'm glad I ended up with two beautiful and smart daughters."

"So how's Kavya's wedding coming along?"

Maa smiled big and began listing all the gory details—and there were many—and then it was almost two-thirty.

Sujata picked up her computer. "Okay, I need to do some work."

"Okay, *beta*. I'll just read my book."

As soon as she said that, Sujata panicked because the book Vivek had been reading must still be out. She scanned the coffee table and the floor around it, but it was nowhere. She looked over at the bookshelf, and to her surprise, it was back in its spot, albeit upside-down, but she wasn't complaining. Vivek must have rushed over there with it while she had been crutching to the door.

Sujata logged into her computer, thinking of the wedding images Vivek had shown her earlier, and imagining Kavya's and Ankur's faces on the bride and groom. Although the ceremony would be different from Vivek's cousin's because they were both Bengali, and wedding traditions varied widely across India.

She opened up her code and started working on the analyzer. She needed to work, and not obsessively think about Vivek and what he might be doing, what he was thinking, and was it about her?

She'd just send him a quick text telling him to text her when he got to Atlanta safely.

Maybe she'd put a few xo's at the end. Was that juvenile? She had no idea how to do this anymore.

But she was weirdly excited to figure it out.

~

VIVEK WAS UNLOADING groceries with his roommates in his new kitchen Wednesday night when his phone chimed again, Sujata's special two-beat chime. The smile and good feeling was instinctive.

"Who is that that keeps texting?" his new roommate Ranjit asked, laughing.

"My girlfriend, Sujata." Saying those words sent a surge of happiness he hadn't felt in a while. Now it was really real—he'd said it out loud to someone.

He looked at the text.

—She's staring at me right now—

Vivek laughed. They were talking about her *maa*, who was playing mother hen and driving Sujata a bit crazy. Sujata had decided to take the rest of the week entirely off rather than try and fail to work because her *maa* wouldn't stop talking to her.

—Does she know who you're texting?— he responded.

Amir—his other new roommate—handed him a large bag of rice and he had to put the phone back in his pocket. He was far more interested in his phone than his new roommates. "Where does it go?"

Ranjit spun the lazy Susan around and pointed to the bottom shelf.

Vivek squeezed past him and set the rice down. His phone was burning a hole in his pocket.

"We usually take turns cooking, Vivek," Ranjit said.

"Okay. What's the schedule?"

They went through the plan, which basically meant they each cooked solo two nights a week and handled Sunday either by getting takeout or something from the pantry. They all had to make enough for leftovers for everyone to have lunch the next day.

That wasn't too bad.

The phone chimed again.

"Sujata needs your attention," Amir joked.

Vivek blushed, but he was more happy than embarrassed so he checked the message.

—It's like being a teenager again. You're just a friend, sorry—

—I'm not offended, since my family don't even know you exist—

She sent a laughing emoji. *—If she were a cool western mom, she'd be happy I'm giving men a chance again—*

—Please don't give men a chance again— he said.

Sujata responded with several more laughing emojis. *—I only need one—*

—Good—

He sat at the little table next to the kitchen and looked at her new message.

—I can't think of anything to say, but I'm sending you this message because I don't want to stop texting—

Vivek laughed. He'd better respond so she could keep going. With both of them not working this week, they could text all day, with just *maa*-related interruptions.

It now occurred to him that he should have just stayed there with her. But she'd dumped the whole "let's try this" thing on him so last-minute. And then her *maa* showing up right when she did threw them both for a loop.

Ranjit and Amir were both looking at him, clearly about to tease him again.

"She hurt her foot right before I left and her *maa* is there to help out. She's complaining about her." This was obviously not true, but it was too complicated to explain everything.

Ranjit finished putting away some packets of frozen food for Sundays, and Vivek composed his text.

—Why don't you tell me about one of those romance novels you appear to be a fan of—

—Oh, that's good. I'll leave out the spicy bits, but there's a lot to say. I'll tell you a new one. Some other time, I'll tell you the whole story of the one you picked up—

Ranjit and Amir moved out of the kitchen, everything put away, and Ranjit and Amir sat on the couch. Ranjit turned the TV on. Voices speaking Hindi filled the room.

Vivek stayed at the little table next to the kitchen, eyeing the bag of samosas they'd picked up at the Indian restaurant next to the store. He pulled one out and took a bite. The apartment was tiny, just like his last apartment in Portland. But he had his own room, so he would not complain.

—I'm waiting— Vivek texted, even though he could see the dots on the bottom of the window so he knew she was typing.

—Patience— she responded, then the dots reappeared.

His new roommates seemed nice enough. Ranjit seemed to be the outgoing one and Amir the quiet one, rather like Kiran and Ishaan in Portland. How could something be so much the same when everything else was so different? He was now in Atlanta, he was starting a new job, and he was finally in a real relationship with Sujata.

"Oh, bring the samosas over here!" Ranjit said. "I forgot them. You can sit here if you put your phone on mute, Vivek."

He muted his phone, grabbed some plates, and ended up between them on the couch. They passed around the samosas and sauces while a picture got started.

—So here's the story— Sujata texted. *—Two engineers, a man and a*

woman, meet at a tech company and immediately like each other. But she is a woman scorned and is too scared to do anything about it—

Vivek smiled—was she really going to talk about them? She was typing more. Never did three dots make him happier.

—But the man is so hot that she has trouble saying no, but she is very, very stubborn. But he's patient and keeps trying to help her see that they belong together, without being a creeper, though—

He felt like his heart must be glowing. The part about him not being a creeper made him smile.

The picture was playing, but he was watching the dots on his little screen in his hand instead of the big screen across the tiny room.

*—It is especially difficult for her after an incident in the office where they *REDACTED* and almost got caught by their boss—*

Vivek chuckled out loud and desire coursed through him at the memory of that very first kiss.

Ranjit looked at Vivek, eyebrows raised.

"Sorry," he said, not at all sorry.

"Are we going to meet this woman?" Ranjit asked.

It was a good question. Was she going to visit? They were together, yes, but what did it really mean? They were doing the long-distance thing, but was that with or without visits? "I hope so," he eventually said.

He decided he'd ask her once she finished her story.

—Then there was an incident where they ran into her ex, and she pretended they were together, which was very mean of her and she is still sorry to this day. But she stayed stubborn while he stayed patient. Fortunately, her resolve started to crumble—

He couldn't get the smile off his face. Although that had been a tough night. He watched the TV a bit, a band of police trying to take down the coal mafia. It was a car chase scene which could never happen in real life because there was always too much traffic in cities in India, but everybody loved a car chase scene.

*—Some other stuff happens and there's an incident with a pasta-like substance and they *REDACTED* again and she's on the verge of giving in*

to what she wants, but now it seems pointless since he's moving away, like a jerk—

She was hilarious.

—But then she suddenly turns into a damsel in distress and he has to rescue her, a classic move in any romance novel, and she finally changes her mind. They are both very happy—

He watched the screen for a bit. Where were the dots?

—What happens after that?— he texted.

*—I haven't finished the book yet, but it's a romance, so they obviously live happily ever after and have lots of *REDACTED*—*

He laughed out loud again, loving that she was thinking far ahead, even though she was joking around. He answered *—What? Babies?—*

—Maybe as a side effect—

He put his fingers to his forehead to stop himself from laughing and annoying his roommates too much. Ranjit and Amir were understandably eyeing him at every sound he made.

But thinking about acts that have to be censored in front of anybody's mother, when would that happen? Surely the first time one of them visited, assuming her ankle was better.

He sincerely hoped her ankle was better very soon, and that she could spare some vacation. He didn't know what his would be like.

Once the picture was over, he'd ask Ranjit because he also worked for Irish.

He and Sujata needed to figure out how they were going to do this, because he didn't think she wanted to keep it long-distance for too long. He definitely didn't. They'd figure something out—he was sure of it.

~

MAA WAS MAKING dinner Thursday night. She had bemoaned the state of Sujata's fridge and cupboard and taken a Lyft to the Indian grocery store. She'd come back with pollock and all the right stuff to make macher jhol, a hot and sour Bengali fish curry that their whole family loved. She'd bought several other things, but Sujata was looking forward to the curry today.

She'd set up in the kitchen after putting everything away—Sujata would probably never find anything in the kitchen after her *maa* went back home—and started on the curry. The pungent scent of the mustard oil Maa was frying the curry paste in reached Sujata, and her stomach growled in anticipation.

Her phone vibrated in her hand as she stared at the screen, and she felt that familiar rush of excitement. With both her and Vivek not working, the texting was pretty much nonstop, even under her *maa*'s watchful eye, and every text came with a kick of serotonin. They were currently having a deep discussion about the best spices to use with dal. Sujata didn't like lentils as much as most Indians, and needed the right spices.

—Okay, so how do you feel about potatoes?— he asked.

—All Indians love potatoes, Vivek— She shifted on the couch to get more comfortable.

—Not this Indian—

—How is this possible?— She was genuinely surprised.

—They're okay. I like aloo tikki, but not when the potatoes are really identifiable. You know they weren't a part of Indian cuisine until the British, right?—

—Okay, so maybe potatoes aren't politically correct. But they are so good—

He just sent a bunch of laughing emojis.

Sujata looked over and saw Maa leaning against the wall next to the kitchen, watching her. She was embarrassed about how happy texting Vivek made her, but it didn't take the smile off her face.

"What are you and your friend talking about now?" Maa asked.

"She doesn't like potatoes!"

Maa made an exaggerated shocked face with overly wide eyes and put her hand to her chest. "And you said she's Indian? This friendship will never work, *beta*."

Then they both laughed.

—My maa says it will never work between us. But she also thinks you're a girl, sorry—

More laughing emojis.

"Food's almost ready," Maa said. "It's simmering with the tamarind." She disappeared back into the kitchen and Sujata's stomach growled again.

—I'm about to eat macher jhol, with potatoes. Yum—

—I'm supposed to cook tomorrow night—

—What are you making?—

—No idea yet— He added the shrug emoji at the end. *—I also still have no idea what I'll be doing at work—*

The nutty smell preceded Maa as she carried in two plates, each with a bowl of curry and a batch of rice on it.

Sujata quickly texted *—be back soon—* and took the plate handed to her, along with the paper towel under the plate. "Thanks, Maa."

"Of course, *beta*." She sat down carefully and they dug in.

Sujata was going to have to leave the phone alone for a bit. She might lose her mind.

20

Vivek caught the bus with Ranjit to head into the office Monday morning. It was only a thirty-minute bus ride in, which was not too bad. But there would be no Sujata to look forward to every day, as he had at InfoQuest.

The company was in a tall building with an entirely glass facade.

"We've got floors three and four," Ranjit said as they walked through the front doors. Ranjit showed his badge to the guard at the security desk and Vivek showed him his license for a guest badge, which he clipped to his polo collar.

His phone dinged as they stepped into the elevator.

"Your girlfriend again?" Ranjit asked.

Vivek's smile would have given it away if Ranjit hadn't already guessed.

—Best of luck!!!—

—We're heading up right now. I'll let you know how it goes— he responded.

"Actually, Vivek, you should mute your phone. Nirish doesn't like phone noises. He doesn't like us on our phones at all, actually."

Great. "A tech leader's anti-tech ethos."

"Yeah, pretty much."

Vivek wasn't just imagining his uncle's unpleasantness. Nirish had been in America since Vivek was very young, so he didn't know the man very well. But he'd never liked him the few times he'd met him. He was always a show-off. *Look at me, I'm helping family out.* It worked on his parents, but Vivek himself not so much. He switched his phone to mute.

Ranjit scanned in through double doors and Vivek got a first view of his new office. There was a reception desk with a curved counter and a wall behind it, with aisles leading into the office on either side. A young Black woman sat behind the desk.

"I've got our new hire, Talia," Ranjit said.

"Oh, hi," Talia said, her not-so-subtle southern accent shining through her friendly smile. "What's your name?"

"I'll see you later, Vivek," Ranjit said before heading off to the right.

"I'm Vivek Aachari," he said, thumbs behind his backpack straps.

She typed it into the computer. "Here you are. Nirish said he wanted to welcome you himself. You must be special."

"He's my uncle." He was embarrassed. Plus, saying it made him dread meeting Nirish again.

"Ah, that makes sense. I've just pinged him. Let me get your photo right quick and I can get your badge printed."

This was supposed to happen last Friday because he was going to get his new computer and fill out paperwork, but the HR woman was out sick so Nirish told him to just wait until Monday.

Talia snapped his picture with her phone and he sat down in one of the orange chairs against the side wall.

"Vivek!" His uncle's booming voice filled the space. "I'm so glad you decided to join us. Let me show you around. Is his badge ready, Talia?"

"No, Mr. Iyengar, I'm uploading his photo right now."

"Faster, Talia. Always faster."

Vivek did not miss the annoyance in her smile. Nirish clearly didn't care.

Vivek's stomach was full of lead. This whole thing was probably a mistake. He should have tried harder to stay in Portland. Bowing to family pressure shouldn't be his style. His heart became a well of desperation. Could he just stay long enough to get his green card and then take off? It would take forever.

"Come this way, *marumaan*," Nirish said. He was using the Tamil word for nephew. Vivek hoped he didn't do this in front of other people.

Vivek followed him off to the left, trying to push down the negative thoughts. His phone vibrated in his pocket. He knew better than to check it out now, but he was desperate to see if it was from Sujata. It had to be.

Nirish first pointed out his own office, which had expensive-looking cherry furniture. The rest was underwhelming: a few offices for directors and then utility tables with computers on them, crowded together three to a row. It was obviously ridiculously cheap. Apparently he'd run out of money after decorating his office. They walked the rest of the floor—more of the same—and ended up in a small kitchen.

"Now for the best part," Nirish said, leading Vivek to the reception area again. As soon as Talia saw them, she put the badge on the counter with a clip. He didn't think that his uncle meant this as the best part, though.

They went down to the third floor, where the devices lab was, the most interesting thing so far. It took up half the third floor and was where the electrical engineers worked on the various sensors and GPS devices the company used. They did logistics for trucking companies.

Vivek had hardly said a word, just trying to stay under the radar, wondering the whole time what his actual job was going to be. They finished the third floor, and Nirish still hadn't shown him where he was going to be sitting.

"What do you think, *marumaan*?" Nirish gave him his glowing smile, knowing exactly what Vivek would say.

"It's very impressive, Uncle-ji." He just hoped he'd start

addressing him with his name, not keep calling him "nephew." "I am wondering, though, where will I be sitting?"

Nirish nodded importantly. "I will introduce you to the team."

They walked back toward the lab and ended up in a section with two tables that had been empty when they'd passed by before. Now, there were five men, all looking to be in their twenties—three Indian, one Chinese, and one white. Two of the Indians were chatting animatedly about something.

Nirish cleared his throat and they all turned, the two who were talking suddenly quiet.

Nirish had obviously gotten worse with more power. Vivek's stomach twisted. He really didn't want to be related to the tyrant they all worked for.

"This is Vivek," he announced. Everyone smiled or gave a friendly wave, but they all retreated to their spots at the tables. Nirish walked to the middle spot on the right one and tapped his finger on the MacBook Pro sitting there. "This is yours."

"Thank you, Uncle-ji." There were also an Apple keyboard, two monitors, a docking station, and a mouse.

"I'm going to send IT over here to help you get set up. HR will be by at eleven to finalize your paperwork. For now, get to know your teammates."

Nirish strode away and Vivek went to his desk, dropped his backpack on the floor, and sat down. He pulled his phone out of his pocket, his heart skipping when he saw Sujata's name on the notification.

—*I can't wait*— she'd said.

—*I think I have made a mistake*— he responded. He plugged the computer into the peripherals.

"Nirish is your uncle?" the white guy said, from the chair on Vivek's left. He was leaning forward and toward Vivek.

Vivek turned and nodded, feeling his upper lip quirk a bit. "He still hasn't told me what I'll be doing here." He started to put his phone on the table, but it vibrated again.

—*Why?*— Sujata asked.

The guy laughed. "I'm Brian." He stuck his hand out and Vivek shook it, a decent grip. Brian rolled his chair around so Vivek turned to look. The Indians at the other table had all turned their chairs to face them, so Vivek joined them, typing a quick message that he'd respond in a bit.

The Indians all introduced themselves and one said, "Come on, Michael, join the party."

The Chinese guy finally rolled his chair around and into the circle, giving Vivek a shy smile but saying nothing.

"We're the embedded prototyping team," Manu said.

That was a surprise. Usually embedded programming was done with lower level languages that were doing things like turning specific electronics components off and on, which Vivek had very little experience with. And no interest in. "Do you use Python?"

"Some," Deepak said. "But we also do a lot of our work in Apex, our custom prototyping software, which is written in Python, and which we also support."

"What else?" Vivek asked. He heard his phone vibrate again and wanted to check it, but obviously couldn't.

"Some C, and we use Verilog for custom design," Manu said.

"Oh." A small pulse of anxiety hit Vivek. He'd never used Verilog and had only really basic experience in C, and they were very different from Python and the other object-oriented languages he knew.

A throat clearing made them all look to the aisle, where a large white guy with thick square black glasses stood. A chain ran from his belt to his back pocket, a bunch of keycards dangling off it. "I'm here to help you get logged in," he said to Vivek.

Everyone else turned back to their desks. Once Vivek was set up, he turned to Brian and asked if he knew what he was supposed to be doing.

"I'm not sure. I'd show you Apex, but I'm on a tight deadline today. But I can get you set up in it and send you some links for our documentation. It's not great, but not terrible."

"Sounds pretty good for internal software documentation," Vivek joked, which made Brian laugh.

Okay, at least there was one guy he'd get along with. Well, he'd be fine with the Indians, too, most likely. He just hoped people weren't too serious.

A bit later, he filled out some remaining paperwork with the woman from HR, and spent the rest of the day fiddling around in Apex and reading documentation, which was almost incomprehensible without more context. He'd taken one embedded systems class during his Master's, but they'd done very little programming and had used C++, so this was going to have quite the learning curve.

His phone vibrated with another text from Sujata.

—How are things going?—

—I think it's going to suck. I won't even be doing much Python— He explained more about the work, his heart filling with dread with each typed word.

—I'm really sorry, Vivek—

—I'll live—

He still had to slog through more documentation. All he wanted was to get back home so he could talk to Sujata. She was also back at the office, which meant he'd have to wait for her to get home, too, which would be after ten his time. He was worried about her getting there and back. She'd been planning to take the bus, but he convinced her to Uber in. He hoped she really would. He knew she didn't like to spend money, but it was too dangerous to go around on city buses on crutches. He'd bug her about it tonight and make sure she really did it.

~

"No *WAY*!" Sujata said into the phone as they were FaceTiming, snort-laughing. Her feet lifted off the bed from her stomach contracting as she cracked up. "Internal documentation is crap? I can't believe it!"

"Did you just snort?" Vivek asked.

And that got them both cracking up. She was laughing so hard that she had tears in her eyes. She never would have known how much fun Vivek could be if she hadn't finally opened up to him.

"That was my one allocated snort-laugh for the year," she said as they calmed down, with only a few giggling fits along the way. She was hiding in the bedroom from her mom, who was there for a few more days.

"Okay, I won't keep track or anything." His smile had lit up his eyes.

"Anyway, tell me what you'll be working on exactly." She really wanted to know how he'd be spending his time so she could picture what he might be doing at any moment she thought of him.

It was so weird that she'd resisted him for so long, and now she was near-obsessed. Just not in an unhealthy way. But actually, this was the reason she'd resisted—because she was already so far gone that if they were to break up, she would be heartbroken again. But if they didn't, she would be eternally happy.

She trusted him.

"Basically I'm part of the firmware team, designing and prototyping sensors that go on the trucks and stuff like that." His voice was flat.

"That's kind of cool."

"Not really," he deadpanned, a bemused look on his face.

"Okay, maybe not. I've never done anything with hardware. Well, except for that time I did Lego Mindstorms in eighth grade."

"Robots, huh? I wouldn't have guessed. I never even did that."

"It was part of one of those 'let's get the girls into STEM' programs," she explained. She'd just done it to make her parents happy, but she ended up liking the programming part. "But nowadays, give me databases all day long, not silicon."

"Yeah. I don't know what I'm going to do. And my uncle. Sujata. I can't even tell you. Just thinking about him is stressful. He's horrible."

"I'm sorry." That really did suck. She'd never had a bad job, well, at least not until her project was rejected. But it still wasn't that bad day-to-day. "Will you see him a lot?"

"I don't know. He's so arrogant. He might come by to tell me all the amazing things he does in the hopes that it will get back to my family." His voice was disdainful.

"Ugh." Sujata hated the special brand of arrogance some older men had. Especially ones who'd had an overinflated sense of importance from mothers overfeeding their egos when they were growing up. "I hope your coworkers won't think you're like him."

"I think they will notice I'm not. My immediate team seems pretty nice, and I think they could sense I didn't love the fact that I'm working for my uncle." He sighed. "I am sure they are waiting to see if I'm any good at coding."

"Well, then you should be good."

"Maybe. As long as they give me Python work first."

"So it might not mostly be Python?"

"I'm not that lucky." He sounded a bit beat down. "They do have a system they use for design that's written in Python, and we maintain it. So I'm going to try to be custom design system maintenance and developer guy. The rest is C and Verilog."

"Gross, C. What's Verilog?" She was so glad she'd ended up in her situation, but feeling lucky didn't change how bad she felt for Vivek. But she also couldn't help but notice how much better he was taking it than Rajeev would have. Rajeev was pouty when he didn't get his way, but Vivek was pretty much taking it in stride.

She could no longer remember what she had seen in Rajeev. This was probably the first step in truly getting over him.

"It's a hardware description language that looks a lot like C," Vivek said.

She blew air out through narrowed lips. "Ugh, C again. It's sounding inescapable."

"Enough about my day," he said with finality. "Tell me about yours."

"Nothing really out of the ordinary. The Indians did ask me if I'd heard from you yet. They say hi."

"Nothing exciting is just fine for a work day."

"But it's so weird with you gone. Plus, there's this obnoxious, loud guy in your cube now."

"They already replaced me?" He sounded offended.

"He's actually from a different team that ran out of space."

"Oh, okay. That's better."

"Yeah." She told him about her lunch with Theresa, and the bug she spent two hours on before taking a break to make tea, then spotting it the second she sat back down and unlocked her screen.

"Isn't that always the way."

"But, you know, Vivek, I'm only half tuned-in anymore at work. All I can think about is the data quality project." This was absolutely true. She got butterflies in her stomach thinking about what she was stepping out to do. She was really going to do this thing.

"That is how it should be. Just do what you need to do to keep the job, and no more. They don't deserve your overcommitment."

Sujata's heart warmed. She loved how much he was truly on her side. So many men would be dismissive or maybe give lip service, but she knew Vivek believed what he was saying. But she was still struggling with whether to include him in the project or not. Even though she didn't consider what happened with the VPs his fault, it had gone all wrong, anyway.

"Oh!" Vivek exclaimed. "I just realized I didn't ask about your ankle. How are you doing?"

"Now I'm crutching around like a pro." She already had good core strength, so moving around wasn't hard.

"That's good, but that is a really weird word used that way."

"Crutching?" she asked, laughing. People had commented on it being weird before. "When Kavya was ten, she broke her foot, and that's how my family talked about her moving around. Walking didn't seem right, and she definitely wasn't gliding, scurrying, or prancing from place to place. There's no judgment in it, just precision."

"If you say so," Vivek said, smiling. "So how much longer are you on them?"

"I'm not seeing the doctor until Tuesday in three weeks. I'm hoping the cast can come off then, but I don't know. I won't be back in dance for a while, though. He said he doesn't know how much longer I'll have to wait. Nilani is peeved."

"What else are you supposed to do?" He was obviously offended on her behalf.

"I know, she's not the most empathetic person on the planet," she said wryly. "You know how those highly respected genius-types are."

Vivek laughed. "I do."

"But really, I'm dying to get back to everything. I'm not even supposed to do yoga right now."

"Yeah. Is your *maa* still there?"

"Until Saturday. I love her, but oh, my God."

"I get it. It's the same with my parents."

"I tried to give her my bed, but she's insisting on sleeping on the couch because of my injury. I feel really bad about this. The truth is, I don't really need her help anymore. I've become a pro at wrapping my cast in plastic before showering." She paused, smiling to herself. "However, being able to keep my bedroom is definitely convenient since I have a door I can shut so I can talk to you with some level of privacy."

"I hate that I'm not there to be able to help you out. I abandoned you."

She laughed. "That's not at all true. You left me in the very capable—and talkative—care of my *maa*. But she cooks every day. It's worth it."

"Yum. We split the cooking up in my apartment. One of the guys is actually a really good cook. He even makes his own ghee."

"Ooh, nice."

The fact that they were talking about making ghee made Sujata weirdly happy. She and Vivek could talk about anything, and she still loved it. Did she actually love him already? She wasn't sure—it was too scary to think about—but she had a sudden desire to see him and kiss him.

"When are you going to visit, Vivek?"

He cocked his head to the side and said, "I wish tomorrow. I will have to ask Nirish when I can take some time off. I don't know how much vacation I will have, or when I can take it. But you know, Sujata, you could visit me. I'd still have to work, but you could come over a weekend."

"Oh, yeah." She hadn't even thought about it, since in her head, Portland was their place. "Let me talk to David about taking some time off."

"Perfect."

Maybe it *wouldn't* be a while, after all. And Vivek had his own room at his new place, a major upgrade from his couch in Portland.

A shut door and a bed. That was what she was thinking about right now.

21

On Saturday, after his first full week at work, Vivek sat at his desk in his apartment, phone propped up against some books so he would be able to see his parents in WhatsApp. He tried to get cozy in the wooden chair, but it wasn't happening. He should buy a decent desk chair, since this was his home now. The streetlamp just outside his window was shining through the blinds into his eyes because it was still dark out, even though it wasn't as early as he'd had to call in Portland. He was three time zones closer to India now. But he was definitely going back to bed after this, because he'd been up late talking to Sujata..

Thinking about Sujata of course made him smile, and also made his whole body warm up. She was supposed to be coming to Atlanta for the weekend in three weeks, from Thursday night through the Sunday. This stirred him even more.

He closed his eyes to relish the thought for a moment, and then tried to shift into family-appropriate feelings.

He dialed on WhatsApp and waited for someone to answer. Three weeks was a long time when it meant waiting for Sujata and what he assumed would be a lot of kissing, at a minimum. Hopefully more.

"Vivek, hi!" his sister Mishti said.

He was not ready for that, with thoughts of Sujata right at the front of his mind. He closed his eyes tight and reopened them to reset.

"Sorry," Mishti continued, "the phone was in the other room and we didn't hear it right away. How are you?" It looked like she had flour on her chin. It made her adorable, even if she was older than him. She was looking more and more like their *amma* every day. The two of them were working in the kitchen as per usual.

"Good."

"Didn't you start working at Nirish's company this week?"

Vivek grimaced and nodded.

She curled her lip, which made her nose ring move. "I'm sorry. Why didn't you try to get out of that?"

Yes, why hadn't he tried much, much harder than he had? It was Sujata—it had felt pointless to stay in Portland for her. But he had many other reasons to try to stay there. He shouldn't have made it all about her.

"Sometimes you have to fight back, *thambi*," Mishti said, looking down.

He narrowed his eyes. "The same could be said for you, Mishti."

She eyed him. "It's different for women. You know that."

Vivek nodded. She wasn't wrong, but still. He hated her husband, a jerk who thought women shouldn't work, even though he made enough to hire a cook. He wanted Mishti to do it because that was the "natural" order of things. The guy's personality was like Nirish's.

Someone called Mishti's name from the background.

"Oh, that's Amma. Let me tell her you're on the phone." She looked off to the side. "It's too loud in there. I'm going to leave you here. Love you."

He said it back as she disappeared.

"Vivek!" his *amma* said, her round face on the screen. "Nirish said you are great at your job. What took you so long?"

Before he could answer, his father's face appeared on the screen.

"Yes, why did you take so long?" he asked.

"I was trying to finish up my work at InfoQuest. You know I take my commitments seriously, Appa."

"Of course you do, *wā-pā*," his father said, a proud smile on his face.

"You are a very honorable boy, it is true," his mother said.

Any second now, they were going to bring up the girl with nice skin. Mishti's marriage was the exact reason he didn't want to do an arranged marriage—you couldn't really know the other person until you'd spent a lot of time with them.

"When are you going to visit?" his mother asked. "Adya's parents are looking forward to meeting you."

Well, now there was no chance whatsoever. He'd have to steer clear of India for a while. "You know I just started a new job. I need to learn more about the vacation policy."

Why hadn't their parents gotten the message? Young people didn't want arranged marriages. He wasn't the only one.

"Nirish will let you come see your family," she said, eyes glowing with that annoying pride in her big brother.

"I don't want special treatment, Amma. I have to find out what everyone else is allowed to do first."

His mother sighed. "How are your new roommates?"

"Everybody's really nice." This seemed to be true, fortunately. "Ranjit works there, too."

"I will talk to you later, *wā-pā*," his father said before leaving.

His mother shared neighborhood gossip and he managed to avoid any of the more annoying topics. He let his mind wander to Sujata, who would definitely still be in bed, since it was only four-thirty in Portland.

After they hung up, he climbed back into bed and sprawled out comfortably. He didn't have much planned for today, except for one very nice thing—he and Sujata were chatting at three about the crawler. He was still going to offer to do it for free for her.

Hopefully she'd take him up on the offer, because then she could focus on the other parts and get the whole thing done much more quickly.

He so wanted this to work for her. He knew it could, but he still had to wait and see it play out.

~

SATURDAY, Sujata grabbed her laptop and settled into her couch, her ankle still sore but vastly improving. She would have to do physical therapy before she'd be cleared to go back to dancing, though.

Her heart was beating fast in anticipation of talking to Vivek in three and a half minutes.

She opened the laptop and went to her calendar, clicking on the meeting link, which brought up the Google Meet pre-login screen. Vivek wasn't in the meeting yet. She joined it anyway.

Then the window popped up saying Vivek wanted to join—that's why he wasn't in there yet, because she had to let him in. He was obviously as anxious to see her as she was him. She felt her smile all the way to her belly. She clicked Admit.

As soon as he was in the meeting, a grin stretched across his face, which she returned. She was so smitten by him, feeling joy in her whole body just from seeing him.

"Hi," he finally said.

"Hi." Never had the word Hi been suffused with such emotion.

"I've been looking forward to seeing you again. I can't wait until you visit."

"Me too." She thought about finally having sex with him. It would be the first time in such a long time. Her cheeks had warmed right up with her thoughts.

They continued staring at each other, and her cheeks just got warmer, and the rest of her body got into the game.

"Are you ready to talk about the crawler?" he asked, not sounding very ready himself.

"Sure. Let me get VS Code up." She started opening the programming environment on her computer.

"Actually, I wanted to talk to you about something."

She looked up. Was he going to break up with her? Her stomach roiled.

"I want to write it for you. It will be so fast and easy for me, letting you concentrate on the other parts." He raised a finger. "But I won't take any credit. It will just be a gift for you."

She was touched that he'd offered, but she wasn't totally surprised. "I don't think that's a good idea. It's my idea and I need to do it all."

"I wouldn't request any ownership of it at all. It would be a gift." He obviously meant what he said, from the earnest look on his face.

"Well," she started. "So, I think maybe we could do it. But I don't want it to be a simple gift. I can't pay you for it now, but maybe you could have a stake in it if we get it officially off the ground. But we need a contract. Casey told me she could get a recommendation for a lawyer from a friend of hers. So I'm going to ask for that, and then I'll talk with the lawyer to see how things work."

"But it isn't really necessary."

She shrugged. She was going to have to be smart about this, because every decision she made now would have consequences down the line. "I think any time you mix business with personal life, it gets sketchy and complicated."

Vivek cocked his head to the side. "I guess that does make sense."

"But I also don't want you writing off in some dark, secret corner. I want to really understand what you're doing."

She wasn't a control freak, but she did struggle with asking for help. She had her whole life.

"We should start a GitHub repository." He grinned. "We can totally do formal code reviews. I've never gotten to review your code before."

Sujata laughed. GitHub was a website to store and collaborate on code, with versioning built in so you could roll back to earlier versions if a bug got introduced and there wasn't time to fix it right away. "You might find out I'm a terrible coder."

"Not a chance," he said. "I would never believe that. Your standards are high in every part of your life."

"Oh, actually—I don't want the code to be public."

"They allow private repos even on the free plan. We'll be fine."

She got butterflies in her stomach. This would make it feel even more real. She really was going to do this. "This is so cool. We're actually doing a Thing."

"I know, I can't wait to see what happens." Vivek's grin was infectious, even though she needed to be practical about this.

"Don't start writing anything yet, but let's talk about it now, so as soon as we have a contract in place, you can start." She started digging through some of her documents.

"That sounds good. It will be interesting to have a legally binding contractual relationship with you." His eyes twinkled.

Her eyes widened and she had a quick thought that he was moving too fast, but it was just a joke. And obviously she did want to get married some time.

"Let me share the design doc with you," she said, presenting it on the screen. "I'll also share this with you in Google."

Vivek nodded, leaning forward to read the document. "This is a rather familiar format," he teased.

She smiled. She'd used the same structure for the design document they used at InfoQuest. "I'm not embarrassed. It's what I know."

"And we know it works. Seems logical to me."

They started going over it, making tweaks along the way, but really fleshing out the entire system. With his help, she got a bunch more specifics in the section on the crawler.

"Are we done?" Vivek eventually asked.

She looked at him on the screen.

"Because I want to talk to you about other stuff. Like your upcoming visit." He waggled his eyebrows, which made Sujata burst out laughing.

"I've never seen you do that!"

"I learned it from TV last week," he said, still grinning.

"But yeah, let's talk about that." Her heart was already starting to race, imagining being there with him. He was so adorable. She really could not wait to see him. She assumed he was feeling the same anticipation. "Three more weeks."

"I know." His grin was infectious and she felt it straight to her heart.

"We haven't really talked about the logistics. Am I staying with you—would your roommates be okay with that? Or should I get a hotel?"

"You can stay with me. It will be fine. I'm going to get some interesting things to do around town from my roommates. I will have to work Friday, but I can sneak out of there at a decent time so we can have more time in the evening."

"I don't need you to entertain me, Vivek," she said. "I just want to be with you."

His cheeks flushed in response, and that shy smile she remembered from their earliest interactions came back. "I feel the same," he finally said.

They grinned at each other stupidly again for a bit.

She truly couldn't wait to get to Atlanta, even though it would already be hot there and she'd been so spoiled by the weather in Portland.

But she'd be with Vivek, so nothing else mattered.

PART III

SUMMER

22

Sujata passed Arrivals at the Portland airport yet again, comfortable in her new Audi, which she'd only had for two weeks now. No Vivek, so she went for another loop. Her pulse was going a mile a minute because this was going to be the first time they'd seen each other since he left for Atlanta over four months ago. Every attempt they'd made to get together had been foiled by work. His uncle was a jerk and he was on a big project that was requiring overtime, and things had exploded at InfoQuest and her vacation had been cancelled three times. She'd finally managed to get these two days off, and Vivek was taking three days of sick time, which was obviously a big risk.

It was hopefully going to be worth it. As much as she was excited to see him—and she was very, very excited to see him—their main reason for taking the risk right at this moment was their trip to San Francisco. They were catching a flight tomorrow and presenting their idea in front of several potential investors the next day, then flying back. She'd brought him on after arranging for a lawyer to draw up a contract, so they were both protected from any wrongdoings of the other.

Not that that was going to be a problem. But you never knew for sure. He could get a head injury and become a different, evil person. That stuff happened.

But hopefully not to her Vivek, because that would be terrible in so many ways.

Sujata's phone rang and her heart trilled as she answered it through her console. "Vivek!"

"I've finally got my bag. I'll be outside United. I cannot wait to see you!"

God, it was great to hear his voice. "Me too!" She felt like a little kid with how excited she was. Well, maybe a little kid who'd gone through puberty early, because she wanted much more than to see him right now. Her whole body was buzzing.

There he was! There were way too many cars between them so she kept pulling forward, struggling to take her eyes off his solid frame. He had on jeans and a shirt that she could tell was close-fitting.

A car swung out in front of her and she hit the brakes, but she didn't tear her eyes away from Vivek in time and she tapped the car's bumper, only registering the insistent beeping her car was making after the clunk.

Dammit! She closed her eyes and leaned forward. Now it was going to take them forever to get back to her apartment and bed.

She reluctantly opened the door and saw a white man striding toward her.

As soon as she was standing, she looked over at Vivek again, and he was running toward her, his head bobbing over the tops of the cars against the curb.

"What is wrong with you?" the man shouted.

She recoiled and looked at him, his face red with anger. She was instantly glad for all the other people around.

"Sujata!" she heard, and there was Vivek, coming around the car and hugging her.

They kissed, and it was the biggest relief to finally have him here, and his greedy lips on hers. His arms were around her tightly. Nothing had ever felt so right.

"Fucking foreign drivers!" sounded from behind her, though it barely registered over all the sensations flying through her body. Vivek stopped kissing her and looked over her shoulder at the man.

This brought her back to her senses, and her hackles belatedly shot up. "I'm not foreign, you asshole," she said to the asshole. Somebody honked behind them while other cars squeezed past them.

"Who are you calling an asshole, you bitch?"

He was raging mad and Sujata's heart was beating like crazy for all the wrong reasons.

Vivek stepped forward. "Do not talk to her like that."

Sujata thought he might get in the man's face, and as nice as that would feel, she did not want a fight. She had no idea how that would go. Vivek was solid, but she never imagined him as a fighter.

But instead of approaching the man, Vivek inspected his bumper. "There's not even any damage," he said, obviously disgusted. "Did you even look?"

The man looked at where Vivek was pointing, as did Sujata, and it was true—there was not even a small dent or paint mark. She stepped forward—the same could not be said for her bumper, which had a very noticeable dent. She'd hit the other car's bumper right on the corner.

"Get out of here, since that's what you were so desperate to do," Vivek said.

"Fuck you," said Mr. Charming, but he got back in his car.

Vivek hugged Sujata as the man pulled away. She was all hyped up with muddled feelings.

"Let's go," she said, suppressing a sob that suddenly wanted out from how overwhelmed she felt.

Somebody honked at them again. Vivek let go and ran around to the other side of the car. "Can you open the boot?"

She got in and opened it for him, and soon he was in the car next to her. They instinctively leaned toward each other and kissed again, the taste of him like coming home after a long trip.

Another honk. And rightfully so. They pulled apart. And soon she—carefully—pulled into the lane and they were off.

She glanced over at him and he was just smiling at her, those beautiful dark brown eyes glowing.

"Eyes back on the road, sweetheart." But from his thick voice, he obviously felt the way she did.

"I can't wait until we get home." She glanced over at him and threw him a wicked smile. "You know where we're going first, right?"

"I hope you're planning what I'm thinking."

"From your unusually deep voice, I'd say I am."

He laughed but she kept her eyes on the road as they left the airport.

Also, it just registered that he'd called her sweetheart. He'd never used a pet name before. She liked it.

She wished she lived closer to the airport so they would be home sooner, but there was nothing to be done but drive.

And plan for what she was going to do to him first. Well, first once he was naked.

It involved her tongue and that penis of his that she would finally be seeing for the first time. She'd felt it before and knew it wouldn't disappoint.

~

THERE WAS SO much energy coursing through Sujata's body as they approached the stairs to her apartment that she was barely touching the ground. She guessed Vivek felt the same, because the point where their hands were touching was practically radioactive.

They hurried up the stairs, Vivek's suitcase hitting the steps a couple of times as he dragged it behind him. Her finger got stuck in the keyring when she pulled out her keys and it was taking a million years to get everything untangled.

"Do you need an assistant?" Vivek joked.

"No, I do not." She managed to get the door unlocked. Vivek pushed it open, and they stumbled inside, already all hands. They'd had to wait so long.

Just inside the door, his mouth was on hers, hot and hungry. She had wanted this so much, for so long, that her mind was erased and all she could feel was the heat of his mouth, his hands in her hair, holding her close, their tongues sliding. She forgot to breathe while they devoured each other. She slipped her hands under his shirt in the back, hot skin practically burning her fingers.

Suddenly, he stopped and wrapped his hands around her butt and lifted her up. She wrapped her legs around him and just managed to swing the front door shut before they headed toward the bedroom. The click sounded just as they reached the corner.

Vivek dropped her on the bed and she held on, bringing him down with her. His mouth was on hers again while she tugged his shirt up his back. He yanked his shirt over his head while she sat up to pull hers off. She reached for his jeans and unbuttoned them. He reached around and unhooked the red lace bra she'd worn, while she unzipped his jeans and pushed them down over his hips, exposing his black boxers. He took her breasts in his hands. She spared a glance at his face and he had a small smile, even though his eyes were flashing with lust.

Sujata pushed the jeans so they fell to the floor. He stepped out of them and reached for her yoga pants and had everything off her in a second. She was fixated on the front of his engorged boxers, anticipation about to explode in her belly. He was looking down at her, all desire, and they pushed his boxers down together.

There Vivek was in all his glory. Big, but not too big, and glistening at the tip. She leaned forward, intent on doing what she'd been imagining since long before he got in the car at the airport.

He pushed against her forehead. "Not that, not right now." For a millisecond she wondered if he was going to be like Rajeev about it, and not like it because it was "gross." But Vivek's husky voice turned her on even more, if that was possible, and her mind went back to where it should be. Vivek.

"Scoot back," he said.

Sujata pushed herself back until her head was on a pillow, and he followed her and straddled her, then leaned down and started kissing just below her ear. She ran her hands across his firm chest, enjoying his slight intake of breath when she brushed his nipples. This felt so right, like it was the most natural thing in the world, the two of them together.

Vivek was working his way down her neck, the gentle sensation giving her chills and melting her heart. He held himself above her, the need for him to be inside her increasing by the second, and she arched her back and brought her hips up so that his cock brushed her stomach. He inhaled again at the contact and sucked on her neck before returning to her mouth. She was desperate for him. Starved. She focused on their mouths existing as one hotbed of sensation and ran her hands down the strong muscles on his back, reaching his taut butt. All those hours playing cricket had paid off.

Sujata closed her eyes and lost herself in the kiss. She couldn't think of anything when his mouth was on hers. He sucked on her lower lip and she wondered why that felt so good, and then she dove in with her tongue and they were entwined again.

When he broke the contact, their breathing was ragged.

"You first, Sujata." God, she loved the way he said her name, like she was the only person in the world.

He moved down and sucked on her left breast before moving over to the right, leaving her desperate for more, but then he dragged his tongue down from between her breasts to her stomach and then slowly moved lower.

The fact that he was going to do this was amazing. Rajeev had also thought this was gross, and they'd never tried it. He didn't care about her experience at all.

Jerk.

Vivek was obviously completely different in this way, too. So, so many ways. How had she confused them so much?

Her stomach fluttered in anticipation, bringing her back to the moment.

When he touched her clit, she bucked slightly and he chuckled before latching on and sucking. God, the intensity was overwhelming and she focused on paying attention to what he was doing. She could feel the slight stubble he had from a day of traveling.

He put his palms on her butt and pulled her up for better access, then started on her with his tongue. Her body started building up tension with each flick, until he stopped to suck for a bit so it receded again. But then he started the flicking again and he kept going until she thought it couldn't get any more intense. She moaned through her release, her body falling back to the bed, muscles convulsing while it played out.

He squeezed her butt one last time before removing his hands and placing them on her thighs. His hands we so solid and comforting. But now it was his turn. Plus she wanted more, even though she should have been completely spent.

"Vivek, please. There are condoms in the drawer." She pointed to the nightstand, where she had carefully placed several from the box she'd bought last week.

He pushed himself up and looked at her, eyes nearly black with lust, a smile stretching across his face. "Okay. Are you ready?"

"I've never been readier." This was the truth, the only thing she could think about was Vivek, his cock, her hot core, and how when they all came together, it would be the best experience in the world.

~

VIVEK MOVED OFF SUJATA, his heart slamming against his ribcage, and slid the drawer open to pull out a condom.

Sujata's breathing was as heavy as his and he crawled back over her before ripping the packet open and rolling it on. Sujata watched him with dark eyes.

They had waited so long for this, and it was finally happening. In some ways it seemed so obvious, a given, and in other ways it was like a miracle.

They stared at each other for a couple more heartbeats and he knew she felt the same way he did.

He scooted down and positioned himself against her entrance so he could feel her heat.

Sujata whimpered quietly and shifted slightly so they were touching, and he couldn't wait any more, so he pushed in slowly, savoring her tightness as she enveloped him. He closed his eyes for focus until he was all the way in. Then he opened them and saw Sujata staring at him with such intensity that he thought his heart would burst. He pulled out and pushed back in, watching her eyes widen ever so slightly in response.

He began thrusting, Sujata moaning with each one. It had been so long since he'd done this, and the fact that it was with someone he cared this much about made it the best feeling he'd ever had. He wanted it to never end and focused intently on not going too fast because he wanted Sujata to finish first, if he could make that happen a second time. He'd never been able to do this for a woman, but he'd heard it could happen. Sujata deserved the best experience possible.

She looked depleted, but her pulse told another story. And then she said, "I'm so glad you came, Vivek. I'm so glad I hurt my ankle like an idiot. It may have been the best thing I've ever done."

He was still trying to focus on his movement, but it didn't prevent him from smiling. He felt exactly the same. He was happy she had fully recovered from the injury and was dancing again, but they might have never gotten together if not for that injury. "I agree," he said through slightly gritted teeth.

But an inkling of doubt slipped into his heart. Did she love him? If not, what was this for her?

But lust didn't seem to fit her personality. Maybe it wasn't love yet, but he believed that it was going in that direction for her. They had only been officially together for four months, and she had resisted seeing him as a romantic partner for so long, while he'd been dreaming of it the whole time. He couldn't expect her to fall for him so fast.

Even if he wanted it more than anything.

She smiled at him and ran her hands down his back.

He couldn't quite read that expression, but it didn't feel like only lust—there was some real affection there, at least.

Then she squeezed his bum, which brought him too close, so he kept going but focused entirely on the motion.

Sujata moaned a few more times before her entire body shuddered, and finally he didn't have to hold back. He pounded into her ferociously until he exploded inside her, involuntarily gasping.

Vivek collapsed over her, holding himself up by his elbows, and when he finally came down, he pulled out and rolled to the side so he could put his hand on her stomach.

She rolled toward him and kissed him slowly.

He started to get up, but Sujata put a hand on his hip. "I put a trashcan on the other side of the bed."

He chuckled. "Miss Prepared."

"I had a lot of time to prepare."

They laughed and he rolled over to drop the condom in the trash.

"Way too much time," he said, rolling onto his side and placing his hand back on her stomach.

She nodded. "Let's sleep for an hour and then work on the presentation."

"Hey, the only presentation I want to work on is in this bed with me."

She laughed and rubbed his nipple. "I am divided. I want this business thing to work so well that I'm trying to not let other things distract me. Even if those other things are delectable. Thank you for coming, and for being a part of my life in general."

She leaned in and kissed him sweetly. Then she asked, "Where's my phone?"

"If it was in your pocket, it's somewhere in that general direction." He waved his hand toward the side of the bed.

She slid off and he admired her fit body as she leaned over. She had to have one of the firmest bums out there, but she still looked all woman, and so beautiful.

He was disappointed that she wanted to work on the presentation, but then he felt bad because he wanted her to be happy, and this business was incredibly important to her. Helping her get there should make him happy, too. Plus it would be incredible for him if it worked out.

It would. She was right that they needed to focus on it.

She climbed back into the bed, set an alarm on the phone, and put it on the side table. She faced him and kissed him again. "Wanna spoon?"

He wasn't sure what that meant, but he nodded, and she turned on her side with her back to him, and snuggled against him. He put his arm over her, and after he closed his eyes, he was halfway asleep before his mind started going on about the upcoming presentation. This was a huge deal, and they had no idea how it would go.

23

The next day, they'd hit cruising altitude on their flight and Sujata finally headed to the bathroom. She'd had two glasses of wine while they were waiting for their flight. Not that she was nervous or anything.

When she got back, Vivek was squinting at his computer. She sat back down and buckled up. They'd splurged for first class so they were extra comfortable, and wouldn't be bugging anyone with their frantic back and forth.

"Did we talk about accounting for this?" Vivek asked, pointing to a chart on his screen.

"The attrition?" Sujata asked.

He nodded.

"Yes. Slide twenty-two, I think."

He flipped through the slide deck until he got to it. "Okay, good." Then he leaned in and kissed her, a lingering one she didn't want to end. But they were around all these other people, so they should be decent.

In a minute. His fingers cradled the back of her head as he held her in place while he worshipped her upper lip. He pulled back and they smiled stupidly at each other.

They could behave. They actually needed to, because there was still much to prepare for.

All bets were off when they hit the hotel room, however.

Vivek leaned back in his seat and Sujata did the same.

"Should we go through the sections from the top again?" she asked.

He nodded. They had split the presentation up so they would be alternating over the different topics, taking turns so they looked equally involved and informed.

They had appointments with two different angel investors tomorrow. The first was at eight a.m., the next at one. They'd worked really hard to get these meetings set up and then spread out in case things went long at either of them.

Sujata was assuming that these men wouldn't presume it was all Vivek, but of course she had no control over that.

"Close your laptop," Vivek said, smiling at her.

Sujata nodded and shut the lid, returning his smile. "Thanks for meeting with us today. We are blah blah, and we're here to tell you about our company Data Cata. Data Cata is a smart organizational-level data catalog that includes built-in tools for discovering and monitoring all aspects of data quality, privacy, and security." She continued their well-practiced intro on the need for this system and others like it, with a focus on what made Data Cata different.

She'd had to look at a spot on the wall over his shoulder because his smile was still so distracting. It was hard to know if their business or their relationship was the most important thing right now. It was probably both.

What would happen if they did break up? Would they stay business partners, or would that be the end of it? It would be a nightmare if seeing Vivek after a breakup was anything like seeing Rajeev at the movie theater had been.

She couldn't think about that.

Also, she knew Vivek would never do anything so cruel.

Vivek started in on his spiel on the first data quality dimension, and then they bounced back and forth to cover the other dimensions one at a time. Sujata covered data privacy and Vivek did the data security component they'd added.

As soon as he started, Sujata smiled at him, and his eyes twinkled as he spoke. Security was no longer a sore spot for Sujata, and they had figured out a way to bring it in but keep the tool grounded in data quality rather than slipping into more general infosec. They had a plan for now, and one for later integration with an InfoSec department.

It was perfect. Just like Vivek.

"One second," Vivek said. "Before you start again. What do you think? Is this still good so far?"

Sujata looked up and really considered everything they'd just gone over. "I think so. We sound like we know what we're talking about, which obviously we do, and we're covering all the critical major points. Do you think it's too long?"

"I am not sure. Let's keep it all for now. We can do a full run-through after dinner and time the various sections."

"Okay." She started the next section, which addressed machine learning tools they had already built. This really was a fantastic product they'd created. Their system was solid. Somebody was going to fund them, even if it wasn't one of the two people they'd be meeting with tomorrow. She just had a good feeling about this.

Vivek covered the catalog itself, and then Sujata launched into the business plan, which she thought was completely solid. How could this not convince funders?

Vivek took her hand and squeezed it after the third point, which threw her for a loop.

"Sorry," he said. "It's hard to be near you and not touch you."

They leaned in and kissed slowly, ending up resting their foreheads together.

"Tomorrow's going to be hard," she said.

"It's going to be incredible. It's going to change our lives."

She smiled at him, feeling the same thing.

She couldn't wait.

But there was that little concern gnawing at all her good feeling. Could this whole thing still go wrong?

~

THE LYFT VIVEK and Sujata had taken from their hotel Friday morning pulled up in front of a tall glass building. Vivek grabbed the briefcase they'd bought to look more professional, did a quick visual sweep of the back seat as he got out of the car, and joined Sujata by the front door. She was beautiful in dark trousers and a fitted white top that stretched across her large breasts. They looked at each other. Sujata's eyes were glowing, but he could also see the nerves like tiny cracks in her smile. But only because he knew her so well.

"Ready?" he asked, touching her elbow. He was nervous, too, but it wasn't overpowering. Part of his worry had to do with her possibly changing her mind about this whole thing. Getting spooked by something and dumping him, and then where would they be with the business idea?

She took his hand. "Let's do this."

He steeled himself for the next several hours, but the worry remained in his belly.

They went through the heavy glass doors and encountered a desk with a security guard in a blue uniform. "Who are you seeing?" he asked.

"Jack Forsey," Sujata said.

The guard nodded, his shaved head reflecting the fluorescent light from the ceiling. Pointing, he said, "Take elevator three."

They walked over and got in. It was preset to go to the eighth floor, where Forsey's office was, and Vivek pressed the button to shut the door. The elevator shot up, quickly coming to a stop and pushing them hard toward the floor. All the movement aggravated the butterflies in his stomach.

They looked at each other again, serious this time. "We can do this," he said.

Sujata nodded and the doors opened.

They faced another reception desk, and a young Hispanic woman in a blouse with navy stripes. "For Mr. Forsey? Names?"

They nodded together and Sujata gave their names. The receptionist nodded and handed them each a plastic badge to clip on. "I will take you back."

Vivek motioned for Sujata to go in front of him, and they followed the receptionist down a hall with white walls adorned with art depicting San Francisco landmarks. They passed the Golden Gate Bridge on the right, a streetcar on the left. He couldn't believe this was all happening, and with Sujata. He wanted so much more with her. They had already entered one huge commitment to each other, but he wanted the other one. Did she?

After they passed a picture of a busy pier, the receptionist stopped at an open door leading into a meeting room. She motioned for them to enter, so they went in and sat down.

The woman smiled and said. "Mr. Forsey will be here shortly."

Vivek and Sujata sat next to each other near the end of the table, opposite a screen that was on the wall. They shared another look that was full of encouragement for each other, and then a smiling tall middle-aged white man with short salt and pepper hair came in, casual in a pair of black jeans, followed by a pale younger man in a blue suit.

Vivek and Sujata stood up and they all shook hands.

"This is my assistant, Zachary," Mr. Forsey said of the man in the suit. "He'll be taking notes."

"Great," Sujata said, her voice shaky, but not enough to be noticeable to someone who didn't know her well.

"You flew in from Portland?" Mr. Forsey asked. "Good flight?"

"Yes, no delays," Vivek said.

"Great. Let's get started. I'm excited to see what you've got."

Mr. Forsey took a seat midway down the table and Vivek and Sujata sat back at the end.

"Are we able to show our slides, or do you want us to go through it?" Sujata asked.

"Why don't you just talk through it. If there's something specific you want to share, we can always look."

"Okay." Sujata smiled and opened her computer so she and Vivek could see. And then she launched in.

"Thanks for meeting with us today. We're here to tell you about our company, Data Cata." Then she was off, sounding confident and bold.

They each covered their parts. Mr. Forsey asked for more details on what data quality specifically covered, and of course Sujata had no problem answering that. Vivek was so proud of her. But the best part was that Mr. Forsey really was listening to her and wasn't fixating on the parts Vivek talked about.

Vivek was feeling really good by the time they got to the business plan, where there was a lot of back and forth. Mr. Forsey seemed really interested, but Vivek did sometimes struggle to read Americans —especially rich Americans. He hoped the good vibe he was feeling was real. They wrapped up with the list of companies they would be targeting as potential customers and their long-term plans for the system.

There were some more questions from Mr. Forsey. He nodded along with Sujata's last explanation about increased infrastructure costs when they grew.

He clasped his hands together after she finished. "One concern I have is how you will compete with the other data catalogs out there. There are quite a few. You mentioned machine learning, but explain to me again what parts of your product have an ML component."

"Right now, we are light on the ML, but we do have it baked into an early version of privacy violation prediction. We also use it in the data discovery stage. We have pinpointed several other areas where it can be added."

Mr. Forsey nodded and tented his fingers. "I really like you guys, and I think you have a strong product here. But I am still concerned about competition. I think you need to do more to differentiate yourself. I'm not willing to invest yet."

Vivek deflated, though he kept the smile on his face. He could feel the disappointment rolling off Sujata.

"But," Mr. Forsey continued, "I think you should apply for Y Combinator. You are in a great position to benefit from that, and I think coming out of it, you'll be in an excellent position to secure funding. You can approach me again if you sort out the competitive advantage."

Vivek nodded. As far as rejections went, this wasn't the worst. Y Combinator was a three-month program for start-up development that ran in San Francisco. That was all he knew about it, but some major companies had started off there.

"Thank you for your time," Sujata said. She sounded overly chirpy and Vivek knew she was crestfallen.

Mr. Forsey slid a card down the table toward them. "This is Zachary's card. Feel free to reach back out to him directly if you feel like you're ready with further development."

Everyone stood up and Vivek made sure to keep the smile on his face as they followed Mr. Forsey out.

They'd be able to share their disappointment in the elevator.

And regroup in preparation for their next meeting. Maybe that would be the one that changed their lives.

~

VIVEK UNLOCKED their hotel room door Friday afternoon, and Sujata followed him in, head low in dejection.

Vivek put the briefcase on the desk and they fell onto the bed in unison, silent.

"Well," Sujata said. "At least Mr. Forsey didn't think we sucked."

Vivek chuckled. "I think this last guy just woke up on the wrong side of the bed."

"No joke. 'And how do you expect customers to sign up with a pitch like that?'" Sujata mimicked. "Oh, my God."

Vivek didn't respond. Which made sense, because what could you say to something like that?

She closed her eyes, emotionally drained.

After what seemed like a few seconds, she opened them again, but she knew it had been a while, since the sun was now low in the sky and shining in through their sixteenth-floor window.

Vivek turned toward her. "I fell asleep, too." Then he rolled over and picked her up so she was on her side, and kissed her deeply, sucking all the bad feeling out of her.

She had never known how much nice lips could do, but Vivek's worked magic on her. He ran his hand through her hair and placed her hand on his chest to feel that solid muscle.

As their tongues tangled, she was lost in him, and any bad memories were put in a back corner of her brain, to be dealt with later.

He pulled back and looked into her eyes.

Why had she rejected him for so long? She'd wasted so much time, when she could have had everything she wanted.

He rubbed her upper arm. "What do you think of the Y Combinator thing?"

"Have you checked into it? It sounds amazing, but you have to move to San Francisco for three months. We'd have to quit our jobs."

"I know. My family would be so angry if I quit my job." He smiled. "I would just be relieved."

Sujata laughed softly. "I have a lot of money saved up. I could do it. If things don't work out, I could just find another job. I wouldn't be homeless or starve."

"I can afford it, too. But I don't know about the visa situation."

"Oh, good point." She reached over to squeeze his butt. "We could just get married. Then you'd be legal."

She threw her hand over her mouth. Where had that come from?

His eyes widened, but then he laughed. Hopefully he'd realized it was a joke.

But saying it, it didn't seem like such a bad idea. Not necessarily a good one, but still. Not ... terrible.

This was a disconcerting train of thought. Was she already falling for him that hard?

They'd been staring at each other for a long time now, and he was working his jaw. She needed to redirect.

But before she could, Vivek asked, "Why did you say that?" He didn't sound annoyed, but maybe hurt.

"I don't know." Sujata put a hand to her forehead. "It literally just entered my head as a logistical solution and I said it without thinking. I'm not saying I don't want to marry you. That's not it at all. I wouldn't be with you if marriage was off the table, okay? But I'm not ready for that discussion. Is that okay?"

His eyes relaxed again and he nodded. "That makes sense. I guess I'm just ahead of you."

She brushed her hand through his hair. That was quite an admission for him. "I'm so glad I got past my hang-ups and you were still waiting for me. I'm still so sorry it took so long."

Vivek smiled lightly but didn't say anything.

They needed to move on from this. It seemed too painful for him, and too frightening for her.

"What do you think about looking up Y Combinator and figuring out what we have to do in order to apply?" she asked.

"Sounds like a good idea to me." He didn't sound too disappointed, so hopefully he didn't feel like she was dismissing him. He rubbed her arm some more.

"Let's do it." Sujata rolled over and sat up. She grabbed the laptop out of the briefcase and took it back to the bed, Vivek watching her the whole time. She propped some pillows up against the headboard and got comfortable. She patted Vivek's arm. "Come on, let's get to it."

He chuckled and sat up.

She opened the web page and they started reading through all the documentation, discovering that the organization would even help non-nationals apply for visas so they could stay on through their project, which was amazing.

Although the session they would be applying for would start in January, they would get a quarter of the money right away, enough to cover the move to San Francisco, including some time to get settled, before starting. And also pay for other stuff.

Sujata looked at Vivek. "This is perfect. I want to do this more than anything."

"Me as well. We should start the application."

So they spent the rest of the night filling the application out, uploading relevant documents, and making the mental shift to do something kind of crazy by quitting their jobs and freaking their families out if they were lucky enough to get accepted. Of course, they wouldn't quit until December, but their families wouldn't like it when they actually did it.

At midnight, they had everything filled out and decided to sit on it and each look it over again before submitting after they got back to Portland.

Sujata hadn't been this excited about anything since ... well, since this morning before their first meeting. But, before that it had been a while.

She had a good feeling about this. But was this an accurate feeling? Time would tell.

24

"Yes!" exclaimed Sujata as she sank her putt just behind the glowing wine keg. "Just three shots," she said and wrote it on the scorecard she was carrying. Her white shirt sleeves and collar glowed bright under the black lights that filled the indoor mini golf course with black "greens."

Vivek smiled at her excitement, but he was also annoyed with himself for not doing better. This game shouldn't be hard. He had managed to get his ball on the other side of the keg.

It was Saturday night and they'd finished the Y Combinator application and clicked Submit. They felt like they had to celebrate, and they'd ended up here.

This place was mad—it had a pirate theme, and there were a lot of things that looked like junk serving as decorations. There were pirate skeletons positioned in various places, and the barriers between and around the holes were all in fluorescent colors. There were also other people around, but not too close to them, although he could hear their voices.

Vivek putted his ball to get it in the vicinity of the hole, but it rolled past it and bounced off the angled wall to roll several feet away.

"Ha," she teased.

He tried to glare at her, but he couldn't pull it off, and instead smiled at her as he stepped over to the ball. He couldn't believe he'd be going back to Atlanta tomorrow. He wanted to stay here forever. But his roommate was taking a risk by covering for Vivek, and he shouldn't ask for longer. Nirish would be so pissed if he found out Vivek wasn't really wallowing in bed with an off-season flu.

"Your problem is that you put too much power in it. You need to be gentle." Sujata walked over to stand behind him. "Let me show you." She reached around him to grasp his hands around the putter. This meant she was completely smashed up against his bum and back, which had an immediate stirring effect on him. Why didn't he get more of this? Why hadn't he worked harder to stay in Portland? He had a million regrets.

Her hands were surprisingly warm. He could feel her turn her head to rest her face on his shoulder. "What you want to do is hit it lightly, like this." She pulled to the side, and they hit the ball with only a tap and watched it roll toward and into the hole.

Okay, he obviously had been hitting it too hard. He twisted around to face her, and she dropped her arms. His right hand landed on her hip and he looked down at her.

It was dark in here and there was nobody around, so he kissed her on the forehead, and then moved down. She brought her lips to his and sucked on his bottom lip. Soon it was a full-mouth, hot kiss that made him feel drunk and went straight to his cock. She pushed against him and he knew she could feel him. He needed to stop because of his state. It was too uncomfortable when they couldn't do anything about it here. But there was plenty of time tonight. Even though after tomorrow it would be back to long-distance again.

He dropped his hands and said, "We are not in a good place for how I feel right now. Let's keep going."

"Next hole, then."

He stepped away, carrying the putter to the next hole.

"You forgot something," she said when they got to the next tee. She dropped his ball into his hand.

"Thank you. You first."

Sujata smiled at him and pushed him aside with a hand on his stomach, then put her ball down. She stood next to it, spreading her feet and rocking back and forth in an exaggerated show of getting ready.

Vivek chuckled.

"Don't laugh. This is serious business."

This was even funnier.

It was so unfair that this was one of the last things they'd do together for a while. At least he now knew that this was a serious relationship for her, even if she wasn't in love with him yet.

"Remind me to take you bowling sometime," she said. "That's even more serious."

She putted. The ball hit the wall perfectly to go racing around the bend and stop within two more putts of the hole.

Vivek put his ball down and copied her preparation technique, bouncing back and forth on his feet, making her laugh this time. He loved seeing her so relaxed, since she was usually serious, and he grinned at her. How lucky he was. He putted, landing the ball inches from hers.

Sujata lightly punched his arm. "See, I knew you could do it. You just needed a little help from me."

"That was it." He wondered where they would be right now if she had started dating him long before he left. He would have stayed in Portland, obviously, and he wouldn't have to leave tomorrow to go back to Atlanta.

They walked over to the other side of the green, and Sujata hit her ball perfectly so it fell into the hole. Then he copied her, but his ball stopped five centimeters from the hole.

"Were you pretending to be bad?" she asked.

"No, I learned from the best." He tapped the ball in, and picked both up.

She smiled and squeezed his upper arm.

Vivek was on a roll for a bit. He matched her next several shots, but then started missing again.

By the time they finished, it was nine thirty and she'd beaten him by several putts, so she had her hands in the air and was pushing her palms toward the sky in a celebratory dance.

"Did Nilani teach you that?" he joked.

She fell forward laughing. "No, it's way too sloppy. If she had, I would be precise with each movement."

Vivek glanced around and there was no one in sight, so he kissed her again, and they got lost in each other until someone cleared their throat at the front of the green they were on.

They smiled at the other couple and headed out, dropping off their putters and the balls.

Sujata drove them back—it really was nice to not have to take the bus anymore, even though parking could be a hassle. At a traffic light, she reached over and touched his thigh with her right hand, and he took it in his. Being with her was incredible. The fact that he was leaving tomorrow was already making him sad. He was supposed to play cricket with his old friends in the morning, but now he was rethinking that. Did he want to spend his limited time away from Sujata?

The light turned and Sujata accelerated.

"I'm thinking I won't go play cricket tomorrow," he said.

She glanced at him. "Why? I thought you were looking forward to it."

"I was, but I think I'd rather spend the time with you." He squeezed her hand.

She smiled but didn't look away from the road. "That's sweet, but these are your friends. You should hang out with them. It's only, what, three hours?"

"Yeah, but then I'll be all sweaty."

She squeezed his hand. "Maybe we can take a shower together. I've never done that. It's supposed to be fun."

A jolt went through his core. He rubbed his thumb over the back of her hand. "It does sound fun. I suppose maybe I can still go."

"Besides, I arranged to meet Gwen for coffee at a cafe over by the park you play at. I can take you, go shopping, hang out with her. Text me when you're ready and I'll pick you up and we can race home to the shower." She glanced over at him. "Let's not be that couple that lives only for each other and abandons all their friends."

He nodded, because that made sense. She could still be the most important person in his life, but didn't have to be the only one.

The rest of the drive, all he could think of was tomorrow. Which was stupid, because first there was a few minutes from now, which he assumed was also going to be amazing. When they got to her landing, they were kissing before she'd unlocked the door, which was good because she was leaning against it while he worked over her tongue, his hands on her firm backside. He was fully hard now.

They needed to get through the door.

He stopped kissing her. "Keys."

She fumbled with her purse and eventually got the door unlocked, and they were in, heading straight for the bedroom, his melancholy thoughts washed away from his brain.

~

THEY KISSED their way from the front door of the apartment, catching each other's mouths through heavy breaths, Sujata's heart pounding hard against her ribs like it was trying to make an escape.

Vivek's breath was hot on her neck as they twisted through the bedroom door, and in seconds were up against the bed.

They looked at each other in surprise when they both realized it was his thighs up against the mattress, not hers.

Sujata's smile went wicked, and she reached for his jeans button and zipper, pushing everything down once it was undone. His cock sprang free, glistening, and anticipation doubled in her stomach. Before she could stop him, his hands were at the bottom of her shirt and it was on the floor.

She stopped him and said, "No, you first. Sit." She pushed on his chest until he sat, pulling on his knees so he scooted forward.

She locked eyes with him. His pupils were huge and his jaw was clenched in anticipation. She didn't need him to tell her how much he wanted this, and that fact turned her on even more, which should have been impossible.

He reached out and cupped her chin. It was such a tender move that it melted her heart, but this was not the time for distracting feelings like that, and she sank to her knees, pushing his apart with her shoulders.

Sujata took him in her left hand and blew on the tip before licking it, reveling in his sharp intake of breath. She loved that she could do this to him. She felt powerful, but like she was using her power for good, not evil. Vivek had earned this. She squeezed with her left hand and wrapped her mouth around the head and gave a quick suck, causing a groan from Vivek.

She pulled off and ran her tongue around the head before taking him in again and sucking, and squeezing, and then moving up and down. Vivek's knees pressed on her shoulders, and she looked up at him and saw that his eyes were closed, his face was tense, and his chest was moving in and out rapidly. She mentally smiled and focused on getting the rhythm right. He twitched and she started moving faster and faster.

His fingers pressed on her forehead, inviting her to pull back, but she just sped up until he came. She swallowed while his body jerked until he fell back on the bed.

Sujata leaned back on her calves, just in time for him to sit up and pull on her shoulders, so she stood and stepped into him. He unhooked her bra and she pushed her pants down, taking her panties with them. His hands were on her breasts, kneading until the nipples were rock hard, and then he sucked on each in turn. She threw her head back at the sensation, anticipating what would be coming next.

He slipped his shirt off and pulled her down, their mouths molding together.

Vivek wrapped his arms around her and held her tight. She felt her nipples driving into his chest while he continued worshipping her with his mouth. His hands moved down and squeezed her butt, pulling her in.

After a few more kisses, they rolled onto their sides, Vivek spooning her.

"Vivek. Thank you for waiting for me." She meant more than that, but it was still terrifying to admit how strong those feelings were.

He paused, then smiled. "I think it was worth it."

It surprised her that he'd known exactly what she'd meant. That should definitely be rewarded. She had a plan.

He held her, and she felt his heartbeat slow down to a normal rate.

After a while, she could feel him thickening again, and the desire that pooled in her flared. It was more than desire. She hadn't felt this —what was it?—since the early days with Rajeev. It was connection. It felt like they were one thing and it was the best thing either of them could be.

She rolled over and pushed him down onto the mattress. His dark eyes were questioning.

"Scoot back," she said. "Today is all about you."

He pushed himself back onto the bed until he was stretched across the width, his cock bobbing from the movement. His eyes were dark with lust. She patted his leg so he'd move, and then got herself straddling his hips.

Vivek obviously hadn't expected this and his mouth was slightly open in anticipation. He licked his lips, which made her smile.

"Stay put." She moved over and pulled the bedside table drawer open for a condom, then straddled him again. She held the packet up and waved it around.

"Any day now, Sujata," he joked, but his voice was deep and he was smiling.

She opened the packet and rolled the condom down his length slowly, staring into his eyes. Then she shifted forward until she was just over him, not breaking eye contact. She positioned him at her entrance, closing her eyes as she sank down on him slowly, savoring every inch of his glorious cock.

Once she was all the way down, she opened her eyes and saw him studying her, a soft expression on his face. But then she shifted, and he clenched his jaw again.

She moved up some more, feeling him leave her, and sank back down. Soon she found the right rhythm, her quads heating up with the effort.

Sujata watched him while her own sensation started building, promising an incredible release. His hands were on her breasts, gently kneading, and keeping her buzzing.

After a few more strokes, she felt him go rigid and at the same time her own body released all the tension, and she collapsed on him, his heart beating like a jackhammer against her chest.

She rolled off him and he leaned over to drop the condom in the trash can.

"Here, roll off," she said. "I want to pull the covers down."

After, they got back in and faced each other, sliding their feet under the blanket, and he pulled the comforter over both of their heads, smiling the whole time.

And then it was dark.

"Is this your big boy tent?" she asked.

He chuckled.

"Hi," she said. She felt too much to say anything else. How could she have ever thought this wouldn't be worth it? She'd wasted all that time. It made her want to cry, so instead she made herself smile again, even though he couldn't see it.

He rubbed her shoulder with his free arm. "Hi." His voice was low.

Did he feel it, too? Did she really love him? This fast? Was that even possible? They had known each other a long time, so maybe it wasn't crazy. She wanted to say something, but she wasn't brave enough, not right now.

But he hadn't said anything else, either. Maybe he was feeling the same thing.

He squeezed her shoulder. "I need to get there by ten tomorrow," he said matter-of-factly, running his hand up and down her upper arm.

Her heart sank. That was out of the blue, and besides, she already knew the time. She'd thought he was thinking about her, and what he was actually doing was planning his cricket game in the park with his friends. Maybe she had assumed too much about how he felt.

But he'd hinted that he wanted to marry her. Where was he emotionally? And where was she?

She still had to answer his question. "Sure. I'll drop you off and then I'll go meet Gwen. How long will you play?"

"Maybe three hours? I'll text you when we're close to finishing and see where you are." His hand was still moving on her arm.

"Okay." This turn of conversation made her feel stupid. She was glad she hadn't said anything, not if they weren't on the same page right now. She hoped he couldn't feel the embarrassment seeping off her. She was glad they couldn't see each other.

Maybe she was overreacting. She needed some time away from him to think straight. Tomorrow morning would be perfect. A little retail therapy and emotional stock-taking would be good.

25

There was nothing better than waking up in Sujata's bed. Vivek had awoken slowly, still spooning her. He could smell the vaguely floral aroma of her hair, right in front of his nose. His hand rested on her upper hip, and he could feel her side rising and lowering with each breath.

If Sujata was anywhere close to waking, she'd be feeling his cock resting against her bum. And although he would love a chance to satisfy that part of his body, he was loving this intimacy with her, this closeness he'd waited so long for. He'd been proven right—they were perfect for each other.

Although he'd loved her this whole time, the way he felt now was so much more intense than ever before. His heart felt double its normal size. The idea of marriage kept popping into his head even though it was too soon. And he didn't think she felt the same, not after that weird mention of marrying for a visa. Really, she probably wasn't there yet, but he was so sure she would be one day. At least, if he hadn't messed it up last night.

He'd been so close to saying how he felt last night, but then he'd fumbled it and instead talked about the drive to the park today, which was idiotic.

Still, maybe it was good. He didn't want to pressure her or scare her off.

Sujata stirred and stretched.

"Well, hello, there," she said in a thick but still teasing voice.

Vivek couldn't help but smile. She had noticed. He kissed the back of her head.

She moved her hand back, squeezed him gently, and started stroking up and down.

He closed his eyes, focusing on the mixture of intense physical sensation and his profound affection for her.

"We should do something about this," Sujata said.

"What might that involve?" he asked. There were so many ways to make each other feel good. They would never run out.

"Well, we're both engineers who value efficiency. Why don't we get in the shower? Kill two birds with one stone?"

"That sounds like a great plan."

She pulled her hand back and rolled onto her back so they could look at each other. She leaned in and kissed him, slow and sweet. But then she broke the kiss. "Come on, let's go."

She was off the bed and Vivek scrambled after her. She was being impulsive, and he loved to see her enjoying herself and being playful, just like yesterday. She looked gorgeous trotting ahead of him, her hair bouncing side to side.

"Grab a condom," she called, halfway to the bathroom.

He padded after her, condom in hand, unable to suppress the grin on his face. On reaching the bathroom, he saw Sujata leaning over to test the water she'd just turned on. Her long, slim body was so tantalizing. Her skin was lighter where her clothes usually covered her. Obviously, she wasn't a beach bum. But she was all firm muscle, in a way that made her beautiful.

He approached and leaned forward to set the condom on the side of the tub in front of her. She turned around and smiled at him.

Even though they were close to the same height, she made him feel big, full of life.

He slipped his arms around her and she moved in.

"Is the water ready?" he asked.

She nodded and kissed him again, cupping the sides of his face.

He deepened the kiss and her hands dropped to his chest, playing with his nipples. His need was heightened even more, and he broke the kiss. "Let's get in."

"Open the condom first. It will be hard once your hands are wet." She handed it to him and he tore it open and set it back down, condom ready for quick removal.

They stepped in and he pulled her close, water crashing down on them. She had one of those non-slip mats in place, which was a good thing for them. He slipped a hand down to the warm place between her legs. She spread her legs a bit and took him in her hand. They stroked each other and leaned in for another kiss, which turned intense enough that it was hard to focus on everything at once.

He placed his hands on her hips. "Let's switch so you can lean against the wall."

She knew what was coming, so they turned so her back was to the back wall, and he lowered himself to his knees, the stream of water hitting him on the back like a massage.

Vivek pulled her knees apart a bit more, and dipped his tongue into her heat. He sucked on her nub and felt her body tense. He sucked until he felt her tense again, then began working it with his tongue. The taste of her drove him the good kind of crazy, and he moved his hands to cup her backside. Her thighs squeezed him and he sped up until he felt her release as she fell back against the wall, hand on his head for support.

He leaned back on his calves while she smiled down at him.

Finally she leaned over and pulled on his shoulders. "Your turn."

He pulled himself up and leaned over for the condom packet. He had it in his hand when Sujata said, "Uh, I wonder if the water might make it slip off. Maybe dry yourself off first?"

Vivek laughed. "You're such an engineer. But you're probably right." He stepped toward the back of the shower and dried off with a towel.

Sujata reached for the condom from behind him. He turned back around and she rolled it on, which just increased the tension in his balls.

It was all about to be released.

Vivek reached forward and picked her up by the bum. She guided him into her center and he slid inside, the sensation forcing him to close his eyes. She wrapped her legs around him. He turned sideways so she had the wall at her back and then he lifted her and thrust inside again.

She leaned against him and he started thrusting in earnest, knowing he wasn't going to last too long, but needing to take enough time for her to experience another release.

She wrapped her arms around him and pushed down with each of his thrusts. He focused on holding off as long as possible, but sped up. The second he felt her whole body melt against him, he let himself go, leaning forward so her back was against the wall so they could stay upright.

He rested his forehead against hers and her legs slid down his hips until they were both standing, breathing hard while the water pounded his shoulder.

"Why does this feel so right?" Sujata asked in a faraway voice.

Vivek's heart nearly burst. He touched her face. "I don't know, but I feel it, too."

"Let's get clean and I'll make something for breakfast. You need some sustenance if you're going to run around chasing a ball."

He laughed. "Don't you need sustenance for that serious shopping you're going to be doing?"

She playfully pushed on his chest. "Don't mock me."

"I would never." The smile was stuck on his face. He grabbed the soap bar on the wall and began rubbing it over her upper chest.

Sujata raised her eyebrows at him and they both laughed again.

"Do you even know what time it is?" she asked.

He shook his head. "Not really."

"We should work on that efficiency we talked about earlier, especially so we don't run out of hot water with shampoo in our hair."

"Good point."

"There will be more good to come later," she said.

He knew she was right, and he couldn't wait to see it.

~

SUJATA'S PHONE rang at the cafe, mid-conversation with Gwen, who was regaling her with dating tales.

She didn't recognize the number, but something told her to answer it. "Hello?"

"Sujata, this is Kiran. We've had to take Vivek to the hospital. He hurt his arm and I think it's broken."

"Oh, my God!"

Kiran continued. "We've got him checked in, but we can't stay because of prior commitments. Are you able to come sit with him?"

"Yes. Which hospital?"

Kiran gave her the details and she hung up.

"Is everything okay?" Gwen asked, face worried.

"I think Vivek broke his arm. I have to go to the hospital. He's there alone."

"Oh, no! Please, get out of here. Poor guy!"

"Okay." Sujata stood up and grabbed her purse. "I'm sorry to cut this short. Let's meet up again soon."

"Definitely." Gwen also stood and collected their dishes.

"Talk Monday." Sujata took off, half running to her car, parked over two blocks away. When she finally got there, she scrambled inside, set up her GPS for the hospital, and took off. The whole way there, she was imagining the worst—his bone sticking out, multiple surgeries, months in casts.

Once there, she still had to deal with the stupid parking. Why did they always make parking at hospitals so difficult? When you were going to a hospital, you had bigger problems and shouldn't need to deal with something as trivial as parking.

Sujata finally found a spot and jogged inside.

She scanned the waiting room, eventually spotting him in a

corner, staring straight ahead. He looked awful, rather gray and completely unmoving.

Vivek glanced up when she stood in front of him, made the biggest failure of a smile ever, and tried to speak, but nothing came out.

She studied his forearms, a small bruise on his right arm. "Vivek, that looks bad."

He said something along the lines of, "Mmm."

He had to be in a ton of pain. "How long ago did you hurt it?"

"I don't know, an hour." He was totally shut down, obviously in excruciating pain.

She sat next to him and they were quiet for a moment. She wasn't sure he'd be able to talk, but she thought she should try to get info from him.

"So what happened?" Sujata asked, hoping to distract him from his misery.

He exhaled. "I slipped in the grass trying to make a catch, and the ball hit me on the side of the arm."

They were in for a long wait. Sujata played a game on her phone and held his left hand while he stared ahead in silence. The area where she'd first noticed the bruise was even redder and darker now.

She knew it wasn't hurting any less by this point. Vivek wasn't himself at all.

Finally, after what seemed like forever—four hours, give or take —a nurse finally called him back to a room. Sujata went with him, thinking the nurse looked familiar.

"Get up on the bed, hon," a small, blonde nurse said. Georgie, read her name tag.

Vivek climbed into the stretcher, holding his arm to his chest.

"You've injured your forearm?" Georgie asked.

"Yes," Vivek croaked, staring at the floor.

"Well, Vivek," Georgie started, "You're already wearing short sleeves so you're ready for the doctor. He'll be in shortly." She moved the curtain to the side and left.

Sujata smiled and sat down in the chair next to the stretcher. She patted Vivek's leg. They waited a few more minutes.

"Hi, I'm coming in," said a voice from outside the curtain.

A familiar voice. She turned. No ...

The curtain parted and there was the doctor.

Rajeev. His mouth parted in surprise.

Her heart instinctively twisted and all the hurt rushed back like dirty floodwaters. She had a sudden urge to burst into tears as worry for Vivek combined with anger and hurt at seeing Rajeev. She didn't want Rajeev treating Vivek. He could be vindictive sometimes, and jealous, something she always tried to deny when she was with him. How had she stayed all that time? Who he really was becoming clearer for her every day, especially when she had a much better version of a boyfriend to compare him to. Right now, she'd storm out if she could, but Vivek couldn't wait any more.

Rajeev said, "Sujata."

She didn't reply and instead turned to see Vivek's face. His jaw was clenched and she didn't think it was from pain this time. Did he recognize him? She realized she'd never told Vivek exactly what had happened with Rajeev. He just knew Rajeev had hurt her badly. And now here he was, in front of her again. She forced herself to stand up, despite her core feeling like lead.

"Which arm is it?" Rajeev said as he stepped forward, avoiding looking at her.

"This one." Vivek pointed to his right arm.

Sujata stepped back and let Rajeev do what he was going to do. He was the doctor, after all, and Vivek obviously needed help. But this was bullshit, a nasty trick by the universe.

"Tell me what happened," Rajeev said.

Vivek went over the cricket mishap, and Rajeev inspected his arm, causing Vivek to inhale sharply. It looked like Rajeev was handling Vivek's arm more roughly than he should.

"It's definitely broken, but I'll need an X-ray to confirm and see the exact configuration. I'll send the technician by and be back afterwards."

Then he looked at Sujata one last time, eyes dark and narrowed, and pulled the curtain to the side to leave.

Sujata wanted to run and push on his back to make him leave faster, but then he walked off.

She moved to the spot between Vivek's knees and rested her hands on his thighs. "I'm sorry he was hard on you. I would have taken you to a different hospital. I knew he worked here."

He touched her face. "Some day you have to tell me what he did to you."

"He doesn't like you," Sujata said, stating the obvious. She wasn't ready to talk about it, not right here, when Rajeev would be back in a bit.

"No. I do not like him, either."

He leaned forward and kissed her on the lips quickly. "Thank you for coming. I didn't want to deal with it, but it feels like I'm dying."

"Are you feeling better now?"

"No, but at least it's going to be fixed soon."

They waited another fifteen minutes for the X-ray technician, who finally came in the form of a young man in blue scrubs. He took Vivek away after getting him out of his t-shirt and into a hospital gown.

Sujata picked up Vivek's shirt and sat down, holding it in her lap. She lifted it to her face. She somewhat regretted this because it was all sweaty, but at least it also smelled like him, which made her feel better. Despite what that asshole Rajeev might have wanted, Vivek was hers, and he was a stand-up guy. Unlike a certain doctor.

Without warning, the man in question appeared inside the curtain.

"What do you want?" she asked, more angry than upset at this point.

"Isn't he a bit young for you?" Rajeev asked.

"What do you care? You have no claim over me." Who did he think he was? Why did men always do this? He'd left her in the cruelest way possible, and he still thought his opinion mattered.

"I just want what's best for you, and this clown isn't it."

"You have no reason to be in here."

His tone softened. "Sujata—"

"I don't want to hear it, Rajeev. You dumped me in the name of some antiquated type of family honor. I *despise* you. Your opinion means less than nothing to me. Go away." The horror of the moment she learned he'd abandoned her, and the emptiness of their apartment, hit her again. Her voice cracked when she said, "You didn't even *tell* me."

"I know. Look, I'm sorry. We need closure."

"Why?" She held up her hand, making herself exude strength while she was crumbling inside. "Really, Rajeev, there's nothing to explain. I know what happened. I no longer care why. Please leave."

He looked at her, jaw clenched, and eventually turned and left.

As soon as the curtain stopped swinging behind him, she put her face in her palms and felt the pain all over again. How could he have done that to her? She'd thought he loved her.

Could she ever truly trust anyone again? Was she right to trust Vivek? How would she ever know?

Vivek came back soon after,and the certainty that he could—and should—be trusted returned to her heart. He would never do what Rajeev had done. She held his hand while they waited.

Rajeev returned with the X-rays. "Yes, it's broken, but you don't need surgery. We just need to get you in a cast after I make some adjustments. We'll numb the arm first."

He looked over at Sujata. "The nurse will come in to give him the injections, and I'll return after they've taken effect."

He left and Sujata looked at Vivek, who was still suffering greatly.

Georgie was back with a tray of needles. "I'm sorry, but this is going to hurt, hon. But a big strong man like you can take it, I'm sure." She winked at Sujata, but Vivek still looked gray and Sujata knew he was dreading this.

Georgie gave him several shots in different places on his arm. Some color came back into his face after she'd left.

"Are they taking effect?" Sujata asked.

"Yes," Vivek said.

But then Rajeev was back. "This is still going to hurt, but not as much as it would without the numbing."

Sujata watched in horror as Rajeev manipulated Vivek's arm, looking back and forth between the arm and Vivek's face, who looked like he might throw up.

"Okay, all set," Rajeev said, like he'd just set a table, not tortured her boyfriend. "A technician will be in to do the cast. She'll also bring you a prescription for medication for the pain."

Rajeev left and Sujata looked at Vivek, gray again. "How do you feel?"

"Okay as soon as he was done. But it throbs. You handled this much better than I am."

"This is a much worse injury than mine was, and I'd taken some ibuprofen."

"Maybe." He didn't sound convinced.

She wanted to lighten the mood and get his mind off the pain. "What color cast are you going to get?"

"I have choices?" His eyes had widened. "What do they have?"

"Well, I don't know for sure, but maybe you should get light blue for India cricket."

"Really?" He actually smiled a teeny, tiny bit at that.

Georgie came in to ask the very question about color, and luck was with them as they did have light blue, so that's what the technician came back in with.

Once he was all casted up, they stopped by the pharmacy and headed back to her place.

By the time they got home he was rallying from earlier. The shot they'd given him before putting the cast on was obviously helping. She ushered him toward the bedroom.

"I should shower first," he mumbled.

"No, let's get you your first dose of the medicine and you can just rest. I'll lie in there with you. We can watch TV or you can just sleep. Whatever you want."

He stripped down to his boxers and she helped him get into bed, and then went to get some water. She changed into pyjamas and got into bed with him. Wearing pyjamas with him seemed weird, but she didn't know the protocol. He took his first dose and she pulled the comforter up over them.

"Look at us, a couple of accident-prone people. And both of us with sports injuries, the second most noble way to get injured."

"What's the most noble way?" he asked, sounding amused.

"War, at least if you're on the correct side."

He smiled, but it was weak. "Sujata, will you tell me what that man really did to you?"

She looked at him looking back at her. He clearly wanted to know, and given the way Rajeev had manhandled him, she figured she should tell him. So she gave the summarized version, answering some of Vivek's questions. He looked suitably horrified when she explained how Rajeev had ghosted her.

"How could he do that?" Vivek asked. "It's not 1900."

Sujata nodded. "I thought the same thing."

"Fish. He's a."

"What?" she asked.

"He's a jerk. Like a boat thing." His eyes were no longer focused on her.

"Are you okay?" The meds must be kicking in. That had come on quick.

"There's ample time."

"Okay, buddy. You just go to sleep now."

They were quiet for a while and she thought he'd fallen asleep.

But then he suddenly said, "Sujata, I really love you." Her heart nearly stopped. But it would have been more convincing without the slight slur. The meds talking, then.

"Shh, no you don't." She reached up to squeeze his hand.

"No, I do. Always. My parents are crazy to think I'll marry her."

Sujata's whole body tensed. "What?"

"I will never." It was stretched out like verbal taffy.

"What are you talking about, Vivek?" The panic was stirring.

He didn't respond. She moved his arm and sat up to turn and look at him. His mouth was hanging open slightly and his eyes were closed. He was totally out. She touched his forehead, the attractive hard lines of his face taunting her with their appeal. "Oh, Vivek, what have you done to me? What are you going to do to me?"

Her phone said it was after one, so she turned the light off and lay back, now with something terrible on her mind.

26

Vivek woke slowly, fighting his way out of some serious grogginess.

He was still at Sujata's, but something was off. She wasn't here with him, and the light was on in the hall. His nose itched and he reached up to scratch it, whacking himself in the nose with an unexpectedly heavy arm. "Ah!"

Oh. He'd broken his arm. Now that he'd become aware of it again, he could really feel a dull throb emanating from it.

"Vivek?" he heard from down the hall. He scratched the stupid nose itch with his left hand and massaged the bridge of his nose, which had received the brunt of the cast punch.

Sujata appeared in the doorway. He smiled stupidly at her.

"What happened?" She stepped in, a worried look on her beautiful face.

"Oh, nothing. I hit myself in the nose with my cast. I didn't remember it was there."

"Ouch. Did you hurt yourself? How's your arm feeling? Do you want your next pill? Are you hungry? Do you need more water?"

"Okay, let me think," he said. He held up his left fist and counted off on each finger, "No. Okay. No. Yes. No. Was that all of them?" He waggled his fingers at her, which made her laugh.

"Now I don't know what to do. I didn't write my questions down in order. Let me know if you need something. I was about to make lunch. Do you want to come eat with me?"

"Yes. I am really hungry."

"Okay." She tossed him some shorts that were hanging on the back of the desk chair.

"Oh, is it a formal dinner?"

She laughed again. "Just shorts. Otherwise, no shirt, no shoes, happy service."

He shifted and turned so he could drop his feet to the floor. He worked on getting the shorts on, which was a bit difficult since moving his right fingers hurt, but he managed it and stood up.

"Are you okay to walk? I know the meds are throwing you for a loop."

"Yes, but I think I can walk." He let go of the bed and made sure he had his balance. "Yes, I'm okay."

She led him to a chair at the little table on the other side of the kitchen. But then she narrowed her eyes and leaned in toward his face. "Oh, my God—you did hit your nose! It's red."

Vivek rubbed it again. "Yeah, I was half asleep and didn't know my arm was going to be so heavy, so it flew at me like a cannonball."

She leaned forward and kissed his nose. "Poor nose. Poor Vivek." She kissed him on the lips and his heart started right up, but then she abruptly pulled back.

Sujata opened the freezer. "I have a cauliflower curry I'm going to reheat."

Why did it feel like she wasn't looking at him? His heart stung from the quick rejection.

She pulled two plastic baggies full of curry out and put them on the counter.

Had something just happened? It felt like something had changed. The pit of his stomach flared.

She opened the baggies and dropped them into a bowl in the

microwave. Still not looking at him. Once she had it going, she got some cooked rice out of the fridge and put it on plates. She just went about her lunch-preparing business like she was all alone.

It made him nervous.

"Are you working today?" he asked.

"Yeah. David was fine with me working from home." She filled a glass with water.

"Did you tell him why?"

She finally looked at him, a wry smile. "You are 'a visiting friend.'" She made air quotes around it when she said it.

"Well, I think we are friends. In addition to being more than friends."

She nodded, expression inscrutable, and returned to filling the second glass.

Something was definitely wrong. But he had no idea what it was, so he had no idea what to do to fix it. He stayed quiet while she finished preparing everything and brought the plates and glasses to the table.

The first bite landed heavy in his stomach. "Sujata, what's wrong?"

"Oh, nothing. I was just thinking about a work thing. I have a lot to do this afternoon."

"You seem mad at me." Mad wasn't the right word, but it was simple, and the feeling he was getting from her wasn't.

"No, everything's fine. Is your arm still hurting? I can get your next pill if you want it."

"My arm is fine at the moment. If I've done something, please let me know." He watched her until she looked back.

She took a deep breath. "I'm just feeling ... a little overwhelmed at the moment, with work and everything."

She obviously wasn't going to tell him what was really wrong.

"Does everything include me being here?"

"Everything's okay. I'm glad you're here. I'm glad we went to San Francisco, even though they turned us down. We got our application in to Y Combinator. Everything's great." She stood up and walked over, leaning down and kissing him for real this time. It was deep and raw.

He felt connected to her again. She was smiling when she pulled away.

He was still confused, but it didn't look like she was going to break up with him. She just needed some time to be ready to talk to him. Maybe it was seeing her ex. She'd obviously been really upset about that.

He'd just have to keep talking to her to see if he could get her out of her funk.

But if she broke up with him, this would be the last time. He couldn't take any more of this from her, especially with her not telling him what was wrong.

~

"I THINK YOU'RE OVERREACTING," Kavya said Tuesday night, while Sujata lay on her bed. Vivek was in the shower and had an early flight to Atlanta tomorrow.

"Maybe." She kept her voice low in case he left the room with the water still on. "It just made me panic. And I can't stop obsessing about it."

It was constantly on her mind. She was trying to act normal around him, but there was so much negativity in her mind that it was hard.

"Vivek has never done anything to betray your trust, has he? I mean, even you decided the bogarting your pitch at work thing wasn't really his fault, right? Rajeev used to keep things from you all the time."

That was true. Rajeev was often cagey about info. Sujata nodded to herself. Why did it take her until now to see what a jerk he was?

Kavya continued. "Like, there was that time he went to his friend's birthday in New York. I mean, why didn't he tell you about that in advance? I never liked him." She didn't hide the disgust in her voice.

Usually this made Sujata feel good, but now she felt stupid, and the pain she'd felt when she'd realized he'd left her bloomed fresh in her heart. Seeing him had really messed with her.

"I have a good feeling about Vivek," Kavya concluded.

"I'm just feeling way too many feelings right now," Sujata admitted. She could still hear the shower running.

"I can't believe Rajeev was a jerk to Vivek. You should file a complaint."

"They'd just dismiss it when he tells them I'm his ex."

"True." Kavya sighed. "I don't want you to mess up this thing with Vivek because of your insecurities. I get it, but you need to be brave here and try to forget Rajeev. Don't let him mess this up, too."

"You're right. I should be happy Rajeev dumped me. He would have gotten even worse once we were married." Sujata closed her eyes and tried to squash her doubts.

"Yeah, because then he would no longer have to be impressing you," Kavya said.

"True." It was always hard to get opinions on her relationship questions because she rarely opened up about it. She wasn't even sure why. She was open about other things.

Sujata pressed her fingers to her eyelids. "Kavya, it's so weird. I never noticed any of his flaws, but all of a sudden, recently, it's becoming obvious that he was pretty horrible. Why was I so stupid?"

"*Beta*, you were young, and then it was familiar."

She was right. But it was time for a subject change. "So tell me what's going on with Ankur."

"Oh." Kavya's blush somehow came through the phone.

"Well, you know, our parents are planning everything. We're just letting them. *Maa* is obviously very excited."

"Have they picked a date yet?"

"They're looking at March. We aren't going to wait until grad school."

"Really? That's awesome! I can't wait to see you get married. I'm so excited!" And she was. She had no doubt that Kavya and Ankur were perfect for each other.

She heard the water shut off in the bathroom. "Oh, hey, Vivek's finishing up. I'd better go."

"Okay. Love you, *shona*."

"Love you, too."

She set the phone down and just thought about Vivek. And how he'd waited so long and patiently for her. He'd never crowded her. He was the most unstalkery guy ever. He was thoughtful and always cared about her feelings on things. This was all so different from Rajeev, who was never wrong and never interested in her view of things. Why was she only now seeing this?

Vivek was just a better person. He was a much better boyfriend, even though they hadn't been together that long. She'd obviously been subconsciously thinking about marriage, even if saying it out loud in San Francisco had surprised even her. She should trust him. She wanted to trust him.

He walked into the room, his wet hair glistening in the hall light, glorious chest on display.

Lust exploded in her core, heating right up.

He was watching her watch him. She couldn't hide the lust from her face. Or from her heart. Really, she had nothing but good feelings looking at him. He wasn't Rajeev. She would ask about the other girl, but not now. Now she was going to screw his brains out.

27

Vivek was back at work, trying to write code one-handed, or more like one-and-a-half-handed. They were working on testing a new GPS device they were considering purchasing, and he and one of his colleagues had been assigned to making a few prototypes.

The more interesting part of his day was texting with Sujata. He couldn't leave his phone out because of Nirish's issue with people being on their phones, so Vivek kept it in his pocket on vibrate. Every time she'd ping him, he'd get a physical burst of sensation.

Nirish was already pissed at him. He was suspicious of the broken arm, but they just said that he fell in the apartment. His parents were really worried when they found out about it and they were basically insisting that he come home for a visit. His mom had gotten in touch with Nirish—which was rather mortifying, really—and he'd agreed to let Vivek take the trip, but he would have to work over some of it. So he was working on picking the dates—soon, but he was still figuring it out.

Oof, there went his phone again. He looked around to make sure Nirish wasn't walking around, and pulled his phone out.

—Kiran just came by and asked how you are—

—you can tell him I'm fine—

She sent a laughing emoji. *—I did, and then I had to stop myself from telling him you're more than fine—*

—lol—

Whatever had upset Sujata before seemed to have passed. Tuesday night in her bed had been amazing. He had the feeling she was kind of making it up to him for being mad about whatever that was.

He looked around again.

—so my parents are all worried about me and now I have to go back home for a few weeks— He rolled his eyes. Sometimes parents were really annoying.

—you're going to India?—

—yes, for about 3 weeks. but I have to work a lot of it— It was going to be a hassle.

—when?—

He looked round again. *—we're still figuring it out—*

—are you sure Nirish is ok with it?—

He wished he wasn't. *—yeah. I'm not going to be able to chat or talk as much while I'm there, too—* He just wasn't going to be able to tell his parents he had a girlfriend. It would cause even more trouble than turning down Adya would.

She didn't reply right away so he tucked his phone back in his pocket. Nirish was supposed to get back to him about acceptable dates before the end of the day. Tonight he'd have to check flights and figure everything out.

But for the moment he had to at least try to focus on this prototype, and not think about starting a company with Sujata. Or a family. Or anything to do with Sujata.

~

SUJATA and her fellow dancers changed back into their comfortable clothes after their practice. She sat on the bench in front of the cubbies, beat. The other women had cleared out, but Paree and

Kaarikaa were still there, excitedly talking about Paree's sister being pregnant, because Kaarikaa's brother was the husband and father. They'd only gotten married in May.

Normally, Sujata would have thought about how that was fast, but today all she could think about was Vivek and his trip to India. Her head had been spinning since he'd sent that text yesterday afternoon. She'd made excuses for not talking on FaceTime last night, but if she did again tonight if would be weird.

But she could not turn off the panic. This was too much. It wasn't déjà vu—it was real and exactly the same as what had happened with Rajeev. Before he'd left, they had joked about the girl his family wanted him to marry. He thought it was ridiculous. Or she'd thought he did. Who knew what had really been going on in his head? Sujata still didn't know what had convinced him.

She put her hand to her forehead.

"Are you alright, Sujata?" Paree asked, her smile replaced with concern. "Nilani was rough on you tonight."

"Yeah, she should have been. I was a mess. I'm just stressed out about something."

"Anything we can help with?" Kaarikaa asked.

Sujata shook her head and stood up, trying to look relaxed. "It will be fine. Things always work out."

"Okay," Paree said with a sympathetic look. "See you next week." She and Kaarikaa left, and Sujata grabbed her duffel and trailed behind them down the dark stairs to the street level.

She had to walk a couple of blocks to get to her car. When she got there, the small dent from the guy she hit at the airport glared at her, reminding her of how happy she had been to see Vivek that day.

She did have an appointment with the car shop next week, so it would soon be fixed.

Unlike her situation. She got in the car, pulling the door shut and locking the doors. She closed her eyes and rested her head on the steering wheel.

The thing was, she should trust Vivek. He would be hurt that she didn't. But she hadn't seen the signs that Rajeev wasn't trustworthy, at least, not back then.

Vivek and Rajeev were completely different men. Rajeev had always been cagey about things, but it hadn't seemed to matter back then. She'd never doubted that he loved her. And then in the blink of an eye, he was married to someone he'd first met two weeks earlier.

Vivek was different. He'd always been open. She always felt like she knew what was going on in his world, since he hid nothing.

Except this other woman. He'd never told Sujata about her. Sujata knew stuff about his family, but he'd never mentioned his parents wanting to set him up with someone.

Why hadn't he told her? This was the part that set her nerves most ajitter. What did it mean that he hadn't told her?

She sat back up and started the car. She backed up and carefully pulled out from between the cars, then onto the road.

She navigated through the back streets on the way to the main road, pondering Vivek's failure to tell her.

She should just ask him. That was the adult thing to do. But what if he lied about it?

But why would he? What would he gain by tricking Sujata into thinking he loved her—or close, if not all the way there—if he planned to go home and marry someone else? It would just be cruel, and she knew Vivek was not cruel.

She stopped behind another car in a left-turn lane, waiting for the light.

Sujata wouldn't make an excuse for their evening talk. She would just ask him. She needed to stop panicking and just get the story from the horse's mouth. And ask him to cancel the trip. Surely he could at least delay it so they could talk more about it.

Once on the main road, she passed a lot of fast-food restaurants and it got her thinking about Rajeev, and how he'd broken her college habit of hitting up the Taco Bell.

But thinking something positive about him was almost as painful as remembering the bad stuff. Every day they'd been together over those several years had been an utter waste because it had always been going to end the way it did.

What if she'd never dated him? It was a white coworker of hers at the library who'd introduced them. She was on a group project with him, and probably didn't know how to read an Indian man, not knowing the culture well. The woman also ended up being kind of horrible, and they'd had an ugly falling out. Sujata had always thought afterward that at least one good thing had come out of their short friendship—namely Rajeev.

But that was rotten the whole time, too. She pulled up to another red light. For some reason the wasted time was so intense in her mind that she actually started tearing up. It was too much. Seeing him the other day had been excruciating. And he had the gall to be jealous? How had she never seen who he really was?

She could not make that mistake again. She would talk to Vivek tonight and convince him not to go.

28

Sujata was sitting on the couch, her iPad propped up on the table. Vivek was about to FaceTime her. She was nervous, but also felt her normal excitement over being about to see him.

She would be utterly heartbroken if they didn't work out. After all she'd done to protect herself, she was already a goner.

The phone rang.

"Hey," she said when she answered. She was smiling stupidly, and could hear his smile in his own greeting.

They switched over to FaceTime and she got the iPad in the right position, now able to actually see his happy face on the screen.

But then she abruptly remembered what she needed to ask him. Her stomach roiled and she felt the color drain from her face like a misbehaving fake beard.

"How was your dance class?" he asked.

"Good." She needed information, even if she was afraid of how the answer might affect her. "Do you have your trip planned yet?"

"Yeah, I leave tomorrow evening. I just want to get it out of the way and get my parents off my case." He gave her a wry smile.

She nodded. She should just get this out of the way. She was way too queasy. "Listen, I need to talk to you about something."

He instantly looked serious. "Okay."

"Why didn't you tell me about the woman your parents want to get you married off to?" She was about to throw up. She looked around for a receptacle in case that really happened.

His eyes widened in surprise. "How ... did you know about that?"

"That's not the right answer." She surprised herself with the sudden anger. She needed to calm down. Why was she pushing to see the worst in him instead of the good? "But you told me when you were stoned on pain meds."

"Oh. Look, I'm sorry. It's such a stupid thing—I would never marry this woman. I know who she is from school, but she's not you so it doesn't matter. That's why I never mentioned it, because it's nothing. There are a lot of things I haven't told you about my family. Just like you with yours."

Okay, that was a good thing for him to say. "Thank you, Vivek. But this still has me reeling. It's too much the same."

"As what?"

"Do you not remember this?" she asked.

"What? No?" His brow was furrowed.

"I told you the full story of Rajeev the night you broke your arm. I thought it was before your brain was out to lunch."

"I'm sorry." He shook his head as he said it, still looking worried. "I don't remember. What exactly did he do?"

She took a deep breath and looked up. She steeled herself to say the words again. "Okay, here's the summary." She gave the basics. "Before he left, we were even joking about the fact that his family had found a girl they wanted him to marry. Then he never came back. He never even told me. I was so worried. I found out when his mother—who'd always hated me—sent me a wedding announcement after it was over."

She finally looked back at her iPad and saw that Vivek's mouth was hanging open in shock.

"I would *never* do anything like that," he exclaimed. "Sujata. You can't think I could do that."

She nodded. "I *know* that. But I can't quite *feel* it, because I didn't think Rajeev would do anything like that, either. I don't know how to completely trust anybody. I don't know if I can. It completely blindsided me."

"He never talked to you?" Vivek sounded confused.

"Yeah. He never came back to the apartment, not even once. He sent a friend to pick up some of his stuff after a couple months, after I'd found out what happened." She felt raw, thinking back to those hellish days.

"I just ... How could someone do that?" Vivek said, shaking his head. "I believe you, but it sounds unbelievable."

Sujata just nodded, feeling too many feelings again.

"Do you really think I'm going to do the same thing?"

She wanted to cry. "I don't *think* it. It's like intellectually, everything is fine, perfect even, but I can't get control of my emotions, which are telling me to freak out." She took a breath. There had to be a way past this. "Can you ... delay the trip? Give me some more time?"

He blinked in surprise. "Okay, I understand your fear here. I do." He narrowed his eyes. "But I am not Rajeev."

"I know." She put her fingers to her forehead. "You can't ... delay the trip?"

"Sujata," he said in clear exasperation. "I understand your fear, but even you know it's not entirely rational."

She felt her eyes widen, even though she couldn't even really get pissed at that.

He put up his hand. "That was harsh. I don't think you're mad. But Sujata, seriously. I do think you're being unreasonable. I have the right to go visit my family. They want to see me now because they are worried about the broken arm, which I have right now, and I haven't been home in two years. It's a good time to go."

"A couple more weeks?" She sounded so pitiful.

Vivek looked up, his mouth in a line. "If you don't trust me when I've never done anything untrustworthy, that is your problem to fix. I don't know how I can help you."

She couldn't stop the real tears from forming. Soon they were rolling down her cheeks and she was humiliated, but didn't know what to do.

He grimaced. "I'm sorry, sweetheart. I'm just so frustrated. Don't cry, Sujata. It's not worth crying about. Nothing is going to change. I'll get back and it will be back to normal."

Sujata wasn't hysterical, but the tears would not stop. It was just too much. She believed him—she really did—but she couldn't turn off the panic. But she had to say something. "I know."

"I think you know you can trust me. Maybe you just need some time to convince yourself."

How would he know? "Stop mansplaining, Vivek," she shot back.

"Wh—"

"Who are you to tell me how to feel?" Suddenly she was pissed again.

"Sweetheart, I didn't mean it that way. But I think I do have a stake in this. You asked me if I could delay the trip to give you more time. I assumed time is really what you need. That's all."

She deflated. She wiped her eyes and looked back at the screen.

"I'll text you when I can." He was being so serious. She should be able to trust him.

"Okay." Her voice cracked and she cast her eyes down.

"Sujata."

She looked back up. "Yeah."

"It's going to be okay." His voice was soft but he sounded sure of himself.

She hoped he was right. If she could just silence the panic.

~

SUNDAY EVENING, Sujata couldn't take the stress of their last conversation and called Vivek.

"Hi, how are you?" he'd started, probably unsure what she was going to say.

"Please don't go," Sujata said.

He sighed. "We talked about this. I need to go. It's not a problem. Everything will be the same when I get back if you want it to be."

"I just … can't." Tears pricked her eyes again. "This is too hard. It's too similar to what happened before."

"Except it's with a completely different person, so it's not the same at all. I am not your ex. I'm guessing he's the only one who's ever done that—it's not normal."

"I know." She was ashamed of the desperation in her voice. "It's just …" She didn't know what to say. It was just what?

"Sujata, if you can't trust me here, then I don't know if we can be together. I have never done anything to make you question me, because I have never been anything but devoted to you. It's always been you and only you."

She couldn't say anything, even though the panic was a whirlwind in her mind.

"I'm going to have to hang up soon. They're about to close the plane door."

"You're on the plane already?" Her voice was high. How could he already be on the plane? He was really going to leave her.

"If you can't trust me, then I don't know what to tell you." He was obviously pissed. "I'm going to hang up. I said what I said. Think about it."

And then he'd disappeared off her phone.

Sujata wanted to scream. Had they just broken up before he hung up on her? How could he hang up on her? He didn't sound anything like himself.

She needed to go on a run to push out all the horrible feelings. She put her shoes on and was out the door. She turned out of her apartment complex, needing the feel of her feet pounding the pavement. It should help level her. She focused on the slight scuffing sound her shoes made on the ground, trying to think of it as rhythmic and calming.

But it wasn't working. She may have just made the biggest mistake of her life.

Not may. She *had*.

She crossed the street and headed toward a street that stretched the length of the neighborhood.

Vivek was going to be in the air any minute now.

Sujata turned onto the long road. Had he definitely broken up with her? She wasn't sure, but the question just made everything worse.

She'd been so set on avoiding getting hurt, but she'd walked right into excruciating pain, anyway. Why did it have to be Rajeev who was the doctor when Vivek broke his arm? It could have been anybody else. She might have been able to handle this trip if it had been someone else.

Not to mention that the broken arm was the whole reason he was going home now. They'd gotten together because of her broken foot, and now they were going to end things because of his broken arm? This was insane.

Why did he have to slip in the grass? Why did the universe hate her? What had she ever done to deserve this?

She'd made the mistake of not bringing her earbuds, so she was stuck in her head.

Sujata started listening to her feet again. Shush-shush. She decided to try to clear her head with simple meditation techniques. She paid attention to each foot as it landed, and then her knees, and her hips. Her arms moved side to side in sync with her stride. She could even feel the contact from each step in her shoulders.

Paying attention to each separate thing helped. Maybe if she applied the same idea to her life, that would help, too.

Of course her mind went straight to Vivek, sitting in a giant metal tube shooting through the air.

It struck her—if she looked only at Vivek as a singular thing, not how he related to Rajeev, it was obvious the two of them were completely separate entities. There was no logical reason for anything Rajeev had done to influence—or have any connection to whatsoever—anything Vivek would do.

She'd always known this, but she finally felt it. She had made a huge mistake. There was no denying it.

Why had she conflated the two of them so thoroughly? Well, she knew—it was all about her experiences. Her experiences were what connected everything. But her devastating experiences hadn't just happened—someone had taken action to give her those bad experiences. Namely, Rajeev. Not Vivek. Vivek had never done anything untrustworthy. He had waited so patiently for her to come around, never pressuring her, but he never wavered in his devotion.

How had she been so blind to the differences? Rajeev was always doing little things to control her—he discouraged most of her friendships with people who weren't Indian and made it clear that he thought her degree was stupid. He made her question everything about herself. Nobody in her family had liked him, but even they didn't know how bad it was to deal with him day-to-day. He expected her to ask him all about med school and then his residencies, but if she tried to talk about her work, once she'd gotten a real job after graduating, he didn't even feign interest. And she'd always made excuses for him. He's tired. What he's doing is more important than making computer chips.

The best thing she'd done after he left her was move. A total life reset.

She was only now seeing it clearly. He'd demeaned her for years. He'd never hit her, but he was emotionally abusive. That was not too strong a word for what it was.

But that was in the past. What mattered now was Vivek and how she had ruined that. Was it fixable? How?

A sense of panic returned, but this time it was about figuring out what she could do to fix things. She had to text him. If he'd paid for the Wi-Fi, he might even be able to get it while he was on the plane.

She stopped running, leaning forward to catch her breath. She hadn't brought her phone, so she'd have to go back to the apartment. She turned around and started running back.

Dammit, she hadn't realized she'd already run this far. She was anxious to get back but it was going to take a while. She sped up.

She started composing her text in her head. Or multiple texts.

I'm so sorry, Vivek. I finally believe you. I got it out of my brain and into my heart.

I finally convinced myself that you and Rajeev are totally separate people, and I know you're not like him

I trust you. I really, really trust you now

If you can, call me when you arrive

Sujata had more to say, but she'd write it in the moment. She hoped he'd respond soon, but if he didn't, she would just have to put up with the situation her stupid fear had put her in.

Was there anything else she could do? She had to think about this.

29

The flight attendants were preparing the cabin for landing on Vivek's uncomfortable flight into Germany. He'd be glad to be on solid ground again, even if it was going to be for way too long.

Then he thought of Sujata. Had they broken up? He didn't think so, but he'd basically given her an ultimatum. It was up to her if she would respond to that, or if they really did break up. Had that been a mistake? But really, if she couldn't trust him with something as mundane as visiting family, they would have bigger problems.

But that thought completely broke his heart. He'd been too hard on her. This situation was really similar to the one she'd been through with Rajeev, and they had just run into the man again.

Had she texted him? The Wi-Fi was out on the plane the whole flight, so he hadn't been able to get texts.

As soon as they landed, he took his phone out of airplane mode, and there was an influx of texts. The relief washed through him. Unless she was angry at him? Anger wasn't the right word for her. It was one of the right words for how he'd felt yesterday, however. Something he regretted.

He opened the first text and his heart lifted. He read through all of them. She had finally come around. He'd started to worry that she had just been hurt too much to ever trust again.

Her last text was the best, though. *—I love you, Vivek. I'm so sorry for doubting you. I had no reason—*

He smiled and his heart skipped. She loved him. Those words had been on the tip of his tongue but he'd been too afraid to say them. Now he wanted nothing more than to talk to her.

He wrote up a text and sent it.

—I love you too, sweetheart. Are you still up? I've just landed in Germany—

—Yes! I can talk for a bit.—

—I'll call once I'm off the plane, okay?—

She sent a heart emoji. He could picture her lying in her bed, tucked under the covers because she kept the room cold, holding her phone in anticipation. He loved that image. She had finally come around. Part of him still worried that she'd get spooked again by something, but he was going to ignore that doubt for now. Just for now. When they were together again, or maybe before, they were going to talk about it. He needed her to commit to stop being hot and cold on him.

They opened the door and Vivek got his carry-on suitcase and backpack and filed off the plane with everyone else, anticipation building in his own stomach. He wanted to be somewhere comfortable to talk to her. And he needed some kind of food. But they'd talk first.

Vivek walked a bit until he found a coffee shop with a miraculously empty table and fell into the seat. He dropped his backpack in the chair next to him and yawned. But he didn't care how tired he was.

He dialed Sujata's number.

"Hey." The smile in her voice woke his heart up.

"Should we FaceTime?" he asked.

"Yeah."

They switched over and stared at each other happily for a moment.

"I'm sorry, Vivek. I finally convinced myself, so even my emotions are on board. I don't know why it was such an internal fight." She was still smiling, but shook her head at the last part.

"Sujata, what he did to you was really terrible. I do understand, especially since we just ran into him. But I'm not him and would never betray you like that." Frustration that she hadn't trusted him settled in his stomach. He should be honest about this. "When you think I'm like him, it really upsets me."

"I know." She obviously didn't know what to say.

But he gave her time.

"I promise the doubt is over. I had an epiphany. I know it sounds stupid. But I realized that Rajeev was basically emotionally abusive the whole time we were together. He just made me feel like nothing. I know it's going to sound stupid, but I think my unwillingness to try a relationship was a step I had to go through to recover from him. Because it meant I valued myself enough to know that I don't deserve to be treated badly. But like a lot of emotional coping strategies, it was flawed. I couldn't separate Rajeev from all men. It finally, finally feels like my brain is fixed. I'm sorry it took so long. I should have gone to therapy or something. My sister did suggest it, but I was like, it's just a breakup, no big deal. Which obviously was not true."

Through her whole monologue, Vivek had watched her intently.

She grimaced. "Sorry, I guess I had a lot to say."

He nodded. "You did. I'm sorry you went through all that, and I see your logic. But Sujata, maybe some therapy right now wouldn't be a bad idea? I've heard it can be really helpful."

"Maybe." She nodded. "Maybe they could get me to not fall into stupid thinking again."

"I'm glad you changed your mind. I was really upset that it seemed like we'd broken up. I wasn't sure if we had."

"Me neither. And I was also freaking out the whole time you didn't respond to my texts. I thought maybe you just hadn't paid for Wi-Fi, but I was all stressing—What if he did pay for it and got my texts and still wants to be broken up?"

"Yeah, the Wi-Fi on the plane wasn't working so I just tried to sleep. But of course I didn't, because I was worried about what I'd said."

"You were right, though. How long is your layover?"

He rolled his eyes. "Over ten hours. There weren't many options left on short notice."

"Aw, that's awful. Is it direct from there?"

"I wish." He laughed, his voice cracking. He really was tired. "I have a layover in Muscat, but fortunately it's only a couple hours."

"It will be Tuesday before you get there."

"Yes, two p.m." Just thinking about it made him even more tired. He yawned again.

"You look beat." She cocked her head. "Long trips suck." She frowned. "I should go to sleep soon. I have to go in for an early meeting tomorrow."

"New project?"

"Yeah, we took on a new big-name customer—I can't even say who it is yet—and they're based in London."

"Well, good luck. I love you, Sujata, and sleep well."

She smiled so big that his heart lit up again. "I love you. I'm so glad I finally got over being an idiot. This is much better."

He laughed. "Get some sleep."

"I'd say, you too, but then somebody would steal your luggage."

"Hopefully I don't fall asleep while walking to my flight tonight," he joked.

"Don't do that."

He didn't want to hang up, even though he was hungry. But what he most wanted in the world was on his tiny phone screen.

"I love you," she said again.

"Love you, too. I'm going to go now so you can sleep."

"Okay. Bye."

They stared at each other for another moment until they both laughed. Vivek waved and they said, "Bye," at the same time. He ended the call, still grinning.

But then he yawned again and his stomach rumbled in the middle of it.

He needed food and caffeine. And he could spend the rest of his time here thinking about the woman he loved, who loved him back—and finally trusted him.

~

SUJATA WAS FRAZZLED AT WORK, feeling way too many feelings, all around the facts that she and Vivek had said the three little words to each other, and he was now half a world away, and she desperately wanted to see him.

So she jumped at the chance to go to lunch with Theresa and Casey and run her idea by them. And to get away from the computer, which taunted her with work she was struggling to get done.

They met up outside Casey's office.

"What are you all up for?" Theresa asked as they walked to the elevator.

"What about Vin's Deli?" Casey asked.

Sujata could not have cared any less, but she nodded in agreement because she wanted to get going.

Theresa was happy with the choice, so they headed onto the street for the short walk. Theresa and Casey were chatting about a project, but Sujata wasn't involved in it so she was stewing. What exactly did she want to ask them? The idea wasn't fully formed.

"You sure are quiet, Sujata," Theresa said when they got to the first street they needed to cross.

"So, yeah. I have a dilemma. Or something. You are going to think I'm crazy."

"Does this have something to do with Vivek?" Casey teased.

Sujata put a hand to her forehead. "Of course. Everything is more complicated now. But not bad, just, yeah. I'm struggling a bit."

"Is something wrong?" Theresa asked.

The Walk sign came on so they started crossing.

"So you both know he was just here so we could go to San Francisco." She'd already told them about what happened, and applying for Y Combinator. "He broke his arm while he was here and his family is all worried about him, so he decided to go home for a visit."

"Okay," Casey said, sounding curious. They'd come to another intersection and had to wait.

"I told you both a while back about what my ex did to me." She shook her head, reliving everything, even though it was vague and nonspecific bad feelings.

They nodded in response.

She explained what had happened at the ER with Rajeev, and how he was all dismissive and jealous.

"Jerk," Theresa said. "What business is it of his?"

"Exactly," Sujata said. "I sent him away, but seeing him really did a number on me." She grimaced. "And then ... Man, this is bad."

Casey and Theresa looked at her as they crossed another street, and Sujata explained Vivek's whole revelation about the woman in India his parents had picked for him.

"Oh, crap!" Casey said.

"Let me guess, you freaked out?" Theresa asked.

"Let's say yes." She put her hand to her forehead, trying to push the humiliating memory back in. "I kept trying to talk myself out of being worried, but then I was wondering why he hadn't told me."

"Yeah, I'd wonder that, too," Theresa said. "But is this a common thing?"

"Parents trying to marry their kids off to specific people? Not as much nowadays. With our grandparents very. But it still happens. A lot of people just go with it, but willingly. My sister is going to marry the guy whose parents my parents schemed with."

Casey and Theresa nodded.

"She actually really likes him. We all do. But anyway, I know that parents do this and usually the kids aren't interested, but I couldn't stop freaking out. At first it was just a general freak-out, but when he was suddenly going to India right now, I just basically went all meltdown."

Theresa rubbed Sujata's shoulder as they neared the deli and Casey opened the door.

"Okay, I'll finish when we sit down," Sujata said. Theresa smiled at her and they got in line.

"I'm just impressed you're talking so much," Theresa said.

"Yeah, usually you keep things really close to the chest," Casey added.

"Yeah. I'm very emotional right now. It's kind of weird. It's like this sustained intense feeling. I don't know what's going on."

They got through the line, Sujata with a grilled cheese—it was a splurge kind of day—and found a table in the corner.

She finished up the embarrassing story of the conversation when he was on the plane, and her epiphany during her run. "I finally realized I was being a total idiot. Like, it finally, finally sank in."

Sujata took a bite of her sandwich.

"Sometimes it's hard to change the way you perceive bad experiences," Casey said. "It's kind of like getting rid of a victim mentality, which is usually a distorted way of looking at things, even though it's easy to fall into."

Sujata nodded and swallowed. With Rajeev, she had definitely been in love with who she thought he was, not who he really was.

"So what did you do?" Theresa asked.

"I sent him a bunch of texts, which he didn't get until he got to Europe, because of course the Wi-Fi was not working on his flight. But then he called me, and everything's great now. But this gets me to my question. Sorry it took so long to get here."

Theresa and Casey just gave her encouraging smiles and worked on their own sandwiches.

Sujata took a breath. "I think I'm going to go to India and try to meet up with him. I can't go to his house or meet his family—we really don't tell our parents when we're dating people, and his are set on this other woman. He will have to tell them later, like maybe if we get engaged. But anyway, so I can't go to his house."

"Okay ..." Casey said. "You are still able to text him now that he's there, right?"

"Yeah, so I'm thinking of just turning up in his city and then arranging for him to come to a cafe for a 'surprise.' I mean, he'd guess that I was the surprise, but it would still be a bit of a grand gesture."

"You're prepping your story for a romance author to write up," Theresa joked.

"I know, I actually thought of that. I'd considered meeting him in Europe, like having him stay in Paris or somewhere else and meeting him there. But I'm the one who made this whole thing difficult, so I want to make it up to him and show him I'm finally really all the way there."

Casey and Theresa both nodded thoughtfully.

"So that's not a too crazy plan, is it?" Sujata asked.

"No way, that would be awesome," Theresa said. "I'm sure he'd love it."

"You are going to tell him, though, right?" Casey asked.

Sujata nodded.

"Then yeah, that's not actually crazy," Casey agreed. "Well, it is a little crazy, but in the spontaneous, fun way people mean. The kind of crazy everybody admires in other people."

They all laughed.

"Okay, I'm going to tell him," Sujata said, glad for good friends and good advice. "I hope he says yes."

"I'm sure he will," Casey said. "He'd do almost anything for you. Except completely abandon his family. That's a great sign."

"He's a good guy," Theresa said. "I hate how we view shy people as lesser."

"Yeah. He's not really that shy, just a bit uncomfortable around people he doesn't know." Sujata chuckled. "And apparently also around women he has a huge crush on."

She felt good. She just needed to tell David she had to take some time off, and since all the fire alarms had finally been dealt with, he owed her some vacation time.

Now she had to plan a trip to India.

30

Vivek was exhausted when he got to Hosur, but he made himself stay up so he could get up for breakfast like he'd never left. Breakfast was as great as he remembered—his *amma* made such good dosa, a crepe-like dish stuffed with potatoes. And her coconut chutney was amazing. But the best part of waking up was plugging his phone back in, since he'd forgotten to charge it and it had died overnight, and seeing more texts from Sujata.

For the rest of the morning, he had to talk with his family in the sitting room, with other family members coming and going. Lunch was another lovely meal—vendhaya kuzhambu, a curry with tamarind, and rice. His little cousins came over after school, and then he hadn't been able to wriggle out of this visit to the house of Adya—the woman his parents wanted him to marry. It didn't matter in the big picture, and it would keep them off his back, at least for a bit. But thinking of the woman just made his mind go to Sujata and how much this stupid thing hurt her.

"You need to put on some nice clothes, Vivek," his *amma* said. It was nearing the time they had to leave to go to Adya's house.

"I didn't bring anything very nice," he said.

"I can find you something." His *amma* disappeared into the back of the house.

"This is important, son," his *appa* said.

"I know you want this for me, Appa, but you know I am not ready to get married." This wasn't strictly true, but a white lie would just make things easier. But if Sujata said, Hey, we should get married, for real, he wouldn't hesitate.

"Just meet her and you can decide. You went to school together."

"I remember her."

Amma appeared bearing an old dhoti and shirt, something he'd worn rarely even before moving to the U.S.

The long shirt was blue and the dhoti was white. "Will that fit me?" He hoped it would not. He did not want to dress up for this.

Although he did wonder what Sujata would think of him dressed up.

"It is fine," his *amma* said. "Go put it on."

Vivek got up and took the garments from her, heading back to his room to change. As he was putting the dhoti on, he realized he was nervous after all, despite having no intention of marrying anyone any time soon. Well, except maybe Sujata, but there was no rush there. But there were no stakes with this meeting, except maybe hurting Adya's feelings and frustrating their parents.

No, what was bothering him was that he hadn't told Sujata about this meeting. He wasn't going to tell her in advance, no. He'd tell her afterward, though. After he'd officially said no.

Okay, now that the dhoti was on, it was tighter and shorter than it was supposed to be. He looked in the mirror. These were flowy bottoms that ended mid-calf, with a lot of fabric on the top half. He'd had grown a couple of inches since his early college days. He looked ridiculous.

Maybe this would be a good thing, actually. It might put Adya off.

Just then his phone buzzed with a text.

—*How would you feel if I surprised you in Hosur?*— Sujata texted.

His heart leapt when he saw her name, but her question threw him. —*What do you mean?*—

He stood there, shirtless in tight but flowy bottoms, watching the three dots on his screen, and scratched his head. Was she saying she was coming here?

—I really wanted to just surprise you by showing up, but then I thought it might be stalkery and look like I didn't trust you, but that's not it—

She was going to come here. That was a little mad, but he'd love to see her. As long as it didn't cause any problems. *—I would love to see you. But you can't meet my family—*

—Obviously! lol— She knew as well as he did how Indian parents were. This wasn't something worth messing around with.

He was still confused, but smiling. *—What are you planning?—*

—Why don't we pretend it's a surprise, but we know I'm not a creep. I'll text you a location and time in advance, and as long as that works for you, let's do that— She added several heart emojis.

His smile widened. *—It's a plan—*

She just texted back with a grinning emoji, something that was echoed on his face, but less yellow.

He threw the long shirt on. It was also tight, and getting his cast through the sleeve was difficult. He hadn't really gotten fat, but his chest had widened.

Maybe Amma would see it and not approve and he could go back to normal trousers. He could compromise by wearing the traditional shirt.

As he left the room, he could feel the bounce in his step, thinking of seeing Sujata soon. He had to wipe that off his face before he got into the front room. Once he was there, instead of disapproving, Amma smiled in happiness. "So handsome!"

Great. He'd been in the U.S. long enough to wish he was an American who could say no to his parents without causing all sorts of trouble.

But that was not his situation.

Now there was more sitting until it was time to leave.

Once at Adya's house, all the formal greeting stuff took a while. He finally saw Adya herself—she was pretty now, and did, in fact, have nice skin, and she'd had makeup done and was wearing a nice sari. But she still was not Sujata, so it did not matter.

They sat in the front room, both sets of parents, himself and Adya, the families on opposite sides of a small table with a tray of tea on it. It was awkward—Adya didn't look particularly happy to be there, either. Her parents started listing all her great attributes, and then his parents did the same about him. They all had a laugh at his sports injury. This part was awkward, but fine, but he knew it was reasonable to ask to talk to Adya in private. He was looking for an opportunity to do this, when Adya rather politely cut her *amma* off and asked that very question.

"Oh," her *amma* said.

"That is wonderful," her *appa* said.

So, soon they were sitting in the room alone while the parents hovered outside the room trying to listen.

"I was trying to ask them for that, too," Vivek said as quietly as possible.

Adya nodded.

"Listen, I can't go through with this," Vivek said. "I have a girlfriend." Sujata's beautiful face filled his mind and his heart skipped. He'd be seeing her soon.

The relief on Adya's face was palpable. "Oh, thank you. I can't either—I have a boyfriend, too."

Vivek laughed, and she followed suit. He was so relieved. Completely off the hook.

"They're going to be so disappointed," he said.

She nodded and smiled. "Yes."

They looked at each other, and then she reminded him of some ridiculous antics his friends had gotten up to back in grade school, and they laughed about that and some other stories. They talked a bit about their jobs. She was working as a statistician—what was it with him and really smart women?—and sympathized with him working for his uncle. He laughed at something funny she said about not mixing family and work, and then all the smiling parents burst into the room and Vivek and Adya looked up in surprise. The conversation was over and the parents surely all thought everything was great. Vivek and Adya looked at each other, both with subtly amused expressions. The parents were not correct.

It would remain to be seen how they would handle that.

ON WEDNESDAY EVENING, Sujata got to the airport early and was soon waiting in the gate for the quick flight to Seattle, where she'd catch a direct red-eye to London, and then fly to Muscat. From there, she'd have another flight to Hosur, just like Vivek had. She'd never been to south India so it was all new. But her layovers weren't terrible. Long enough to not be stressful as short connections, but short enough that she wouldn't feel like she was camping at the airport.

She took a sip of her coffee and looked around. It was a good mix of people. Plenty of business men and women. Families. Young twenty-somethings off for some kind of adventure. The smattering of Pacific Northwesterners with all their outdoor gear.

She'd brought several things to entertain herself on the long journey, including a couple of new romances on her Kindle, her laptop, and sudoku, which she only ever did when she was traveling. She couldn't imagine doing any of them right now because she was so hyped up about the mission she was embarking on. Casey was right that it was a tad crazy, but a lot of people would admire the bold step.

She wondered what Vivek was doing. Then she realized he was obviously sleeping. Or at least lying in bed. Maybe thinking of her like she was thinking of him?

God, she missed him, even though it actually hadn't been that long since she'd seen him. Everything had changed now, though.

The airline staff called for pre-boarding so Sujata took off her jacket and ran it through the handle of her large purse. She got up to stand with the cluster of people waiting to officially line up.

She spotted an Indian couple in line, with two little kids. That was her future, she just knew it. The glow in her stomach flared.

Soon, they were boarding. She found her seat, stowed her carry-on bag, put her phone in airplane mode, and stuck her earbuds in. Some ambient music to calm her nerves would be a good thing.

She spent the entire flight—and the next, longer one—listening to beats, thinking about Vivek, and trying to calm herself from said thoughts. She couldn't wait to see him, even if it would only be in public, so there were be no real opportunities for PDA. That didn't keep her mind from imagining all sorts of exceptional scenarios where they were alone with a bed.

After they landed in London, she waited at another gate and eventually got settled in for her overnight flight. She was stuck in the middle of the four-seat-across section, so nobody had to crawl across her to get in or out of the row. She read for a while and even did some sudoku. After they turned the lights off, she read some more before deciding to sleep a bit. She wasn't a great sleeper on planes, but she could at least get some partial rest so she wouldn't be completely exhausted when she arrived.

After a few hours of on and off snoozing, they were preparing to land. She was going to be in the same continent as Vivek again, like she should be. Her heart sped up just thinking about him.

More waiting and a lot more flying and yawning, and they were touching down in Hosur. She'd been to New Delhi and Bengal several times when she was growing up and while she was in college, but it had been a while. But she'd never been to south India at all, so she was curious.

After navigating taxi selection and then the chaotic roads that defined India—this was no different from the north of the country—she made it to her hotel room. She needed to get some real sleep, and then she'd scope out places they could meet up.

Sujata couldn't wait to see him. She knew he'd be as excited to see her, even though it might be difficult for him to get away. But she was sure he could make it work.

"When are you going to tell me what this is about?" Guru asked. Guru was an old school friend Vivek had roped into driving him to a cafe in south Hosur, where the "surprise" was waiting for him, according to Sujata's hilariously cryptic text that morning. He was playing along with the idea that he didn't know who he was meeting.

"Afterward." He'd had to have a friend pick him up from his parents' house because otherwise he had no excuse to be out. He certainly wasn't telling anybody he was meeting his American girlfriend. They were still mad at him about Adya, even though she also had said no.

"I'm going to a picture, so I won't be able to pick you up until it's done," Guru said.

"That's fine. I think it's up there," Vivek said, pointing ahead. "On the right."

"Okay."

"Let me out here." Vivek's heart was picking up the pace in anticipation of maybe—definitely—seeing Sujata in minutes.

He walked the half-block to the cafe, peeking in the windows, but he couldn't see anything. He pushed the door open. It was a long room with tables spread out. He first looked left, then scanned to the right, before heading farther back.

Then he saw her. Sujata, the love of his life, smiling at him. Sujata, who had been almost too broken by an ex for this to work. But she was here now, and everything was going to work out. He couldn't stop his mouth from stretching into a huge smile.

He strode toward her table, and she stood up so they could hug. They weren't going to be able to kiss in public like they could in the U.S., but hugging felt good enough, and he breathed in her familiar lavender scent.

It was a long hug that still managed to draw some disapproving looks, and then they sat down across from each other. His heart was so full that he must have been radiating happiness, bringing smiles to faces on everyone within a six-foot radius.

Sujata touched his hand, leaned toward him, and quietly said, "I love you so much, Vivek. I'm sorry for everything I put you through to get us here. But I wanted to tell you to your face. I love you."

Vivek couldn't get the happy grin off his face. "I love you. I've loved you almost from the moment I first saw you, as you know, and I always knew it was supposed to be us together forever."

They just smiled stupidly at each other for a moment.

"Did you come here just to tell me this?" he asked.

She nodded. "If you had finished that book you started reading at my house, you would have learned about a plot device in romance called the grand gesture. But it works in real life, too. Basically the person who caused the breakup or crisis does something big to make up for it. So here I am." She held her hands out.

Vivek laughed. "I'm glad you came. What's next?"

"Well, how much time do you have? I have a hotel room."

"Shall we go there?" Vivek said. "I had a friend pick me up, so my family think I'm with him, but he went to see a picture so he's occupied for a while."

"It cracks me up how we have to sneak around like teenagers. But we can also be occupied for a while," Sujata said, putting on a sultry look.

"Let's do it."

They stood up and walked out into the sun, hands brushing against each other.

"You know we're going to have to tell our parents eventually," Sujata said while Vivek scanned the street for an auto-rickshaw.

"I know. Let's do yours first. I think they'll be easier."

"I think you are right." Sujata bumped his shoulder and he spotted their ride.

He waved his hand for the approaching auto-rickshaw.

He helped her onto the seat before climbing in himself. The driver took off and they were thrown back.

Vivek gripped her shoulders to steady her. "On the way to our destination, I'm going to tell you about Adya. I think you will find this funny."

She looked at him, eyebrows arched, but there was a smile on her face.

He knew she truly trusted him now. And now they were really on their way.

PART IV

EPILOGUE

Vivek came into the den with a bowl of popcorn. Sujata took it and put it on her very pregnant belly, which doubled as a table right now.

Their seven-year-old twins sat on either side of Sujata, so Vivek sat next to Samira. Arya leaned into Sujata. She put her arms around both girls and squeezed them tight. She had everything she'd ever wanted. Those many years ago, when she and Vivek were still at Info-Quest, she would never have imagined this perfect future. But here it was.

"Ready?" she asked.

The girls both said "Yes!" and Vivek smiled and nodded. "Let's see how cool we really are."

Sujata hit the play button on the remote and a white balcony appeared on the screen, with about fifteen of Data Cata's top people filling it up. The Data Cata logo appeared on the wall behind them. They were mostly standing there, occasionally saying things to each other, but facing forward. Sujata was in the center, in front of a giant bell that hung on the front of the balcony, Vivek to her right and Theresa to her left, with Conall next to her. They were all grinning.

She looked at all the other smiling faces and remembered the day she hired each of them. They were a great team.

Vivek tapped her shoulder and she turned. He was grinning just like on the video, and she realized so was she.

This was them going public at the New York Stock Exchange. It was incredible that her little rejected project proposal had turned into something this big. Casey said some of the leaders were talking about it when they got wind of what was happening—a lot of the employees were following it. Many of Sujata and Vivek's former colleagues were still at InfoQuest. The company had pretty good retention since it was easy to move between jobs to keep an upward trajectory. But even with that, if the two of them were still there, their lives would be nothing like they were now. Their time with Y Combinator had changed everything. They'd quit their jobs and moved to San Francisco to go through the program. Their parents all freaked out, but the two of them never wavered, despite how hard things were at the beginning. And, of course, now their parents bragged about them to everyone they met.

In the video, the crowd on the trading floor—not visible in the video—started cheering and everyone on the balcony began clapping, all of which went on for a bit, and then Sujata watched herself press the button over the bell, and it began clanging. She had struggled a little to get close enough to the button because of her very pregnant belly, but she'd made it work. After stopping the bell, she grabbed a gavel and brought it down several times against the wooden block.

On the couch, Vivek reached over Samira to squeeze Sujata's shoulder. "We made it, sweetheart.

"We did. We got everything we worked for."

"Including a couple of munchkins." He started tickling Samira, and Arya scrambled across Sujata's lap to get in on the fun, almost falling off because there was very little lap left at this point.

"With number three as a surprise bonus. This baby will be the youngest person ever to attend a NYSE bell-ringing ceremony."

Arya and Samira slid onto the floor and started tickling each other, and Sujata scooted over to lean against Vivek.

"When is your *amma* coming again?" Sujata asked.

"Four weeks." He put his arm across her shoulders and pulled her in. The baby was due in three, but she'd be staying for two months to help out. Amma had completely forgiven Sujata the moment she'd produced twins. His mind was going all the way back.

"Do you ever wonder what would have happened if David hadn't assigned me to work with you on the proposal?" he asked.

"It wouldn't have turned out so great, I'm sure. I also wonder, if they hadn't all been so thick—what if they'd actually supported the project? Imagine if we'd done all that work just for InfoQuest to get rich off our big brains." Sujata laughed. "We wouldn't have any of this. And this is way better."

"You're right, sweetheart. Work life and family life always seemed vaguely good when I was growing up, but both are way better than I could have imagined."

Sujata turned her head so she could kiss him, and he obliged, just like she knew he would.

THE END

Now that you've finished *A Quality Man*, please consider leaving a rating or a review—they help indie authors so much.

If you haven't read *It's Technically Love* (Theresa's and Conall's story) or *Finally in Tune* (Casey's and Adam's story), make sure to check them out. They are both available in ebook, audiobook (AI-voiced), and paperback.

If you are interested in staying informed about future releases and sales, you can subscribe to my newsletter from my website, katvinson.com.

ACKNOWLEDGMENTS

This book only exists because of the help of friends and family. My fellow writers Anne Shaw, Gwen Sharp, and Stacia Leigh helped shape the story. Sas Neogi helped me make sure Sujata and Vivek were as authentic as possible (but anything that is wrong about Indian and Desi culture is entirely my fault). Finally, my ever-supportive mom, Kathy Vincent, willingly gave feedback on the for-prudes version that I make just for her.

PREVIEW OF IT'S TECHNICALLY LOVE

It all starts in It's Technically Love, *Coded for Love #1. Here's the first chapter.*

CHAPTER ONE

Theresa Alberts stared at her desk at work, her chest tight, while Mrs. Winters listed suggestions and named specialists on the phone. Theresa's seven-year-old son's struggle with reading had reared its ugly head again. She'd talked a little about it with Mrs. Winters at the last parent-teacher conference, but things had gotten worse instead of better since then. She glanced at the montage of photos of Liam hanging on her white fabric cubicle wall, and her heart twisted with a mixture of apprehension and pride. Then her gaze landed on his drawing of a zebra they'd seen at the zoo. He had an uncanny ability to draw anything—pictures even most adults couldn't manage.

"Okay, thank you," Theresa said after Mrs. Winters finished. She took a deep breath to calm herself. "Could you give me the last one's last name again?"

She wrote it down this time, her hand shaking.

Liam's reading difficulties were putting him at serious risk of being held back a year, as well as simply being heartbreaking to watch. They went to the library regularly, and he always fought her when she tried to get him to read, because it was so hard for him. His long pauses between words, entirely wrong words or sounds... everything. Somehow, she had to get him beyond this. Being held back would destroy his self-esteem. He was too sensitive.

Plus, what would Michael say? Her ex blamed her for everything that went wrong with Liam. And her mom—she usually echoed Michael.

Theresa headed over to Casey's office. Casey was one of her best friends in Portland as well as her boss. The white door stood open, and Theresa leaned against Casey's doorway. The tall woman sat behind her two giant computer screens with a frown, her dark blonde hair messy like she'd run her hand through it.

After saying hi, Casey asked, "Find anyone for your mother-in-law?"

Theresa had an ad for the finished basement unit under her house hanging in the company's kitchen. "Nope, not yet."

"Maybe some studmuffin will want to rent it."

"Ha. No men for me. You know I don't want a repeat of Michael." Out with the girls one night, she'd made the mistake of saying it would be nice to have a man around to help at home. They wouldn't let her live it down. But she hadn't meant it.

Casey nodded. "Yeah, I get it. You can't trust them not to become cavemen."

Theresa cocked her head in agreement and leaned against the door. It was complicated, but that was the crux of it. Michael had made her feel like the worst wife and mother in the world. He'd basically taken any confidence she'd salvaged after growing up with her disapproving mother and thrown it out the window.

Casey added. "But even I don't think they're all like that."

Theresa shrugged. That might be true in theory, but the problem was that you could never tell until it was too late. So, she'd sworn off all men since her divorce. Michael had turned out how he was despite having been a stellar boyfriend. She wasn't at all sad that he'd stayed in Seattle when she'd moved to Portland. She stretched the elastic cuff of her red shirt, and let it pop back to her wrist.

"You okay?" Casey asked.

Theresa shook her head. "I have to take Liam to a specialist to get him tested for a learning disability."

"Oh, man, it's not getting better?"

"Nope." She told Casey about the conversation with the teacher.

Casey raised her eyebrows. "The school won't test him?"

"It will just take too long. I want to get started."

"Well, maybe they'll find something you can work with. They know a lot more about that kind of thing now."

"Yeah, you're right." Theresa sighed. What would she do if he really had a learning disability? She'd have to manage by herself. It would be so hard. Thinking about it had her heart speeding up again.

But Casey could be right. "No, it's true. Maybe it won't be so bad."

Casey lined up a programming book with the corner of her desk. "Maybe you can help me out and take your mind off this."

"What is it?"

"We've got an interview loop going on, and Guru can't make the two o'clock slot—can you fill in?"

"For a software dev position?" She could do it, but who truly enjoyed doing interviews? Awkward people, time away from real work. The last guy she'd interviewed had worn a sweater vest inside out, and she couldn't stop staring at the seams.

"Yeah. Nobody on their team can fill in, so they asked me to find someone." Casey led the data engineers and data scientists, but they all had expertise in software development, too.

"Tag, I'm it?"

Casey laughed. "Something like that. Are you able to do it?"

"Yeah, of course. Which interview is it?"

"Team suitability."

Theresa's least favorite part of the interview loop. Technical interviews were easier because they were black and white. This one was fairly subjective. Would the candidate be a good fit for the company?

Casey smiled sheepishly and reached for some papers on the other side of her desk before handing them to Theresa.

She read the top of the resume.

"Conall O'Donnell?" Theresa giggled. "Seriously?"

"Rhyming names aren't your thing?"

"No. But seriously, who could look at a tiny baby and write that on the birth certificate?" She glanced further down. "M.S. from Stanford. Nice."

"He definitely looks good on paper."

Theresa rolled up the resume, and they made plans for lunch before Theresa got back to work.

~

Conall leaned forward in the white task chair—everything in this office was stark white and modern—and rested his left arm on the edge of the meeting room's table. He studied his red and blue argyle socks. A bit too bright? A tiny leaf stuck out from the side of his shoe. He pulled the it off and let it sink to the floor under the table.

No, the socks were fine. Everyone he'd seen in the office so far was dressed very casually. Most in jeans and sneakers, and he'd seen several ThinkGeek t-shirts. But he'd followed the advice he'd read online about software job-hunting on the west coast: dress a little better than everyone else at the company.

His HR contact had said business casual. His khakis weren't overly casual, and he'd worn a simple pale blue button-down shirt. He was good.

So far he'd had two of the four interviews planned for today. He was waiting on the next interviewer, who was running late. This was the behavioral interview.

He thought the others had gone well. It was standard computer science fare—data structures and algorithms. How do you reverse a string? How do you avoid deadlock in a transactional database? Et cetera.

He heard a rustling sound and raised his head to see a woman wearing a long denim skirt and a red shirt standing in the doorway scanning papers in her hand. She had shoulder-length ash blonde hair pushed back behind her ears, which were strangely enticing. Delicate.

"Conall, I'm so sorry I'm running late. I—" She looked up, and their gazes locked.

It was still her turn to speak, which was good because he couldn't think of anything except how pretty she was. She might be average height, yet the rest of her was anything but.

Her eyes were velvet brown, and they had widened ever-so-slightly as they gazed into his.

"I—" she continued, still staring at him. She looked away, blushed, and confidently said, "I'm Theresa. It's nice to meet you."

She extended her hand, and he finally remembered his manners, so he stood and shook it, catching a whiff of mint mixed with citrus. Her grip was respectably firm, and touching her was a treat that he felt all the way past his belt.

"Nice to meet you, Theresa." He focused on being calm and not gripping her hand too firmly.

Theresa. A classy name. He imagined whispering it into her ear.

Nope. Focus. This was a job interview, not a night club.

They both sat down. She glanced back at him and blushed slightly before her gaze settled on some point over his shoulder.

"So," she began while setting his resume on the table. "This part won't be too technical. I'm just going to ask you some questions so I can get to know you a little."

"Sure." He gave her a smile, thinking it might be nice to get to know her, as well.

She asked about his experience at Stanford and then had him talk about the job he'd held for a while in Hawaii before moving to the mainland for his Master's. He watched her mouth as she talked, noting that her lips were full and red. She kept tapping on her chin with her matching fingernails.

"Can you tell me about a time you had to deal with a difficult coworker?" Theresa's eyes flitted to his for a second before returning to the spot over his shoulder.

"Fortunately, I haven't had a lot of that. But during my first month on the job, I worked with a woman who grew frustrated with me because I had trouble explaining to her the way the system would to work. And she said, 'You're not very good with people, are you?' That was a little awkward."

Theresa laughed and glanced at him again. "What did you say to her?"

He noticed a blush creeping up her cheeks. Cute.

He put the thought out of his mind. "I think I stuttered and then continued explaining, and she finally got it. I mentioned it to my boss because I was worried she might be right. He told me she had a reputation for being difficult to work with. Still, I worked on getting better at translating technical speak to customer speak."

Theresa nodded, and her shiny hair moved gently over her shoulders. "That's always difficult. In this role, you won't be interfacing with the end customer, and everyone here is very technical, all the way up to the CEO, but it's still good to have those skills."

They went over a few more behavioral questions, and then Theresa rose and said, "It was nice meeting you, Conall."

He stood and stuck his hand out, wondering if touching her would again bring on that internal fire. "You, too."

As soon as her palm touched his, there it was. He watched her watch him with her mouth hanging slightly open.

She turned, and rushed out the door.

Her fingers and head appeared inside the door frame. "Sorry, I forgot. Your last interviewer will be in here shortly. Then the hiring manager will be in to have a quick chat with you."

"Great."

Theresa's gaze fell on the papers she'd left on the table. She rushed in to snag them and disappeared again.

Wow. If he worked here, he'd get to see her all the time. Every day. In the break room. At the holiday party. Everywhere.

Conall wasn't sure if that would be a good thing or not. Besides the distraction, it could never lead anywhere. He sensed that she was the type to marry and have kids, if she hadn't already. If they dated, she'd eventually dump him—just like Clarissa had.

His ex-wife was the reason he'd left Honolulu to attend grad school in California. After the divorce, he couldn't go anywhere on the island that didn't remind him of her. He wouldn't go through that again. But his mind threatened to go down the old rabbit hole.

He needed to get his shit together. He was in the middle of an interview loop, for fuck's sake.

ABOUT THE AUTHOR

Kat Vinson writes contemporary romance for adults, featuring women who aren't going to do all the compromising. She grew up in Oklahoma and now lives in the Seattle area, working as a data scientist. She has many cats, each of whom is her favorite. Her short story "The Lie That Binds" can be found in an anthology called Lake Covington and the three books of her series Coded for Love, featuring women who work as engineers and data scientists at a tech start-up, are out now. Find Kat at katvinson.com and @kvbooks on Instagram.

ALSO BY KAT VINSON

The Coded for Love Series

It's Technically Love

Finally in Tune

A Quality Man

Made in United States
Troutdale, OR
04/14/2024

19115589R00192